Dangerous Destiny

A Suffragette Mystery

Chris Longmuir

To Audrey

Enjoy

Chris Longmuir

B&J

Published by Barker & Jansen

Copyright © Chris Longmuir, 2020

Cover design by Cathy Helms www.avalongraphics.org

Edited by Rachel Natansen

Dangerous Destiny is a work of fiction. Names, characters, places and incidents are the product of the author's imagination or are used fictitiously. Any resemblance to actual events, locales or persons, living or dead, is purely coincidental.

ISBN: 978-0-9574153-8-6

DEDICATION

This book is dedicated to the memory of Dundee suffragists.

1

Tuesday, 23rd June 1908

Victoria bent forward over the table, pretending to be busy.

'You go on ahead,' she said to Martha, who stood in the doorway. 'They'll be waiting for the news-sheets.'

The heap of papers in Martha's arms slipped, and she clutched them with a firmer grasp.

'I suppose I should. The crowds will be gathering, and Christabel will arrive soon.'

'Go on,' Victoria said. 'I won't be long.'

The door slammed. Victoria waited a few minutes to make sure Martha would be out of sight before she left the office. She couldn't risk her finding out about the rendezvous to collect what she needed to carry out her plan.

Excitement rippled through her as she peered into the street before leaving, locking the door behind her. The sound of her footsteps on the pavement beat a staccato rhythm in time with her heartbeat, while her blue, green and gold sash, signifying the Women's Freedom League, fluttered in the breeze. Soon, if her plan was successful, she would exchange it for a purple, white and green one. But she needed to prove her worth first, and that would depend on the success of what she had been working on. If it happened as she hoped, they would hail her as the suffragette who brought militancy to the streets of Dundee.

Barrack Street was quiet. She'd hoped to enter the Howff graveyard by that entrance, but she was out of luck; the gate was padlocked. The clank of a tram rattling along Meadowbank reminded her how close she was to Albert Square, where suffragettes were gathering to welcome Christabel Pankhurst. She hadn't wanted to use the main entrance to the Howff – it was so close to the square it posed a risk someone would see her; she wanted to avoid any awkward questions. But it was too late to turn back now.

Despite an increase in the numbers walking along Meadowbank, no one paid her any attention apart from a group of boys who sniggered and pointed their fingers at her. All eyes were focused on the crowded square ahead and she joined the flow of people heading in that direction. When she came to the main entrance to the Howff, she slipped through the ornate, iron gates into the graveyard. Once inside, she followed the path to her left which led to a secluded area, populated by older gravestones. There was less chance of anyone tending a grave here.

He was there already, lounging on a flat-topped gravestone.

'The preparations,' she began, 'did you get what I need?'

'Everything you require is under here.' He pointed to the hollow space beneath the stone and she bent to look.

It only took a moment for the blade to slice into her and for her to topple forward with the smallest of gasps.

Meanwhile, a short distance away, excitement mounted. The buzz of voices increased, rippling through the crowd gathered in front of a ribbon-bedecked cart. They had been gathering in Albert Square from early morning, jostling and pushing to find the best view; ladies in their finery rubbing shoulders with shop assistants and mill girls, along with a scattering of men, some of whom appeared embarrassed and some belligerent.

Martha Fairweather adjusted the sash across her body to make the words, *Votes for Women*, stand out against the background of blue, green and gold. She had opted out of her membership of the Women's Social and Political Union when Emmeline Pankhurst demanded their motto, '*Deeds not words*', meant members should use more violent tactics. But today, the WFL was out to support the cause alongside their more militant colleagues adorned in the purple, white and green of the WSPU.

Christabel Pankhurst's visit to Dundee in September 1906 had resulted in many more women joining the movement; she would be expecting the same result today. Martha had to admit that, even though she had no great love for the woman, Christabel was a talented speaker and audiences loved her.

Martha stared out over the crowd from her vantage point on the steps of the Albert Institute. Where was Victoria? When Martha raced out of the office, clutching the news-sheets, Victoria had said she had something to finish and she would be right behind her. That was half an hour ago. She should have been here by this time. Martha tutted with annoyance.

She looked around the square, but the other WFL members were either busy or nowhere to be seen. It would be difficult to cover the whole area herself and she needed help to hand out the news-sheets.

'Ethel,' she called to one of the girls standing beside the cart. Most of the women hung back at the rear of the crowd, allowing the men to take up spaces nearer the front, but the working-class girls had no such inhibitions.

'I've noticed your enthusiasm for women's suffrage,' she said as Ethel approached her, 'and I wondered if you'd like to help, distributing our literature.' She gestured to the stack of news-sheets.

The girl nodded, her cheeks pink with pleasure.

'I'd love to help.'

Martha handed her a bundle of papers.

'I'll do this side of the square. You can start at that side.' She nodded to the left. 'That would really help, thank you.'

Ethel grasped the news-sheets. Her obvious delight charmed Martha, who wished other young working girls shared her enthusiasm.

Ever since she'd first met Ethel, the girl had attended meetings and even gone out chalking pavements one evening. With encouragement, maybe she could be used to generate interest in the cause among her fellow workers. It would add vigour to their campaign if they involved more of the working class.

Ethel turned to start her task, but Martha laid a hand on the girl's arm before she walked away.

'Some men might be rude to you but pay them no heed. Smile and pass on to the next person.'

'Don't you worry about me, Miss Fairweather. I get plenty of lip from the men in the mill. I know how to handle them.'

'I'm sure you do.' Martha watched the girl elbow through the gathering throng. Her enthusiasm showed in the way she held her head and smiled as she handed out the news-sheets.

The WFL could do with more younger girls like Ethel. But was she too young? Supporting the cause wasn't an easy task. It came with many obstructions and difficulties, including letters like the one that nestled in her pocket. She hadn't shown it to any of the other women who manned the Women's Freedom League office because this one went beyond the usual bile and hatred – it contained a death threat aimed at all those who supported women's suffrage. The crudity of the message alarmed her, and she wondered if she was doing the right thing by hiding it from the others. More than likely, they would have insisted she take it to the police. But what good would that do? As far as the police were concerned, the suffragettes were a nuisance, women who didn't know their place in society. They would pat her on the head and tell her there was nothing for her to worry about.

A contingent of suffragettes arrived, heralding Christabel Pankhurst's approach, breaking Martha's train of thought. Two women from the WSPU climbed on to the cart and held their hands out in an attempt to calm the spectators. But it was only when Christabel's entourage entered the square and she mounted the makeshift stage to speak that a hush descended. People strained to listen, afraid to miss a single word.

Martha's eyes focused on Christabel's upright form and she pushed the death threat to the back of her mind to focus on Christabel's speech.

2

Ethel Stewart had taken a day off work to attend the rally and if her da found out, he'd likely kill her. She shivered. The memories of her da's fists in her ribs were as painful as the blows he dished out. But she didn't regret tempting his wrath, because Martha Fairweather had acknowledged her and trusted her to hand out the WFL news-sheets.

'A copy of our news-sheet, sir.' Ethel thrust a newspaper into the hand of the nearest man.

He snorted and thrust it back at her.

'You should find something better to do with your time than hand out this propaganda.'

'Don't worry, lass. I'll have one of your news-sheets.' The man standing next to him grinned at her. 'It might come in handy for hanging in the lavatory.'

Ethel shook her head. She'd had worse responses from men who delighted in goading suffragettes. Not that Ethel counted herself a proper suffragette, but she had hopes of becoming one. She carried on moving through the crowd of people, handing out news-sheets to anyone who would take them. The babble of voices quietened, and Ethel stopped what she was doing to push to the front of the spectators where she would be nearer the stage.

Christabel exuded confidence. As she clambered on to the cart, the crowd roared their approval, drowning out the disparaging remarks of a group of men nearby. Removing her hat, she threw it to a woman standing beside the cart.

Martha Fairweather sidled up to Ethel.

'I'm pleased you're here today,' she said in an undertone. 'I'll be nominating you for full membership at our next meeting.'

Ethel's cheeks tingled with warmth. She hadn't been sure

of her acceptance within the group because she was working class. Everyone else appeared to be her betters – posh women who wore fancy dresses and feather-covered hats which swayed in the breeze. Feathers cost a lot of money and Ethel could only dream that someday she might wear them. Women like that rarely welcomed a mill girl to their circles. But Ethel had made a point of working hard over the past few weeks and sought out tasks, no matter how onerous, to prove her worth.

'Ta,' she murmured, hoping her face wasn't flushed.

Miss Fairweather smiled at her.

'No need to thank me. You're a hard worker and I've noticed how committed you are.'

Ethel sneaked a glance at Miss Fairweather who, despite being a toff, didn't seem to have any airs and graces. She must know that Ethel was of a lower order, but it made no apparent difference to her. She had been kind and encouraging towards Ethel.

Christabel's voice rang out, demanding the crowd's attention. They stirred and looked towards the speaker. Ethel found herself caught up in the enthusiasm and she, too, turned to listen. The suffragette's eyes glowed with fervour and her voice had a hypnotic effect as she spoke about women's suffrage and why they should be allowed to vote when men stood for election as members of parliament. Several suffragettes, in their purple, white and green sashes, clustered around the cart, looking at their leader with adoration in their eyes. But the one standing nearest to her looked different. Her dress was not so ornate, nor did she wear a fancy hat. She aroused Ethel's curiosity.

She turned to Martha.

'Who's the woman holding Christabel's hat?'

Martha smiled before she answered. It was as if she found the question amusing.

'That's Annie Kenney. She comes from Manchester and she's a mill girl, the same as you.'

Ethel gasped. It had never crossed her mind that a mill girl could aspire to anything other than a lowly position in the suffrage societies. But Annie Kenney had arrived with Christabel Pankhurst, so she must have some standing in the organisation.

Perhaps, she thought, with Miss Fairweather's help, she could emulate Annie Kenney's success.

In a house overlooking Albert Square, Kirsty Campbell, drawn by the noise, pressed her forehead to the window glass and watched the crowds congregating. It wasn't the first time she had watched rallies and public meetings from her aunt's window, but this one appeared different because pockets of women were gathering as well as the usual men. Unable to see faces from her viewpoint above them, Kirsty studied the hats of the people gathered in the square. Ladies' bonnets of all shapes and sizes mingled with the headscarves of mill girls. Homburg hats, like the ones her father wore, prevailed among the men, although she spotted a few panama hats and a lot of bowlers. Men wearing flat caps – or bunnets, as they called them in Dundee – congregated closer to the cart. These would be the working men, interspersed with some layabouts whose main sport was to heckle the speaker.

The High School of Dundee, with its impressive pillars, formed a backdrop to the gathering crowds, while the grandeur of the Albert Institute, off to the right, made the people congregating appear insignificant. At the centre of the square, positioned between these two imposing buildings, a cart had been rolled into place to act as a stage.

Suddenly, the noise abated and a hush descended. The crowd surged and parted to form a path for a group of women approaching the cart. The tallest one, assisted by the others, clambered on to the makeshift stage and held out her hands to the crowd. She was greeted with a roar of approval. She waved her hands to quieten them and started to speak.

Kirsty fidgeted, trying in vain to hear the speech.

'Come away from the window, Kirsty.' Her mother's voice broke her concentration.

Kirsty frowned. She wanted to ask if she could join the rally in the square but knew her mother would never agree. Frustration overwhelmed her. She gritted her teeth and clenched her fists – why should she have to ask permission? She was eighteen, soon to be nineteen; that was old enough to decide for herself. Her shoulders slumped. As long as she depended on her parents, she could never be free to lead her own life.

Kirsty's aunt, Bea Hunter, ignored the noise drifting up from the square below and concentrated on pouring tea from the silver teapot into the three cups on the table in front of her.

'Sit down, Kirsty. Your tea is poured.'

It sounded like a reprimand. Something an adult might say to a child. But Kirsty wasn't a child. Heat surged through her body, up through her neck, flooding her face.

'I'm going out,' she said, clattering quickly out of the door and down the stairs before she could change her mind.

Three women stood on the doorstep outside, craning their necks to get a better view of Christabel Pankhurst. They didn't move when Kirsty left the building and she had to push past them. One woman muttered and glared at her, but Kirsty didn't care. She was outside! She was free, even if it was only for a short time.

Kirsty squeezed and wriggled through the crowd to get as near to the makeshift stage as she could. Her mother would have been horrified, but she pushed thoughts of her mother and Aunt Bea to the back of her mind. Being part of the crowd was exhilarating.

The voice of the young woman standing on the cart soared above the city noises. It was filled with energy and vitality, enthusing the women around her and the audience she was addressing. These women were *alive*. So different from her own sterile existence. Their enthusiasm for the cause they promoted affected Kirsty, and she felt her spirits rising in a way they hadn't done for several years.

Enthralled by the speaker's voice, Kirsty edged nearer the cart and craned her neck for a closer look.

'Do you think we'll ever get the vote?' The question came from the girl standing beside her.

'It's something I've never thought about.'

'But you're here.'

'Yes, I was watching from the window.' Kirsty pointed to where her aunt's house bordered the square. 'I felt compelled to come outside to listen.'

The girl thrust a leaflet into Kirsty's hand.

'This'll give you information on why women need to be able to vote.'

Kirsty frowned. Members of parliament were a mystery to her and being able to vote for them seemed pointless. As if sensing her doubts, the girl continued to speak.

'The vote's important for us if we ever want to be independent and make our own decisions. If we continue the way we are, men will continue to decide how we live our lives and we'll never gain freedom from their restrictions.'

Impressed by the passion in the girl's voice, Kirsty folded the leaflet and placed it in her pocket.

'I'll take it home and read it,' she promised.

3

It stood forlorn and deserted in the middle of Albert Square. No longer a stage, but a cart that had seen better days. Ethel closed her eyes and saw, once again, Christabel Pankhurst standing on its flat surface to court the crowd with her vision of a world where women could vote for their parliamentary members. Her voice had wooed even the most disruptive amongst the audience; the spell broken now she was gone. No doubt, many of those she'd held spellbound might think differently by tomorrow and return to their original state of scepticism or opposition.

'How does she do it?' Ethel turned to Martha, who was gathering the leftover news-sheets. 'I could have sworn the men would give her grief.'

'Who? Christabel? She's a talented speaker. Men like her because she's young and doesn't resemble the pictures they have in their mind of the old harridans you see on anti-suffrage posters. But she's a Pankhurst, and she advocates more violence than I'm prepared to undertake.'

'That's something I wanted to ask you.' Ethel hesitated, not wanting to admit her confusion over the different suffrage societies.

'What's the difference between the WFL and the WSPU?' Martha predicted the girl's question.

'Yes. We've all turned out for this rally to hear Christabel speak, although we don't support the same societies . . .'

Martha laid the news-sheets on the cart and leaned back against it.

'I suppose it can be confusing. What to remember is the different societies have the same aim – every one of us wants women to get the vote. But each organisation has a different way of tackling it. Christabel's mother, Emmeline

Pankhurst, considered the suffrage movement too passive, so she formed the Women's Social and Political Union. She believed suffragettes should be more militant, and I shared her belief. "Deeds not words," she used to say. And that's why I joined.'

Ethel's confusion grew greater, and she shook her head.

'But you're not a member of the WSPU.'

'I was, but Emmeline Pankhurst expected members of the WSPU to increase their militant activities. It was when they started setting fires and planting bombs in England that I decided it was too much for me. A lot of members felt the same way, so we left and set up the Women's Freedom League – that was just last year. We still believe in using militant methods – petitioning and all that passive stuff doesn't get us anywhere. But we don't believe in using the more extreme methods Emmeline Pankhurst advocates.'

'It's all terribly confusing.'

'Once we gather the news-sheets in, come with me to our headquarters and I'll give you some pamphlets to read. It might help you to understand.' Ethel and Martha, their arms full of papers, walked out of the square and along the street.

'When I put your name forward at the next meeting, I'm hoping you'll join us on a more official basis.'

Ethel hesitated before she replied.

'I'd like that, but I can't be as available as the other members. There's my da, you see.'

They walked on in silence.

'Your home life is not a happy one, I think.' Martha's eyes remained focused on the road ahead.

Ethel blinked and pulled at her sleeve in a subconscious action. She was sure Martha had spotted the bruise on her wrist when she handed her the news-sheets.

She didn't look at Martha but could sense the woman watching her.

'My home is far too big for my needs, should you require a sanctuary.' Martha paused. 'I'm sorry, I didn't intend to intrude.'

'I . . . I don't know.' Ethel gripped the news-sheets closer to her body. Her mind whirled. Did Martha mean it? Was this a chance to escape from her life with a bully of a father, who might turn on her whenever he grew tired of beating on her mother?

Martha stopped walking and turned to look at Ethel.

'I can sense your hesitancy. Perhaps that is because you think accepting my offer would be an intrusion. But, if you do decide to come and stay with me, it will not only benefit you, it will also benefit the Women's Freedom League. You will be more available to take part in our activities than if you remain at home.'

'You really mean it? I can stay with you?' Ethel's pulse quickened.

'Of course, I mean it. I always have rooms ready for suffragettes looking for somewhere to stay.' Martha paused for a moment before adding, 'And, you are a suffragette.'

Ethel's mind whirled. She knew what awaited her when her da got home tonight. Someone was bound to have told him she'd missed work today; if he didn't know by now, he would find out tomorrow. She shuddered at the thought.

'You're shivering. Is something wrong?' Martha's voice was full of concern.

'It's my da; he'd never allow it. And he'll be angry because I missed work today.'

'I see.' Martha paused. 'Will your father be at home when you get back?'

'I don't think so. He usually stays at the pub until closing time.'

'In that case, you must leave while you have the chance. You can move in with me right away.'

4

'It'll be all right, Ma.' Ethel stopped pushing clothes into the bag so that her hands were free to hug her mother. The older woman shrank back – they'd never been a family who touched or displayed emotion. But, after a moment, she relaxed and accepted her daughter's embrace. Ethel tightened her hold, surprised by the sharpness of her mother's shoulder blades and the wave of emotion this provoked within her.

A tear trickled down her mother's face.

'I'll miss you, hen.' She scrubbed the moisture away with a hand as wizened as her cheek.

Ethel turned back to her packing.

'I need to get this finished before Da comes home.' She shivered at the thought. It wouldn't be the first time she'd suffered from her da's fists, but she had no intention of staying and being one more punch-bag for him.

She pulled the top of the bag closed and took a final look around the only home she'd ever known. Two damp, dilapidated rooms, similar in size and layout to every tenement house in Dundee. The front room, known as the kitchen, connected to the front door by a tiny lobby. This was where the family ate, washed, slept and lived. Another door at the rear of this room led into a box-room.

The kitchen was a spartan place, containing a jawbox sink in front of the dingy, net-covered window which looked out on to the shared landing. On the opposite wall, an ash-filled fireplace, in sore need of the black leading brush, held a dead fire that rarely blazed. The table in the centre of the room was strewn with the remains of the last meal. Milk in a bottle, sugar still in its bag, and dirty plates and cups littered the surface, leaving scant space for anything else. An unmade bed, partially hidden in a curtained alcove, awaited its night-time occupants.

Her ma had brought up eight kids in these two rooms while her husband spent his life in the pub. Ethel was the only one who had remained. The rest of them had fled as soon as they were old enough.

Ethel remembered her ma when she was younger. Not that she was old now, although she looked more like a woman of sixty-five than the forty-five she was. Ma had been bonnie then, but Da had beaten that out of her over the years. There was no way Ethel meant to fall into the same trap. Men! She'd see a man in hell before she'd take one.

'I can't come back, Ma. You know that, don't you?' She looked at the older woman with troubled, brown eyes. They were a warmer, deeper, more vibrant version of her mother's.

Margery Stewart nodded.

'He'd have the hide off me if I returned.' She grasped her mother's hands. 'I love you, Ma.' She'd never told her mother this before and it embarrassed her. Hugging her one final time, Ethel ran out of the door, leaving behind her childhood home and all the poverty and dirt and hurt it contained.

She fled along the landing, a stone platform suspended in mid-air which provided a passage from the central stairwell to each individual house. These platforms, known locally as platties, jutted out behind all the Dundee tenements. No one knew what miracle stopped these platties, and the stairs that led on to them, from collapsing; though that was one worry which didn't enter Ethel's mind as her feet clattered along the stone surface.

Several sets of grubby net curtains twitched as she ran past and a new worry took root. What if someone followed her? What if they told her da where she'd gone? It didn't bear thinking about. She didn't stop running until she reached the foot of the Hilltown. Da never frequented the town centre and rarely came this far down the steep hill. He preferred the drinking howffs nearer to home. Ethel leaned against a wall, waiting until she stopped gasping and her breath became more even, then she started to move forward again, walking at a more sedate pace.

Margery Stewart watched her daughter leave the house. Ethel was her youngest child, her favourite, but she wouldn't stop her from going. She'd done her best for the child but knew it hadn't been enough. Ethel was twenty-one now, her own person, and she could do what she wanted. But Hughie never saw it that way. A shudder passed through her slight frame. Hughie looked on Ethel as his possession in the same way Margery had become his to do with as he wished when they married.

Hughie wouldn't like it when he found out Ethel had defied him and left home. Margery clasped her hands around her middle, already feeling the blows to come. If Ethel wasn't here, he'd take it out on her. She moaned gently in anticipation, a wounded sound which seemed to emanate right from her heart. And yet, she was glad for her girl. Ethel had escaped and, so long as she wasn't fool enough to return to this dingy house, Margery knew her youngest daughter would do all right for herself.

Margery stood. She'd best get food ready for when Hughie came home from the pub. It would be one less excuse to hit her. Not that he ever needed one, but it didn't pay to antagonise him. She opened the paper bag sitting on the table. It contained one meat pie. That would do for Hughie; it didn't matter for herself, which was just as well, because she'd only had enough money for one, and Hughie wasn't the sharing kind. She scrabbled under the sink for two potatoes and, running the tap, started to peel them.

Once the potatoes were cooking and the pie was in the oven, she cleared a space on the table for her husband's meal. She threw the dirty dishes into the sink, swilled a dirty cup under the tap and replaced it, sniffed the milk to make sure it hadn't soured and placed a knife and fork at the empty place.

She should tidy herself now but was too tired to care what she looked like. Her dusty, brown hair straggled in rats' tails on her neck, and she spent her whole life in her mill clothes. What was the point of doing anything else? Hughie never noticed, and anyway, it didn't matter if she got blood on her working clothes.

There was a blankness in her brown eyes as she stared at her surroundings. What did anything matter any more?

She sat down and waited for Hughie to come home.

'I thought you were never coming,' Martha said, as she opened the door and took the bag from Ethel.

'It was a wee bit difficult. Ma was upset.'

'Yes, I suppose so.' Martha closed the door behind Ethel. 'It was to be expected. But your father – did you get away without him knowing?'

Ethel followed Martha up the corridor. This house was massive compared to the one she'd grown up in, as well as being a lot cleaner and better furnished.

'Yes. He'll be in the pub until closing-time.' A worried frown creased her forehead. 'I expect Ma will catch the brunt of his temper.'

Martha set the bag on the floor.

'He'd do that, anyway, whether you were there or not. You're well out of it.' She led Ethel up a staircase and opened one of the doors off the landing. 'This is your bedroom. I hope you like it.'

The room was small and functional, with a double bed, wardrobe, chest of drawers, chair, and thick, red, velvet curtains. To Ethel, it was a palace.

'It's beautiful,' she whispered. 'You're sure you won't regret offering to take me in?'

'Regret? Why would I regret it? You're part of the cause and you've already proved your worth.' She reached out and placed a hand on Ethel's shoulder. 'Take your time, get unpacked and join me in the drawing-room when you are ready.'

5

Hugh Stewart drained his glass.

'Give's another wee one before I go home.'

'Can't do it, chum. Closing-time and all that. It's more than my licence is worth.' Charlie rinsed a glass under the tap behind the bar, polished it with a cloth and placed it on the shelf.

Hugh banged his glass on the bar counter.

'Another wee one wouldn't hurt ye.' There was more than a touch of menace in his voice as he glared at the barman.

'No way, chum. And don't take that tone with me or ye can find your drink elsewhere.' Charlie placed his hands on the bar, flexed his muscles and met Hugh's glare straight on.

Charlie was bigger than Hugh, though not as burly. Hugh, with his broad shoulders and long arms, had a threatening, simian appearance, intensified by his shambling gait. The two men squared up. Hugh's unshaven chin jutted; he stared at Charlie with a wild look in his bloodshot, brown eyes. His tension built, and he clenched his fists to prepare for the expected explosion of anger.

'Come on, mate. Wife'll be looking for ye.' His drinking partner, Angus, pulled at Hugh's arm.

Hugh didn't answer for a moment, but the tension in his muscles slackened.

'D'ye think I'm scared of my wife?'

'Naw, I know ye're no feart of her, but I've got a wee something in my pocket.' Angus pulled the neck of the bottle up so Hugh could see.

'Aye, well, then. If ye insist.' Hugh allowed himself to be pulled from the pub.

Hugh gulped a greedy mouthful from the bottle, gasping

as the fire hit his belly.

'Whaur did ye get it, then? Ye'd nae mair money than I had.' The two men hunkered on the grass in the back green, out of sight of any curious eyes.

'Nabbed it from the back o' the bar when Charlie was seeing to yon rumpus.' Angus took the bottle from Hugh.

'Good lad.' Hugh's hands reached for the bottle to be returned and he took a long draw. 'Aw, bugger it! There's nane left.' Hugh shook the bottle. 'What'll we do now?'

'Go hame, like we always do,' Angus mumbled, hoisting himself to his feet with a hand on Hugh's shoulder.

The stairs shifted and swayed as Hugh climbed them. His drunken state wasn't unusual, though, and he negotiated them with his hand clamped to the iron handrail. Hand over hand, he pulled himself upwards until he reached the top landing.

'Nosy bugger,' he roared at one window as he saw the curtains twitch. 'Mind your ain business or I'll come in there and help ye mind it.'

He hammered on his door until Margery opened it.

'Good lass,' he said. 'Have ye got my supper ready?'

Margery placed the plate with a meat pie and potatoes in front of him and stood back.

He looked at the plate.

'What's this?' he roared. 'A burnt pie and potatoes no better than mush.'

'Ye were late . . .'

The fear in her voice fanned his temper. Why would she never stand up to him?

'Shite. That's what it is.' He lifted the plate and threw it at her. Margery sidestepped, and it skiffed past her shoulder, splattering against the wall behind her. The pie slid to the floor, while the potatoes stuck like lumps of white cement.

'Don't just stand there!' he roared. 'Wipe that bloody mess up.'

Margery grabbed a washrag out of the sink and scrubbed at the wall, only widening the affected area and spreading the grease.

'Bloody useless, that's what you are. This place is a hovel.' He watched Margery through narrowed eyes, enjoying her fear. Tension built within him, tightening his muscles and feeding into his rage. It was a familiar feeling; one he knew could only be relieved through using his fists. He clenched his fingers into his palms and hit her on the side of the head with his knuckles.

'No, Hughie, don't,' Margery pleaded. He liked it when she begged, but he wanted her on her knees.

He hit her again and again; she sank to the floor.

'Stop! If I can't work, we'll have no money.' Her voice was barely audible.

'We'll use Ethel's wages.' He raised his hand again. 'She's a good lass, she'll not see us starve.'

'But Ethel's not here,' she said, just before the blow struck.

'What do ye mean, she's not here?' His knuckles were bloody; his fists ached. 'Away with some toerag, I suppose. She'll be having it off up one of the closies. Well, I'll soon sort her out when she appears.'

'She's not coming back.'

Margery looked up at him from bloodshot eyes and he could have sworn a smile twitched at the corner of her mouth.

'She's moved out and taken all her belongings with her.'

'Moved out? She can't do that – I won't allow it.' Heat flooded Hugh's body, spreading up through his neck to his face. The veins throbbed in his temples and a drumbeat of anger pounded in his head. His fists clenched, and he punched his wife until his knuckles ached so much he had to stop. Then he used his feet.

It didn't take Ethel long to unpack the few belongings she had. The board money she paid to her mother swallowed up most of her pay. Although she didn't grudge her mother taking the money for food, she knew her father drank most of her mother's wages and hers, as well. Meeting Martha had been one of the most fortunate things that had ever happened to her.

They'd met several weeks ago at an open-air meeting on Magdalen Green. The speakers that day had been interesting and spoke with passion about women and their rights. Ethel had never thought women *had* any rights, and she had been overcome with excitement at the thought that these women were prepared to fight for what they wanted.

'You seem to be enjoying the meeting,' a voice next to her had said, and Ethel had turned to the lady, nodding in awed agreement. She'd never spoken to anyone like this before, someone fashionably dressed and quite obviously not a working woman.

'My name's Martha Fairweather.' The woman offered her hand.

Ethel stared at her for a moment before responding. Martha was the most beautiful woman she had been this close to – small and delicate, with bluest-of-blue eyes and blonde curls tucked up under her elegant bonnet. Her cheeks held the faintest blush, while her lips had the softest touch of rouge. Ethel touched her own lips. She'd never used rouge, but she liked the effect. An uninvited thought seeped into her mind that she was being propositioned for a life of vice. But Martha didn't seem that kind of woman and Ethel felt instantly embarrassed by her thoughts.

'I can see what you're thinking.' Martha laughed. 'But don't be afraid – I'm one of the organisers of this event.'

Heat suffused Ethel's neck and spread to her face. She hoped she wasn't blushing. Martha ignored her discomfiture.

'Some members of our group are meeting at my house after the meeting. Would you like to join us?'

After that initial, chance encounter, Ethel attended many more meetings and discussions. She even went out with Martha, on one occasion, to chalk advertisements for an evening meeting on the pavements of Dundee. That had frightened her, and she was sure she couldn't have done it without Martha's support. And throughout it all, her friendship with the older woman had grown.

And now, here she was, living with her. Ethel heaved her bag on top of the wardrobe then moved to the window overlooking the Nethergate.

At the other side of the road, she could see the church and its steeple; and if she leaned forward, she could just glimpse the majestic proportions of the Queens Hotel, further up the road to her left. It was so clean and civilised in this part of the town, a million miles from the grime and dirt of the tenements and their backlands.

There was a tap at the door and Martha called out.

'I have tea ready – would you care to join me?'

Ethel turned from the window.

'Of course.'

She walked to the door and grasped Martha's hands in her own.

'I don't know why you're so good to me and I'm not sure how I can thank you.'

'You don't have to thank me.' Martha smiled. 'It's what anyone who supports the cause would do. We're here to help others who join us.'

Ethel slept fitfully that night. Her plush surroundings were unfamiliar and, while the bed was more comfortable than she was accustomed to, sleep eluded her as worries about her mother plagued her mind.

The house was quiet when she rose. Ethel tiptoed around, trying not to make a noise, unable to shake off the feeling she shouldn't be here, even though, the night before, Martha had shown her where to find breakfast things and had helped her make sandwiches for her midday meal.

'It's too early for me,' Martha had apologised. 'But help yourself to anything you need and I'll see you in the evening.'

Ethel struggled into her mill clothes, the stink of jute strong in her nostrils – a peculiar, musty, dust-like smell which clung to everything it came in contact with, although it hadn't been so noticeable in the Hilltown house where everything stank the same. It made her think of Martha, so delicate and beautiful, who always smelled of fresh flowers.

Maybe she wouldn't care for the smell of jute in her lovely, clean house. Maybe she'd change her mind about allowing Ethel to stay.

Aching all over, Margery struggled out of bed. She stood up and promptly slid to the floor, where she lay for a moment before crawling to the door. She had to find help and Hughie was no use, lying on top of a pile of clothes in the box-room, snoring.

It took her an age to get to the front door, and then she couldn't reach the doorknob. She lay, panting, as she tried to summon the strength to pull herself far enough up the door to open it. Several agonising attempts later, she succeeded. But the effort was too much for her and she collapsed on the doorstep, her head and shoulders lying on the stone landing and her feet and legs in the lobby.

'Godalmighty!' It was the voice of her neighbour, known as Nosy Nelly. For once, Margery was thankful for her curiosity, although normally she shunned her.

'A tram hit you, did it?' Strong arms helped her to her feet and back into the house where she plonked Margery into a chair beside the window. Margery could see Nelly's eyes taking everything in, but for once didn't care. 'My, you've copped a wallop. D'you want me to send for the doctor?' Nelly stood in front of her, inspecting the damage.

'No, no. I've no money for a doctor, ' Margery muttered through thick lips. It felt as if some of her teeth were missing. 'I have to get to work.'

Nelly snorted.

'I doubt you can stand, never mind work. You'd be better if the doctor saw you, but if you say no, then no, it is. Here, I'll try to clean you up.'

'Thanks, Nelly.' Margery tried to grasp her hand, but it hurt too much to move her arm.

'I'd better give you a prod or two, make sure nothing's broken. It'll hurt, mind.'

Nelly went to work, feeling Margery's ribs, her legs,

ankles, arms and wrists. There was an unspoken, shared, grim acceptance of the situation between them; so many of the women of the tenements suffered from the same sorts of attention from their men.

'Feels as if it's only bruises,' Nelly said at last. 'But the bruises are worse than any I've seen. You'll be sore for a while.'

Hugh wandered through from the box-room.

'What're you doing in my house, you old harpy?' He glared at Nelly.

'You should be ashamed of yourself, Hugh Stewart. Beating on your wife.' Nelly straightened. She was a big woman, taller and stronger than Hugh. 'You're lucky she's no' deid.'

'Get the hell out of my house!' Hugh roared. 'Always poking your nose in where it's not wanted.' He flailed his long arms in the air, though he didn't move any nearer to Nelly.

'I'll get out,' Nelly shouted back. 'But you'd better look after your wife, and if I hear her scream, I'll send for the bobbies.'

She slammed the door and stamped along the landing to her own house.

Hugh looked at Margery.

'Aw, Marge,' he said. 'I'm sorry, lass. I didnae mean it. Ye know I never mean it, but I was so upset about Ethel going off, I couldna help myself.'

'I know, Hughie.' Margery forgave him like she always did. 'But ye'll leave the lassie alone, promise?'

'Aye, I promise.' The promise was easy to make in Hugh's sober, penitent state. Assurances were harder to abide by when he was drunk and raging against the world.

6

Wednesday, 24th June 1908

Sleep evaded Martha. The streetlight outside her house ensured the room was never completely dark. She stared at the ceiling, watching the shadows flicker, while she thought about the rally. She wasn't a devotee of Christabel Pankhurst, nor her call to women to take a violent stance to further the cause. But Christabel's appearances generated publicity and interest, and even Martha had been surprised at the number of people who'd turned out to listen to her.

She adjusted her pillow and snuggled further beneath the blankets. Ethel had done well. The girl showed great promise; she would be an asset for the cause. Martha's thoughts drifted to Victoria. Where had she disappeared to earlier? It wasn't like her to miss a meeting or a rally. She was one of the foremost advocates of suffrage. What on earth had prevented her attending? It must be something serious.

Martha fell asleep worrying about Victoria, and what might have kept her from the rally.

The clang of a tram passing in the street outside woke her. She struggled to prise her eyes open as the previous night's worries resurfaced in her mind. Determined to find out the cause of Victoria's nonappearance, she sat up with a groan and forced herself out of bed.

Refreshed after a wash and breakfast, Martha donned a short jacket over her skirt and blouse and set out for Perth Road, where Victoria lived with her sister and brother-in-law.

Elizabeth Inglis opened the door to her knock.

'I'm looking for Victoria,' Martha said. 'Can I speak to her?'

Elizabeth slumped against the doorpost and shook her head.

'She's not here. I haven't seen her since the night before last and I'm sick with worry.'

'The night before last?' Martha's mind whirled. That was when they'd been sticking posters all over Dundee to advertise the rally. 'I was with her that evening. I said goodbye to her in the Nethergate and she told me she was going straight home.'

'She never came home. I waited and waited, but she didn't come.'

'Strange,' Martha said. 'The last time I saw her was in the office, yesterday morning. She intended to join me at the rally in Albert Square but she never turned up and I wondered if something was wrong. Has anything unusual happened?'

'Nothing I know about – she's not said anything.'

A worrying thought crept into Martha's mind.

'Have you reported her as a missing person?'

Elizabeth shook her head.

'I keep hoping she'll turn up.'

'Get your coat and we'll go to the police station now.'

They walked in silence until they came to the archway leading into the police quadrangle.

'You don't think something awful has happened to her, do you?' Elizabeth stopped, as if afraid that continuing meant making their fears a reality.

'I'm certain it will be all right. Victoria's strong and able to look after herself. It's probably completely innocuous, but it's best to be on the safe side.' Martha put an arm around Elizabeth's shoulder while she tried to sound convincing. But inside, Martha wasn't as sure as she sounded. Her mind kept returning to the threatening letter pushed through the Women's Freedom League letterbox that same morning, and she regretted not bringing it to the attention of her colleagues.

The policeman behind the counter in the charge-room glanced at them and then looked towards the door as if expecting someone else to follow them in.

Martha cleared her throat.

'We want to report a woman missing.'

The policeman tapped his pencil on the desk.

'If you had a piece of paper, I could give you the details.' Martha was losing patience.

'Perhaps this is something the *man* of the house should attend to? A police station is no place for ladies.' The sergeant's eyes flickered away from them. 'You meet all sorts in here.'

'Such as yourself, I take it.'

'No need for that tone, ma'am.' He placed a ledger on the desk and opened it.

'Name?'

'Victoria Allan. This is her sister, Elizabeth Inglis.'

'Age?'

'She was thirty-two on her last birthday.'

'And you are?'

'Martha Fairweather.'

The sergeant wrote the information in the book.

'When and where was the missing person last seen?'

'It must have been shortly before one o'clock yesterday. I left her at the Women's Freedom League office in the Nethergate. I expected her to join me at Albert Square, but she never turned up.' Martha tightened her grasp on Elizabeth's hand. 'And no one has seen her since.'

'She never came home on Monday night and I've been worried.' A tear slid down Elizabeth's cheek.

The sergeant laid his pen on the desk and closed the ledger.

'So, she's only been gone since yesterday, but she didn't come home the night before and she's a grown woman. It's obvious to me that she must have a man friend.'

'Why is it obvious?' Martha stiffened.

'Sounds to me she's one of them modern young women. No knowing what they get up to.'

'What you mean is that because Victoria is a *suffragette*, you intend to do nothing about this.' Martha pulled Elizabeth towards the door. 'Come on, we're wasting our time here.'

Anger consumed Martha, and she didn't calm down until they'd left the quadrangle and were walking along Ward Road. That was when she realised she hadn't informed the sergeant about the threatening letter in her pocket.

Inspector Hammond pushed open the door from the inner sanctum of the police station. Women always made him feel uncomfortable, so he lurked in the corridor while Sergeant Edwards questioned them.

'What was that all about?'

Edwards snorted.

'Missing person, sir. I've taken the details but – if you ask me – it's a waste of our time.'

'Why do you think that?'

'Well, for a start, she's one of them suffragettes and we know they're all a bunch of unnatural women. She could've run off with a man or taken off for London to cause havoc with the police there. Maybe she's banged up in a cell at Holloway. That's where a lot of them wind up.'

Hammond sighed. He had an unsettling feeling.

'I suppose you're right but keep hold of the details. We don't want them coming back and accusing us of negligence.'

7

Ethel reached the mill a moment before the gates were closed to latecomers. She'd woken later than usual and had to run to get here on time before the gaffers docked her pay at the end of the week.

She joined the queue of workers crowding through the mill gates and tagged herself on the end of the line, to wait her turn to insert her time-card into the clocking-on machine. Women and girls made up the workforce of weavers, spinners and winders, though a few men – mechanics, engineers and box boys – straggled along beside them. She looked for her ma but couldn't see her. A pang of fear twitched at her, and she tried to shrug it away. Her da couldn't touch her inside the mill – the women would protect her. He knew that and Ethel was sure he'd keep his distance. The fear that remained was for her ma and what her da might have done to her.

Caught in the middle of the crowd, Ethel had no choice but to keep moving forward. Once the mill started to hum, she'd have no time to think of anything except work.

The huge wooden doors leading into the courtyard were open. They closed after the last worker was in and wouldn't open again until the bummer shrieked its loud whistle to release them from the working day. Then the hordes of workers would push and clatter through them, glad to escape the drudgery of their daily toil.

Ethel passed through to the courtyard, the uneven cobbles biting into her feet and threatening to unbalance her. The gable ends of three rows of stone buildings faced her at the other side of the yard. Carding and roving sheds lay in the buildings to the left and ran the length of the mill. Spinning sheds stretched all along the right-hand side. The middle building was for the weavers, who wouldn't lower themselves to enter the sheds at either side of them.

The crowd separated. Women of all ages, shapes and sizes made their way, with weary footsteps, to where they worked. Ethel headed for one of the spinning sheds, a large, long room, with a claustrophobic atmosphere owing to all the machinery it contained.

Rows of massive, iron spinning frames extended its length. The roves, spindles and bobbins they housed stood lined up alongside the machines, looking like soldiers waiting for their orders. Workers scurried inside, eager to reach their designated spinning frame before the signal to switch on echoed through the room. Their shoes and clogs clattered in a staccato rhythm on the stone floors and muted the buzz of voices. Soon, even those sounds would be drowned out, replaced by the noise of engines and whizzing spindles beating on Ethel's ears until they ached. Dry, musty dust, filtered into her nostrils, tainted her skin and hair and marked her as a jute worker.

A set of wooden stairs by the door led upwards to a platform that ran the length of the room. This was where the gaffer stood to get a clear view of several frames at a time; by walking its length he could oversee the entire room. At the top of the stairs was a glass-windowed office, where he filled in his time-sheets and kept a note of how many shifts each spinning frame did, keeping track of the number of bobbins available for the weaving sheds.

Ethel walked to her frame and checked every bobbin, making sure they were pressed down so they couldn't fly up and split the jute ends once she turned the machine on, then she waited for the gaffer's signal.

The signal came soon enough, and she switched on the engine of the massive frame, watching as the silvery spindles gathered speed until they whirled so fast they became a blur.

She stood for a moment, watching the thick, woolly thread being pulled downwards from the roves to run through the rollers, transforming it into a finer thread, similar to string. From there, each thread filtered through the spinning top of a flyer, which spun and fed it down through the machine, into the eye of one of the legs of each whirling spindle winding the thread around the bobbins. As the spindles whirled, the bobbins filled with string.

Ethel's job as a spinner was to work the machine that spun the raw jute into string, mend any broken ends of jute after they passed between rollers and spindle caps, and then to shift the full bobbins from the machine and start another new set spinning. At the start of each working day, her prayer was the same as every other spinner's prayer: that not too many jute ends would break at the same time. Too many half-full bobbins led to a reprimand from the gaffer. It was all right for him; he didn't have to halt a spindle and put his fingers between its stationary legs to grasp the thread, while the other spindles continued to whirl their high-speed dance on either side.

There were many injuries in the mill; it didn't do to be careless. Ethel, who had seen friends hurt, feared the spinning frames, imagining they were waiting for their next victim. As a result, she tried to work like an automaton but wasn't always successful at blanking out the task and her fears. She often woke up in the middle of the night, convinced she'd lost her grip on the flyer cap which fed the jute through to the whirling bobbins. In these nightmares, the spinning legs of the spindles trapped her fingers and she always needed to feel her hands repeatedly before she was satisfied they'd only been mangled in her dream-world.

Despite this, she was a good spinner; though more often than not, she counted the minutes until the end of each shift, when she could turn off her frame.

The morning passed in a daze and she tended her machine while her mind was elsewhere.

'You working overtime or something?'

The voice broke into Ethel's thoughts and she started. The spinning frames around her had fallen silent, and hers was the only one still operating.

'You'll be giving the gaffer ideas. He'll think we don't need time to eat. Half an hour's short enough as it is.'

Ethel turned off her machine.

'I was too busy thinking about yesterday's gathering in Albert Square. Martha – she's a suffragette – let me hand out news-sheets. I was so excited. Fancy choosing the likes of me to do that! And when Christabel Pankhurst spoke . . . it fair fired me up!'

The spindles spun to a stop and Ethel opened the box at the end of her spinning frame. After removing the paper bag, which held two cheese sandwiches, she slammed the lid shut and turned to Maisie.

'Let's get a breath of fresh air while we eat.'

Dust motes glittered in the sunshine as they opened the door and left the spinning shed. Ethel leaned against the wall and breathed in the warm air, feeling its freshness after the dust-filled atmosphere inside.

Maisie took up a stance beside her.

'You're fairly into all this suffragette stuff,' she said. 'I'll bet your da hates it.'

'What he doesn't know won't bother him.' Ethel opened the paper bag and broke off a piece of the bread and cheese.

'I've been thinking about them suffragettes. I was at that meeting in Albert Square.' Maisie took a bite of her sandwich. 'I saw you handing out papers. Maybe I could do something like that.'

'Martha says everyone's welcome. I'll bring you some leaflets if you like.'

'Would you? That'd be good.' Maisie brushed the crumbs from her hands. 'Better bring a pile, actually. There's more than me interested, I reckon.'

Ethel pushed the last piece of bread into her mouth and scrunched the paper bag into a ball before shoving it into her pocket.

'I'll see you later, Maisie. I'm worried about my ma. I haven't seen her around this morning.'

She darted outside and over to the winding sheds. Most of the winders congregated at the end of their room, some sitting on stools and others on upturned boxes, but her ma wasn't amongst them.

'You looking for someone, hen?' A big woman in a flowery overall stopped eating and peered curiously at her.

'Margery Stewart,' Ethel said. 'Has anyone seen her?'

'Sorry, love. She's not in today. Heard tell her man beat her up again.'

'Ta.' Ethel's shoulders slumped as she left the winding shed. She didn't know why the news had shocked her; she'd known it would happen, the same as her ma had known. And there was nothing either of them could do about it.

The day ended at last and Ethel switched off her machine, sighing wearily. She untied the hook she used to mend broken ends and hung it from one of the operating switches, ready for the next day's work. Lifting the lid of the box at the end of her spinning frame, she grabbed her shawl and shook the mill stour out of it before shrugging it on to her shoulders. She needed to hurry; she had things to do tonight.

There was a look of wariness in her eyes and she tried to keep to the centre of the crowd as she sidled through the mill gates. She needn't have worried; there was no sign of her da.

All too soon, it was time to leave the protectiveness of the workers and, keeping her head bowed low, she scurried through the streets to the Nethergate. She didn't feel safe until she was inside the house and the warmth of Martha's welcome flooded over her.

'Oh, you poor dear,' Martha said. 'You're exhausted. Let me help you. I'll take your shawl while you go through to the sitting-room and get your feet up for a while.'

'That's all right. I'm dirty. I should wash first.' Embarrassment swept over Ethel in a wave. Martha wasn't used to the dirt and dust brought home from the mill, and then there was the smell. She wouldn't want that permeating the house.

'Hurry, then. I've fetched something nice for your dinner.' She turned aside. 'I'll be in the kitchen when you're ready.'

Ethel watched Martha turn away. She hadn't argued and Ethel took that as an acknowledgement of everything she was ashamed of. Her embarrassment increased. More than ever, she was convinced this arrangement wouldn't work out. But what could she do? Returning home to face her father's wrath was unthinkable.

8

Thursday, 25th June 1908

Kirsty dangled her feet out of bed and wriggled her toes. The air was cool at this early hour, even though it was almost the end of June. Waking early was a habit for Kirsty, who hadn't slept well for the past three years, not since . . . No, she refused to think about it. So long as she didn't, everything would be all right. She could continue to live her comfortable life with no pain, no regret, and no purpose. The last thought crept up on her, unexpected and uninvited, making her sigh. It was true her life lacked purpose, something to make it worth living.

Despite her resolve not to think about it – she always referred to what had happened as 'it' – the suffocating sensation threatening to overwhelm her was familiar. A tear gathered in her eye and she blinked it away. Kirsty hadn't cried for three years. She didn't intend to start now.

Reaching for her wrap, she pulled it over her slim shoulders, stood up, and shoved her feet into her slippers. The house was quiet, a slumbering prison that gripped Kirsty and kept her safe from harm and wrongdoing. She shivered again, not from the cold this time. Was that why she was still here, closeted and cosseted, because she had been guilty of wrongdoing? A small worm of anger stirred within her, wriggling through her body and mind like a hot wire. Lately, she had been feeling these flashes of rage and it was becoming more and more difficult to repress them, as she had done for so long. The doldrums, her parents called it. But Kirsty's doldrums had lasted such a long time she'd thought they would never lift. Maybe, she thought now, the time had come.

Kirsty opened her bedroom door, barely disturbing the

silence. She stood for a moment, breathing in the peaceful atmosphere, before venturing further. Wraith-like, she tiptoed along the passage, across the landing at the top of the stairs and into the next corridor. This was where the nursery was. A safe, comfortable room, containing so many of her happy, childhood memories. She smiled as she remembered how spoiled and wilful she'd been, at a time when she'd had more spirit than she had now. A time when she hadn't been so concerned about conforming or about safety. But it was no longer a happy place for Kirsty; her memories had been replaced by a deep, painful sadness.

The nursery was dim, shadows lurking in the corners and the drapes not yet opened to the early morning light. But Kirsty had no problem finding her way to the armchair beside the fireplace. She curled up in it, in the same manner she'd done as a child, with her feet tucked under her nightgown and her auburn hair hanging in loose waves around her shoulders.

There was a familiarity about the room that was comforting and, as she became accustomed to the darkness, she identified different shapes. The dolls sitting on the shelf above the dolls' house. She'd spent hours arranging and rearranging the furniture inside, pretending this was the house she would have when she grew up. How simple her wishes and dreams had been. Her eyes strayed to Dobbin, her old rocking horse, standing in the middle of the room waiting for his mount. He was the most patient of all the horses she'd ever had, rocking on command and never straying into dangerous places. Not like Velvet, who'd led her into danger. She pushed the thought away, but it was getting more difficult to keep memories from straying into her conscious mind from the corners in which they lurked.

The sleeping child stirred, murmured, and slept again. Kirsty leaned her head against the soft back of the chair and gazed across at the dim outline; a small mound in the bed and a fuzzy halo of hair spread out on the pillow.

Her heart ached with an anguish she couldn't dampen; a pain that intensified as time passed. Tears filled her eyes.

How was she going to cope, watching her child grow and develop when each new change increased the agony? If it was unbearable now, what would it be like in years to come?

Meggie, a small, plump woman who had been part of the Campbell household for the past twenty-two years, pulled her clothes on and combed her light-brown hair. She listened for a moment, but no sound came from the nursery. Ailsa wasn't awake yet. Thank goodness for that – today would be busy enough, so at least she could get on with the things that needed doing just now.

She opened the door into the nursery and crept in. She pulled the bedcover over the child's arm, smiling as she did so. Ailsa looked as if she might sleep for hours. A slight movement attracted Meggie's attention, and she tiptoed over to the armchair. Kirsty's eyes were closed but flickered open as Meggie leaned over her.

'Hush.' Meggie nodded toward Ailsa. 'We don't want to wake her, not yet, anyway.'

'I'm sorry,' Kirsty murmured. 'I shouldn't be here. Mama wouldn't like it.' Her hazel eyes, more green than brown, swam with unshed tears.

'No, I don't think she would.' Meggie's heart ached, knowing only too well what Kirsty was suffering. They were both her girls, in a way. She'd been nursemaid to Kirsty from the day she was born, nursed her through illnesses, covered up for her when she was naughty, cried with her, laughed with her, loved her and mothered her. Now she was doing the same for Ailsa.

Kirsty stood.

'I'd better go. You won't tell Mama, will you?'

'Of course not.' Meggie put an arm around the girl's shoulders. 'But you're cold.' She walked to the door with Kirsty. 'Come on, I'll help you dress and do your hair. It'll be like old times.'

The corridor seemed endless. Kirsty had moved out of the nursery when Ailsa came, as was only right, but the room they had given her was at the opposite end of the house which, in Meggie's opinion, was too far away. If she'd been nearer, Meggie could still have looked after both her girls.

'You're spoiling me,' Kirsty said after Meggie finished buttoning her dress and started to brush her hair.

'Well, what of it?' Meggie replied. 'Haven't I done that all your life?' It was nice to feel the brush in her hands again and she took pride in the firm strokes which made Kirsty's long, wavy hair gleam with its auburn tint. It reminded her of Kirsty as she'd been before, a girl who'd bubbled with happiness and mischief and feared nothing. She sighed as she laid the brush back on to the dressing-table.

'What are you thinking?' Kirsty's green-brown eyes stared at her from the mirror. 'You just came over all pensive.'

'Nothing much,' Meggie responded. 'I was just thinking about the old times and wondering why things can't stay the same and why we all have to change.' She put her arms around Kirsty and hugged her. 'You were never one to brood, Kirsty. It pains me to see you like this.' Her arms tightened around the girl's shoulders. 'Don't you think you've paid enough? Isn't it time for you to live again?'

9

Kirsty couldn't get Meggie's words out of her mind. They whispered and buzzed with an insistence that refused to go away, probing into areas of her consciousness that had long been closed. They were with her as she descended the stairs to the breakfast-room and still with her when she said good morning to her father.

The room was bright with the early sun and Kirsty wished they could eat all of their meals here rather than in the darker, more formal dining-room. The breakfast-room, with its southern exposure and views over the lawns, inhabited by strutting peacocks, was friendlier.

Breakfast was an informal meal in the Campbell household, with family members coming to the table at different times. Robert Campbell, who had to drive into Dundee to attend to his mill, was always first, so it didn't surprise Kirsty to see her father had finished eating and had now turned his attention to the newspaper.

Robert, a tall man with stooped shoulders and unruly, reddish-brown hair, becoming increasingly sprinkled with grey, was a kind man at heart. He knew how to assert his authority, but his workers and his family respected him. He loved his family and considered it his duty to protect them from the evils of the world; he also prided himself on being a conscientious man who worked the same hours as his employees. The option of going to the mill later, because he was the owner, would never have occurred to him.

He looked up from his newspaper and nodded to Kirsty.

'You are up early this morning, my dear.'

'I couldn't sleep, Papa.' Kirsty ladled porridge out of the tureen into a bowl and carried it to the table.

'Mmm.' Her father turned a page in his newspaper.

Kirsty spooned some porridge into her mouth. The silences between herself and her father bothered her; lately, they had become longer and more difficult. She never knew what to say to him, though it hadn't always been that way. There had been a time when they'd had plenty to say to each other, but that, like so many other things, seemed so lost in the past she sometimes thought she might have imagined it.

'Papa,' she ventured. 'I was wondering . . .'

'Yes, Kirsty?' He placed his paper on the table and helped himself to tea from the silver pot.

'Well, it's just that my life is so aimless. I wondered if there was anything I could do. You know, a job or something. I need to get out of the house.' She toyed with her spoon, afraid to look at him. 'Maybe I could do something at the mill?'

Her father laughed.

'Out of the question. I can't have you at the mill. It would not be proper.'

'Why not? You used to take me there when I was a child.'

'That was different. Those were visits to let you see how our living is made.' He sipped his tea. 'No, Kirsty.'

'If I'd been your son, you would allow it.' Kirsty suspected it had disappointed her father that his only child was not a boy.

'That is not the point. You are my daughter and it is not appropriate. I'll hear no more about it.'

'Something else, then? University, perhaps? More women are being accepted now. Maybe I could train to be a teacher.'

'No, Kirsty.' Her father's voice rose and he pulled his shaggy eyebrows together in a frown. 'People would think I couldn't support my daughter. You will stay here in this house until you find a husband. Until then, busy yourself here or do some charity work.' He picked up his paper. 'Discussion closed, and I mean it.'

Angry heat coursed through Kirsty's body. Restraining herself, she laid her spoon on the table. With exaggerated carefulness, she pushed the plate away, her appetite swallowed up by anger.

'Good morning, Robert, Kirsty.' Ellen Campbell, a plump, motherly looking woman, entered the room and, walking over to her husband, kissed him on the cheek. Even at the breakfast table, she was formally dressed for the day, her brown hair pinned up on top of her head. Kirsty had never seen her mother's hair hanging loose, and she often wondered if it was as long as her own.

Robert glanced up from his paper.

'Good morning, my dear. You slept well, I hope?'

'Yes, dear.' Ellen helped herself to porridge and sat. She lifted her spoon and then frowned at Kirsty's full plate. 'Aren't you hungry this morning, Kirsty, dear?'

'No, Mama.' Kirsty struggled to keep her voice even.

'But you must eat something.' Ellen sipped porridge from the end of her spoon. Everything she did was ladylike. 'It was only the other day Maud Wilberforce was telling me that her Janie never eats breakfast and now she's prone to fainting fits. They can't take her anywhere for fear she swoons.'

'Yes, Mama.' Kirsty reached for a slice of toast. 'Will this satisfy you?' She didn't care if her mother heard the resentment in her voice. She was tired of being treated like a child and wished her parents would see her as the woman she had become. But she knew that was a vain hope; in their eyes, she would remain a child forever.

'Is there anything exciting in the *Dundee Courier*?' Ellen never read the newspaper and relied on her husband to provide her with any titbits of news.

Robert Campbell turned over a page in his paper.

'I notice Winston Churchill is in Dundee today. He's speaking at the Kinnaird Hall this afternoon and evening. The afternoon meeting is for women only. Whatever next?'

Kirsty scraped butter on to her toast.

'I've heard so much about this Winston Churchill, I wouldn't mind going to the meeting this afternoon.'

Her father rustled his newspaper and frowned at her over

the top of it.

'Political meetings are no place for you, Kirsty.'

'Why not? Why shouldn't I go to a political meeting if I want?'

Her father slapped his paper on to the table.

'It is no place for a decent woman to be seen.'

'But the meeting is for *women*, Papa.' Kirsty frowned in puzzlement. 'What harm can come to me?'

Robert Campbell's face turned red.

'I will not have any daughter of mine mixing with the type of women who attend such meetings.'

'What kind of women would that be?' Kirsty had trouble controlling her voice.

'Suffragettes, that's who!'

Robert slapped the table with his fist. 'I will not have my daughter becoming involved with those banner-waving, window-breaking, trouble-making –' he was running out of breath and adjectives – 'women.'

'I see,' Kirsty said and left the table before she exploded with rage.

Ellen jumped as the door slammed behind Kirsty.

'Whatever's taken the girl today? She's usually so amenable.'

Robert glowered at the closed door.

'She had the cheek to argue with me. Me? Her father? She hasn't done that since before that bit of bother she got into. But she needn't think she'll get the better of me.'

'Calm down, Robert.' Ellen gazed at her husband with concern. She hadn't seen him so upset since Kirsty had her 'bit of trouble', as he called it.

'I will not calm down. That girl has always been troublesome.' He frowned, his fingers beating a staccato rhythm on the table. 'She says she wants more freedom . . . Well, maybe you can forget the disgrace she brought on this family, but I can't. Mark my words, Ellen – she's becoming defiant, and it spells trouble.'

'But she's been really good lately. I'm sure it's just a little upset,' Ellen soothed, but her forehead creased with an anxious frown and there was a worried look in her placid, brown eyes.

'You must keep your eye on her,' Robert warned. 'We don't want any repeats.' He rose from the table. 'After all, it is not as if we can trust her.' With that final, damning statement, he strode out of the room.

Ellen stared after him. She was a quiet woman who abhorred discord in her family, and this argument between Kirsty and Robert puzzled her. She felt she must have missed something and wasn't sure what. After breakfast, she would have a quiet word with Kirsty and see if she could smooth things out between them.

10

Kirsty clenched her fists, gritted her teeth and fought the urge to scream. She had never experienced a rage like the one surging through her now, and it was a wonder she contained herself until she reached her bedroom. Once inside, she stood with her back pressed hard against the door, gulping air greedily. But that only fuelled the fire. What right did her father have to dictate to her? But she knew the answer. It was because he was her father and she still lived under his roof. She would have no independence of her own until grandmother's trust fund was hers. And that wouldn't be for several years; until then, she was trapped.

Nervous energy coursed through her body in a quivering wave and she paced the room endlessly, faster and faster, but it wasn't enough to get rid of the three years of repressed feelings which all wanted to burst out of her at once.

She wasn't aware of the first thing she threw until the sound of breaking glass pierced her consciousness and she stared, aghast, at the broken mirror.

Shock paralysed her. She'd done nothing like this before. But the need to strike out was overwhelming. She struggled to control herself, but it was futile. Her emotions swamped her with an intensity that frightened her, and she couldn't stop. She wrenched drawers out, upturning and scattering the contents. She stopped only to catch her breath before she started on her wardrobe, tearing dresses from their hangers and hurling them across the room. Wraps followed, until the place resembled a multi-coloured jumble sale.

Her hands grasped the last dress and, half-crying, half-laughing, she collapsed on the bed in exhaustion. It was several minutes before she realised what she was clutching to her body, and by then it was too late to draw back. It had been years since she had seen this gown, touched it, stroked it, held it. Now, it revolted her.

She wanted to throw it from her, destroy it, burn it – anything to remove it from her sight and her mind. The dress invoked too many reminders, awful memories, of something that should never have happened.

It had started after the day Velvet threw her. She'd landed in a heap in front of Johnnie Bogue, whose own mount pranced around her. Instead of laughing, as she'd expected, he'd leapt from his horse and helped her to her feet.

'You're not hurt, are you?' He'd raised his eyebrows in concern, making her blush because this was Johnnie Bogue, admired by every young girl in Dundee.

'I'm fine,' she'd mumbled, brushing grass from her skirt.

They'd said little more than that, but when their paths kept crossing, Kirsty started to think it was more than a coincidence. To begin with, they reined in their horses and passed the time of day before cantering off. Soon, however, when Johnnie saw her on Velvet, he would turn his horse and trot beside her. They became friends, or so she thought.

She invited him to her fifteenth birthday party and her parents welcomed him. They assumed, in time, Kirsty and Johnnie would make a suitable match, and form a link between two important mill-owning families. Kirsty had laughed at the idea because they were only friends.

Her hand tightened on the silky fabric of the gown. The Bogues had held a magnificent ball to celebrate their son's twenty-first birthday, and Kirsty's invitation was the envy of her friends. The dress, made especially for the event, was pale green organza, with a yellow rose on the neckline. At fifteen, it was her first grown-up ballgown.

How proud she had been to wear it on that eventful night. A night which should have been imprinted on her memory as a happy time, something to be remembered with pleasure. Oh, it was imprinted on her memory, all right, despite all her efforts to erase it.

Even now, the scent of full-blown roses transported her to the summerhouse again. That lovely little summerhouse, which was just far enough away from the Bogue mansion to leave her isolated and alone when Johnnie became overly familiar.

Aunt Bea, who thought she was safe in Johnnie's company, sipped wine and chatted to Amelia Bogue in the ballroom. The band played on, but the sound of music drifting over the lawns had seemed to be coming from a great distance. Guests danced and gossiped and drank and ate; but not one of them heard her cries of, 'No! No!' as the young man, of whom her parents approved, tore at her dress.

Painful memories sent their icy tentacles probing into her brain.

'Complain all you like,' Johnnie Bogue had said when he left her crying in the summerhouse. 'No one will believe you.' There had been a contemptuous expression in his eyes; he'd looked at her as if she were something dirty. 'I'll tell them how you led me on, and I'll say I wasn't the first.' He'd left her then, and she had pulled the fragments of her dress around her before walking the two miles home, thankful no one saw her.

It was only later she had found out he had a weakness for pretty, young girls. The younger they were, the more he liked them.

She'd hidden the gown at the back of her wardrobe, hoping her parents need never know. But then, there was Ailsa, and there was no way she could hide that.

Kirsty's hands tightened on the dress. It stood for everything in her past she hated. It had spoiled her life, just as Johnnie Bogue had. She had lost her parents' trust because they hadn't believed she'd played no part in her downfall. And the daughter she lost became her sister, to maintain the family's respectability.

The yellow rose taunted her and she tore it off. Then she ripped the dress down the middle, tearing it into smaller and ever smaller pieces. It was time to rid herself of the past, throw out the memories and start to live again. And if that meant defying her father, then so be it.

11

'Meggie?' Ellen Campbell, normally so calm and collected, looked flustered.

Meggie sat back on her haunches and looked at her friend and employer hovering at the nursery door.

'Just give me a minute to finish wiping up this mess or someone'll slip on it.' She turned her attention back to the pool of porridge on the floor. 'Our wee Ailsa's been throwing it about again. She's a little madam, so she is.' Pulling herself up, Meggie lifted Ailsa out of her highchair and patted her on the bottom. 'Off you go and play with the dolls' house while I talk to your mama.'

Ellen leaned against the door, her hand on her breast.

'I need you to help me with Kirsty.'

Meggie's concern increased as she saw how upset Ellen was and heard the shortness in her breath.

'Come and sit down.' She crossed the room to Ellen and guided her to the armchair.

'What's up with our Kirsty?' she asked, once Ellen was settled.

'Oh, Meggie, she's had some kind of seizure,' Ellen wailed, 'and I don't know what to do. I spoke to her, but she ignored me. It was as if I wasn't even there. Oh, Meggie, what are we to do?'

'Start from the beginning,' Meggie said. 'You're confusing me. Where is she? And why's she in a state?'

Ellen twisted her hands together.

'She's been funny all morning. Arguing with her father, then storming out of the breakfast-room. So, I thought I'd better go and check if she was all right.'

Leaning forward, she grasped Meggie's hands.

'She was in her room, sitting on the bed. Tears pouring

down her face, but she was laughing. She looked mad. And you should see the room, clothes everywhere, a broken mirror.' Ellen raised her eyes to Meggie's. 'She'd even ripped one of her dresses to pieces. You don't think she's gone mad, do you?'

'No, I'm sure she hasn't. Not our Kirsty.' Meggie freed her hands from Ellen's grasp. 'Why don't I go and see what it's all about?'

'Would you?' Ellen smiled through her tears.

'Of course,' Meggie said. 'Will you keep our Ailsa out of mischief until I get back?'

'Yes, yes,' Ellen said. 'This is her time with me, anyway.'

Meggie hurried through the corridors to Kirsty's room. Poor Kirsty; she'd thought the girl had been hurting when she was in the nursery this morning. Were things getting too much for her?

Meggie pushed open the door. Ellen hadn't exaggerated when she described the mess. If anything, it was worse than she'd portrayed. Meggie closed the door behind her, walked to the bed, sat beside Kirsty and took her in her arms.

'Oh, you poor, poor dear,' she murmured, rocking the girl the way she would have rocked a baby.

Meggie's arms were warm and comforting, the way her mother's arms should have been; but then, Meggie understood her, she always had. Not like her mother, who had never understood the depth of Kirsty's anguish when she relinquished Ailsa. As far as her mother was concerned, she'd offered Kirsty the perfect solution when she covered up for her during the pregnancy by having a phantom one of her own and claiming the child when she was born.

'This way is best,' Kirsty remembered her mother saying. 'You can have Ailsa for a sister instead of not having her at all.'

But although Kirsty couldn't have Ailsa as a daughter, this situation was torturous.

Kirsty shifted in Meggie's embrace and looked at the woman who had been better than a mother to her.

'Why can't she understand?' she whispered. 'Is she so unfeeling?'

'Hush now,' Meggie said. 'She loves you and thinks she's doing what's right.'

Kirsty snorted. 'She's doing what she wants to do. She's taken Ailsa from me and she thinks I'll accept it. But I won't.'

Meggie's hands tightened around Kirsty's shoulders.

'You *have* accepted it. Ailsa's growing fast – it's only three months until her third birthday. She believes you're her sister. You can't change things now. Who's to say it's not for the best?'

Kirsty buried her head on Meggie's shoulder.

'But she's mine,' she wailed. 'I can't stand it any more.'

'Think of Ailsa,' Meggie said. 'Think what her life might be like if it became known she was illegitimate.' Meggie paused, seeming to weigh her words. 'You wouldn't want her known as Kirsty's bastard, would you?'

Kirsty tried to wriggle free from Meggie's grasp, but the woman's arms were strong.

'You're right, you always are. My feelings don't matter, what's more important is Ailsa. I haven't been very sensible.'

Meggie's hands loosened on Kirsty's shoulders.

'That's my good girl. Let's tidy up, shall we?' Meggie picked up dresses from the floor and heaved them on to the bed. 'My, you have had a paddy,' she said as she started to sort them out and hang them back in the wardrobe.

Shame washed over Kirsty.

'It was childish of me,' she admitted. 'But I got so angry because they didn't trust me. They think if they give me a little bit of freedom, I'll bring more disgrace to the family.' She shivered before continuing in a low voice. 'They never believed it wasn't my fault.'

'I know.' Meggie patted her shoulder before gesturing to some of the pieces of the green dress. 'I'll get rid of this,' she said. 'It's not something you should keep.'

Ellen and Ailsa looked like a mother and daughter having fun together as they sat on the floor arranging the furniture in the dolls' house.

Meggie hovered in the doorway to the nursery and sighed as she thought of Kirsty, alone in her bedroom.

Ellen scrambled to her feet.

'Is Kirsty all right?'

'She's fine now,' Meggie said. 'It's just that she hurts so much. I think it became a bit too much for her this year.'

'I thought she'd got over it a long time ago.' Ellen frowned. 'What can we do?'

'The lass doesn't have enough in her life to keep her mind off things. Maybe if you gave her a wee bit more freedom?' Meggie let the suggestion hang in the air.

'But her father says she has all the freedom she needs. We provide her with money to spend. And she can come and go as she wants, within limits.'

'Maybe she needs a wee bit more than that.'

'But look what happened last time.' Ellen's eyes moved to look at Ailsa. 'We thought we were being progressive parents, and we were simply being foolish.'

'It wasn't her fault.' Meggie stared at Ellen until she looked away.

'So Kirsty said.' Ellen twisted her handkerchief in her hands. 'But she must have led him on and who's to say the same might not happen again?'

'That was over three years ago,' Meggie reminded her. 'Don't you think it's maybe time you trusted her?'

12

Martha woke early, but Ethel had already left for work. She had high hopes of the girl – one of the best they'd recruited in Dundee. It hadn't taken Ethel long to understand all there was to know about the suffrage cause and she'd already proved her worth at meetings and in some of their more militant activities. Although the Women's Freedom League wasn't as violent as the Women's Social and Political Union, they did their share of fighting for the cause. Ethel was ready and willing. It was just too bad she had to work – that cut the time she was available. As it was, she'd miss the meeting this afternoon at the Kinnaird Hall.

Martha's house, like all the others in the Nethergate, formed the upper storeys of the buildings above the shops. The WFL office was situated in one of these shops. It formed part of the building where Martha lived, and it only took seconds for her to reach it after she'd breakfasted.

'Hello, Lila.' She breezed through the door. 'Is that a new banner?'

Lila Clunas looked up.

'Do you like it? I found a dressmaker who can make them in next to no time.' She held out the flag for Martha's inspection.

'I like the motto underneath the rampant lion, *"Now's the Day and Now's the Hour"*. Yes, I like it.' Martha fingered the banner. 'Good, strong material. It might even survive people trying to tear it out of our hands.'

'How's Ethel settling in?' Lila folded the banner and placed it on a shelf.

'She's at work today. Pity, she will miss the meeting this afternoon.'

'She can join us tonight when we storm the men's

meeting.' She took some leaflets from the shelf. 'They have no right to make the meetings exclusively male or female. They think they're pandering to women, keeping us quiet by giving us our own meeting. We'll have to change their minds for them. After all, we have to consider our sisters who are working women and can't attend afternoon meetings. Your Ethel is a good example of that.'

'I thought, through time, Ethel might make an excellent organiser. She has a good grasp of what it's all about, she's keen and has the spirit for it. It would get her out of the mill, which would make her more available for the cause.'

'It's too early, Martha.' Lila smiled. 'I know she is your protégé, but you know what they say, before you can become a suffragette, there are three forms of baptism – be thrown out of a cabinet minister's meeting, go to prison, and fight in a by-election. Ethel hasn't even passed the first post.'

'I suppose you are right, but don't forget those are the WSPU forms of baptism, not ours. And some of them might be difficult to achieve in Scotland. Ethel is not in a position to travel to London or go to prison because she works.' Martha paused. 'I still think she would make a good organiser.'

A draught of wind fluttered the papers on the table and the two women made a grab for them.

'I say, ladies. Didn't mean to send your pamphlets flying.' The tall, young man placed his silver-topped cane on the shop counter before bending to rescue the fluttering leaflets.

'Oh, it's you, Archie. I assume Constance is still in London?' Lila stacked the leaflets into bundles on the table. 'Have you come to help, or are you just here to amuse yourself?'

'Now, now, ladies. You know I take an interest in everything you do. I can just see it now, women wielding the vote. It'd add a bit of spice to some of the dullards we've got in parliament. What ho?'

'If you want to help, you could take some of the leaflets

and pass them around your friends.' Lila grinned as she challenged him.

'And get myself lynched?' Archie shuddered. 'Tell you what, though. I don't mind scattering them through Dundee as I pass on my merry way. Anything to help the cause, as you term it.'

Martha shoved a pile of leaflets into his hands.

'Off you go, then.' There was something about Archie that unnerved her. It was his eyes – blue and piercing, they always seemed to watch her. She shrugged the feeling away. 'Will you be at Winston Churchill's meeting this evening?'

'I wouldn't miss it for the world, even if only to see what you ladies are up to.'

'It will be an exciting evening, I promise you.' Lila grinned at him.

Martha busied herself stacking leaflets into piles for the volunteers to collect, only looking up again when she heard the door close behind him.

'Why do you think Archie keeps coming here?' Martha watched him as he sauntered along the street.

'That's obvious,' Lila said. 'He's attracted to you. Hadn't you noticed?'

'I don't have time for that kind of nonsense. Besides, he's married to Constance,' Martha snapped, feeling unsettled and annoyed. 'I'm off to hand out leaflets.'

She gathered up a bundle and left the office as the first group of volunteers arrived. Lila would have her hands full preparing them for the demonstrations today but, despite a brief pang of guilt at leaving Lila to do it all, she walked to the city centre to distribute the leaflets.

She enjoyed her job as an organiser for the Women's Freedom League and she liked Dundee. The women here were warm and friendly, though the men were more aggressive. However, that was nothing out of the ordinary because men, in general, resented the suffragettes who aroused violent emotions and reactions from them. Educated men were always the worst because of their own unrecognised fear that women might question the God-given right men had to wield authority over them and change the order of society.

Martha had been fortunate. Her family had never treated the female members any differently from the males. She had been brought up to regard male dominance of women as something to be detested. Unfortunately, many women accepted this dominance as normal having been subservient, first to a father, then to a husband. Martha's mission in life was to educate as many women as possible into believing they didn't have to accept this state of affairs; women had rights. Her involvement in the WFL allowed her a free rein to do this, and she took pride in recruiting as many women as possible to the cause.

She smiled as she handed out leaflets and it pleased her when a woman took time to read what she'd pressed into her hand, frowning ever so slightly when it was screwed up and thrown away. Sometimes, she thought leaflets did no good, although every little thing helped. She was good at the small things but, with something bigger, she was a failure.

Martha never forgot that she'd been tested and found wanting. Oh, she'd done all the things that suffragettes were supposed to do. She'd demonstrated in London, broken her share of shop windows, been thrown out of meetings. Once, she even tried to get into Buckingham Palace to present a petition to the King. She didn't get anywhere near him, but it generated a fair bit of publicity.

Where she had failed was prison. She'd been proud when they arrested her. It had been the apogee of her career as a suffragette. She had held her head high in court and been offensive to the magistrate, who'd responded by sending her to Holloway Prison along with Mary Phillips and Annot Robinson.

Martha could have coped with prison if it hadn't been for the hunger strike and forcible feeding. But she couldn't tolerate the tubes and the savagery of the prison staff, so she'd given up. The Women's Freedom League didn't hold it against her, though she knew if she had been in the WSPU, the Pankhursts would have taken a different view. Still, she felt it was a failure and she had never stopped trying to make up for it.

'Leaflet, madam.' She thrust a leaflet into the hand of a stylishly dressed lady who looked at it in disgust and pushed it back at her. Martha sighed. It was time she went to the meeting. With luck, she'd be thrown out and spark more publicity for the cause.

13

Kirsty lifted her skirts to run across the grass. The house had become oppressive. She needed to escape, and there was only one place to go. The gazebo stood at the end of the lawn, within sight of the house but far enough away to offer privacy. It had always been where Kirsty hid when she needed a quiet place to think; she longed for that now.

She sat, leaning her head against the wooden panels, and looked over at the distant river. A sailing ship drifted seawards on the outgoing tide, a whaler off to the Arctic, perhaps. She envied the men on board, able to go anywhere they wanted; they didn't have to fight for their freedom.

From her vantage point, she could see most of Broughty Ferry. The streets, busy with passers-by, looking more like ants from this distance, horses pulling their carts, a few cars, and a train chuffing and puffing its way out of the station, bound for Dundee. It appeared to Kirsty that everyone in the world had more freedom than she did. She pressed her lips together in annoyance. It was time she asserted herself, but before that, she had to decide what to do about Ailsa.

Meggie's words still echoed in her mind: *'Kirsty's bastard.'* It would tear her apart if that were how her daughter came to be known. But it would also break her heart to deny her.

A peacock strutted past the gazebo, stopping to fan out his tail-feathers in a colourful display of eyes. It reminded Kirsty of all the eyes that watched her and how many more there would be if the truth about Ailsa became known.

She couldn't hurt her daughter. She would have to leave, maybe not now but some time in the future, when she was financially independent. She groaned. The money her parents gave her wasn't enough for her to live on. If she were to survive on her own, she would have to find some way of earning it. But her father was right – there was nothing she was qualified to do.

In any case, the world frightened her. Everything she had ever done involved her family. How would she survive on her own? The peacock screeched. Even he was contemptuous of her ability to win independence, but she determined to assert herself and show them all. Her mouth pursed in a stubborn line. She could begin today and go to the meeting her father had forbidden her to attend. That, at least, would feel like a start. And, when the time came to leave home, she promised herself she would be ready.

The breeze ruffled her hair while she listened to the birds singing in the orchard behind her. The ship in the estuary was moving out of sight now, while the peacock had evidently decided she wasn't worth bothering about and had moved to a different part of the garden.

Distant sounds, voices and hammering, impinged on the quiet of the afternoon. Strange men scurried about the lawn in front of the house, pulling and pushing at a massive red-and-white-striped, tented structure. Workmen hammered guy-ropes into the ground; it wouldn't be long before the marquee took shape. It was the preparation for her mother's garden party.

Kirsty's mood plummeted. She should be there helping, but she couldn't bring herself to do that. She didn't even want to be in the house while the preparations were going on and she didn't want to attend the party. A black cloud settled on her. She had to escape. Gathering up her skirts, she slipped out of the gazebo, around the side of the house, up to her bedroom for a wrap and what little money she had, and left without a backward glance.

Ellen had no time to worry about Kirsty after the men turned up to erect the marquee.

'We'll have it at this end of the lawn,' she had instructed, pointing out the preferred spot. A quick glance told her that

Kirsty was still sitting in the gazebo, so she hurried inside to give cook instructions on how she wanted the tables laid out. Everything had to be ready before the guests appeared and she didn't think she should ask Kirsty for help. The girl might have another outburst; Ellen shuddered at the thought.

Ailsa came running out of the door, her feet skimming across the grass until she crashed into Ellen's skirts.

'Mama, Mama!' the child squealed, her eyes round with wonder. 'Can I come to the party?'

'Of course you can, my darling, but it doesn't start until later.' Ellen swung the child into her arms. 'Come and watch the strong men putting up the tent. Isn't it gay?' She held Ailsa close to her as they looked at the red-and-white-striped canvas tent, Ellen with critical eyes while Ailsa's grew even rounder.

'Will there be ice-cream, Mama? And cakes and jelly and sweets?'

'All that and more.'

Meggie panted her way towards them.

'I'm sorry,' she said, 'the little minx ran away from me.' She held out her arms for Ailsa. 'Come on, we have to get you cleaned up.'

'Not dirty.' Ailsa wriggled.

'Yes, my love, but what about your pretty dress? The one your mama bought for you. Don't you want to wear that?'

Ellen watched them return to the house before she continued with her inspection. Once that was done, she would join Kirsty for a short time so they could chat.

She strode towards the gazebo, but Kirsty was no longer there. Neither was she in the orchard nor any other part of the garden. A tiny pang of fear fluttered in Ellen's breast and she tried to fight it down. Kirsty must be in the house, there was nowhere else she could be. Still, the niggle was there. Kirsty had been strange today, talking about freedom and being cooped up here with nothing to do.

'Meggie will know where she is,' Ellen muttered aloud.

But Meggie hadn't seen Kirsty. Together, they searched the house but there was no sign of her.

'Where do you think she can be?' Ellen wailed. 'She couldn't have left home. Where would she go?'

'She's probably just gone to the town,' Meggie soothed. 'She wasn't looking forward to the party, and she said something about a meeting today.'

'But her father forbade her to attend it.' Ellen's voice held a tone of horror.

'In the mood she was in,' Meggie said, 'that's probably the reason she's gone. Don't worry about her. She'll be back.'

'I suppose you're right.' Ellen twisted her handkerchief between her hands. 'What on earth am I going to tell her father?'

'She'll probably be back home before he is, so don't concern yourself too much,' Meggie said. 'Let's just concentrate on the party.'

14

Kirsty sped down the drive, determined to continue on her way even if she were challenged. But the drive was quiet; everyone was busy at the other side of the house. She supposed she should have told her mother what she intended to do, but that didn't fit in with her mood of defiance and act of rebellion. She would face her parents when she came back. They couldn't keep her captive any longer, though she had to admit, at times it had been a willing captivity requiring neither lock nor key.

The walk to the railway station was invigorating and her mood soon lifted. She had never travelled alone on a train before, but it couldn't be too difficult. Other people did it every day. When she got to the station, though, it felt strange and alarming. Men and women bantered with each other on the crowded platform while Kirsty hung back and listened. She had never been part of such a group before and their sidelong glances convinced her they had marked her out as different.

When the train chugged to a stop at the platform, it frightened the life out of her with its puffing and blowing out great clouds of steam, smoke and sparks. She almost regretted not telling her mother and arranging for their carriage to take her to town. She told herself not to be silly. If it was independence she wanted, she'd have to face up to a lot more than this, so she gathered her skirts together and got on the train.

Mama, Aunt Bea or Meggie usually accompanied Kirsty to Dundee, so it was strange being in the town centre on her own. Strange, but exciting. The crowds thronging the pavements were daunting at first, but Kirsty soon became used to them and walked among them as if she had been doing it all her life.

Now and then, she stopped to look in shop windows and even ventured into Draffen and Jarvie's department store, where she fingered fabrics and considered the latest pattern designs. Maybe Mama would allow her to have more up-to-date fashions the next time the dressmaker called for orders.

It was still early, so she walked to the Queens Hotel in the Nethergate. This was always where Mama went for tea and scones when she was in Dundee. Kirsty had never entered a hotel on her own before and wasn't sure if that was what ladies did. She inhaled deeply, pasted a confident smile on her face and climbed the stairs to the dining-room, even though her insides were quaking. Several tables were occupied; with her confidence waning a little, she allowed herself to be led to a quiet one in the corner. She peeled off her gloves for, even though it was a warm June day, ladies always wore gloves. The waitress hovered at her side, making her nervous, but she steeled herself.

'Afternoon tea, please,' she said, in her best imitation of Mama.

'Certainly, madam.' The waitress appeared almost immediately with a three-tier cake stand filled with dainty, triangular sandwiches on the bottom plate; scones, pancakes and muffins on the middle one; and, on the top, the most delightful variety of iced cakes.

Kirsty, feeling independent, poured tea from the silver teapot and helped herself to one of the floury scones for which the Queens Hotel was renowned.

She left the hotel more confident than when she first arrived. With a spring in her step, she walked to Bank Street and the Kinnaird Hall, where the size of the crowd gathered outside astonished her. She hadn't realised so many women would be interested in attending, but she supposed Winston Churchill was becoming well-known in politics and it wasn't often he came to speak in Dundee.

As she hovered, uncertain how to proceed, a young woman approached.

'Is this your first time?'

'Yes.' Kirsty nodded. 'It's all a bit overwhelming.'

The woman laughed.

'I suppose it is, but stay with me and I'll see you get in.'

'That's very kind of you,' Kirsty said.

'My name's Martha.' She held out a hand and grasped Kirsty's.

'I'm Kirsty Campbell.' Kirsty returned the handshake.

'Well, Kirsty –' Martha tucked Kirsty's arm through her own '– just follow me and look demure so we don't get thrown out before we're in.' Martha looked her up and down. 'I'm wasting my breath. You don't need to act, just be yourself.'

Martha was a small, dainty woman with dark-gold hair and the most amazing blue eyes. The hat perched on her curls at a jaunty angle was much more fashionable than Kirsty's own bonnet. Her dress was the latest model, and she carried an exquisite, frilly parasol. But she had a gleam in her eyes that Kirsty couldn't quite identify and an air of excitement that seemed totally inappropriate for a political meeting.

Despite Martha being smaller than Kirsty, she pushed her way through the crowd with an expertise Kirsty envied. Once inside, she found them two seats near the front of the hall.

'Exciting, isn't it?' Martha said as she settled in her seat. She looked around, waving to a few women in the audience.

'You know quite a lot of people here,' Kirsty said.

'I'll introduce you to some of them later.' Martha fell silent as the meeting began.

Kirsty was a bit disappointed with Winston Churchill. She'd thought he would be a man like her father, but he was younger and didn't have as much presence.

He'd hardly started to speak when Martha stood up.

'What do you intend to do about the franchise for women?'

Martha's voice was clear and audible, ringing out and attracting the audience's attention, making Kirsty think how brave she was. Kirsty would never have dared to stand up or ask a question.

Stewards, who were parading the hall, descended on Martha, pinning her arms behind her and forcing her out of her seat. Martha kicked and screamed and hit out with her parasol as the two burly stewards attempted to twist her arms up her back. One of the men tore the parasol out of her grasp, tossed it on to the floor and then swiped her face with the back of his hand, knocking her hat off. Her hair, escaping from its fastenings, flew all over the place, cascading down her back and flopping over her face. Two more men descended on her and between them, they manhandled her out of the hall, one of them taking the opportunity to rub her breasts with his hands.

Kirsty stared in horror. She'd never seen a woman treated so violently before and it left her shocked, shaken, and at a loss. She wanted to jump up and protest but feared she might receive the same treatment. The thought terrified her. She gripped the wooden arms of her seat, forcing her attention back to the speaker while Martha's hat and parasol lay at her feet, reminding her of the nice young woman who had befriended her.

15

Martha's face stung from the steward's vicious slap, but he had her arms pinned behind her back and she couldn't retaliate.

'Take your hands off me, you brute.' Martha struggled, feet flailing toward the men's shins as they lifted her from her seat in the hall. 'Beasts, pigs, animals!' she hissed, as her feet struck flesh. 'Although that's an insult to animals.'

'Ouch!' The man who uttered the screech twisted Martha's arm further up her back, making her squeal in pain. 'Kick me again, and I'll break your bloody arm.'

'Oh, come off it, Sid.' The second man twisted her other arm up her back. 'We're only meant to eject them, and if you haven't learned to keep your legs out of the way of their feet, that's your lookout.'

'Too bloody soft for this job, that's what you are,' Sid muttered. 'I'll be glad when we get this spitting cat outside.'

'See how these two brave men treat women,' Martha screamed. Her feet kicked the air with vicious swipes as the two men carried her by the arms out of the hall. They flung her out the door and she tumbled down the steps, landing on her knees in the road. She turned to spit at them, but they grinned at her, dusted their hands and returned to the hall.

'Are you all right?' Helen Archdale bent over Martha and helped her to her feet. 'They threw me out earlier, but they were rougher with you. The stewards who ejected me were gentlemen by comparison.'

Martha winced as she brushed earth from her skirt; her arms and hands stinging from the stones embedded in her scraped skin.

'It's the luck of the draw. Anyway, rough handling hurt no one, and it's all meat for the cause.' Her arms ached from the pressure of the men's grip and her breasts were sore, but she was sure nothing was broken. She would have bruises tomorrow, but she didn't care. She was accustomed to them and it made up for her other failings.

Helen leaned against the façade of the building, turning her face to catch the sun.

'Did you know there's a new reporter started with the *Dundee Courier*? He's moved from a newspaper in Glasgow and he seems more sensitive to our cause than the others.'

'That will make a change. Good publicity instead of bad.' Martha brushed her skirt with her hands. 'Strange, though, coming from Glasgow to Dundee. Isn't that a step down for him?'

'I'll bring him to our meeting on Sunday at the Mathers Hotel if you want,' Helen offered. 'You can judge for yourself.'

After watching how the stewards had treated her new friend, Kirsty cowered back in her seat for fear they would return and manhandle her. It had been her own stubbornness that brought her to this meeting, a petty defiance because her father ridiculed her and forbade her to attend. If it hadn't been for that and her genuine interest in the speaker, she wouldn't have been tempted to come. When she arrived, it had been confusing, not the orderly affair she'd thought it would be, and Martha had helped her find a seat. The young woman had been polite, helpful, kind and not any different from Kirsty, herself. Kirsty had taken to her and thought she seemed nice.

Kirsty couldn't understand it. It wasn't as if Martha had done anything awful. She had only asked a question. And, even though men didn't like women questioning them, Kirsty could see no reason for the rough treatment meted out. Recalling the steward's hands on Martha's breasts brought back memories of her own ordeal and she started to worry what might happen to her new friend outside the hall.

I should have helped her, Kirsty thought. Instead, I sat

here like the mouse I am and did nothing. But it wasn't too late. Sighing at her own stupidity for not minding her own business, she snatched the abandoned hat and parasol from the floor and squeezed her way out of the row of seats before hurrying for the exit.

Clustered in small groups outside were several women, in varying degrees of dishevelment, all of them ejected from the hall. She soon spotted Martha conversing with a tall woman older than herself. Kirsty hesitated, not wishing to interrupt, but she had rescued Martha's hat and parasol and wanted to return them to her.

Martha saw her coming and turned to her with a smile.

'Kirsty, isn't it? Did you get thrown out as well?'

Kirsty handed her the hat.

'No, I'm afraid I didn't,' she apologised, although why she should feel apologetic, she didn't know. Maybe it was because Martha took so much pride in her ejection. 'You lost your hat and parasol,' she mumbled. 'I thought you'd need them.'

'That is exceedingly kind of you. Isn't it, Helen? Few people would rescue a suffragette's bonnet.' She took the hat from Kirsty and tucked her curls underneath until she looked presentable.

Kirsty swallowed. What a fool not to have realised Martha was a suffragette. One of the women her father talked about so disparagingly. But Martha wasn't an ogre or a woman pretending to be a man, she was just an ordinary woman, like Kirsty. The only other time Kirsty had met a suffragette had been at the Albert Square meeting the previous Saturday. Curiosity got the better of her.

'What is it suffragettes do? Apart from getting thrown out of meetings.' She laughed self-consciously.

'It would take a long time to explain,' Martha said. 'Although the main aim is to fight for women to have a vote.'

'What good would that do?' Kirsty had never felt any need to vote, thinking politics beyond her intellect.

'It would give women more independence. We'd have a

right to say who represented us in parliament and we'd make sure we voted for people who would stand up for women and give them a say in their own lives. Men wouldn't be able to control us in the way they've always done.' Martha paused for breath. 'If you're interested, come to our meeting at the Mathers Hotel on Sunday afternoon. Here, I'll write the address for you.' Martha scrabbled in her bag for a pencil and wrote the details on the back of a leaflet.

The thought of independence intrigued Kirsty, fuelling her newly aroused rebellious feelings.

'Thank you,' she said. 'I'll try to be there.'

She scurried off, eager to get home but feeling more alive than she'd felt for a long time.

Martha watched Kirsty hurry away. She had liked the girl when they met in the crowd before the meeting. At first, she had thought Kirsty was a sister, a member of the cause, but after talking to her it was clear she was not. Martha, however, had the knack of spotting women who could be recruited, and she'd taken care to encourage the girl. It had paid off because Kirsty had followed her out of the meeting with her bonnet and parasol.

'I can tell what you're thinking.' Helen also watched the girl leave. 'Why didn't you ask her to come along to the demonstration tonight?'

'I thought about it, but she's very new to all this and I didn't want to scare her. Too much too soon can be overwhelming, particularly for someone like Kirsty.'

'Mmm,' Helen murmured. 'She seemed a bit naïve. But there's also a spark there. Didn't you feel it? Maybe she'll be ready earlier than you think.'

'The meeting on Sunday should be a fruitful one if both Kirsty and this new reporter come along. Isn't it exciting?' Martha jiggled from foot to foot. 'We're really expanding in Dundee. We'll soon have as many members as Glasgow or Edinburgh.'

'Talking about excitement, let's join the others and plan

our action for tonight. I heard tell someone is planning to enter the hall from a skylight on the roof.' Helen tucked Martha's hand into the crook of her arm. 'Come,' she said. 'There's much to do before tonight's little exercise.'

16

The excitement Kirsty felt, generated by her foray into Dundee, dissipated as she returned home. Her mother's party was in full swing and the beat of the music, along with the buzz of voices, seeped out of the marquee, across the lawn.

Several children were playing tag on the grass and a sliver of pain pierced her heart. Ailsa was among the screaming horde, and Kirsty ached to be with her. To take her rightful place as Ailsa's mother. But that role had been usurped by her own mother, and the thought of joining the children's game was too much for her to bear.

She turned her back on the marquee and ran to the house. No one would miss her, nor would they care. But Kirsty's attempt to sneak into the house unseen failed – her mother spotted her before she could slip through the back door.

'Where have you been? You know I was relying on your help this afternoon.'

Guilt swept through Kirsty as her mother berated her. Was she as selfish as her mother seemed to think?

'I'm sorry, Mama. It was all too much for me. I had to get away.'

'Where did you go?' Her mother's voice developed a strident tone, unlike her usual placid one.

'Dundee.'

'You can't have gone to visit Aunt Bea, because she's here. So, where on earth did you find to go?'

Kirsty scowled. This was ridiculous. It was time her mother stopped treating her like a child. Now that she was eighteen, almost nineteen, she was an adult and her parents should treat her like one. She squared her shoulders and glared at her mother.

'I went to the meeting at the Kinnaird Hall. I wanted to

hear Winston Churchill speak.'

Her mother struggled for words. 'But your father forbade you to attend,' she managed at last.

'I think I'm old enough to make my own decisions,' Kirsty snapped. She turned and pushed through the door into the corridor beyond, leaving her mother, spluttering, outside.

'We'll see what your father has to say!'

Kirsty heard the statement echo after her as the door swung shut behind her.

Tears of anger nipped her eyes as she stumbled up the stairs to the sanctuary of her bedroom. Once there, she tossed her hat on the floor and collapsed on the bed in a fit of weeping. Other young women could lead independent lives. They weren't tied down by silly rules. Why were things so different for her? Why was she unable to live up to her parents' expectations?

For the first time, Kirsty began to question if those expectations were even realistic or desirable. Her father expected her to be a lady, to fit into society, to marry well, and be a credit to him. But, if they never allowed her any freedom to mix in society and continued to treat her as a child, how could she achieve any of this? As for meeting young men, that was frowned upon. Not that she was interested in meeting any. Her one, disastrous encounter with a man had killed any interest she might have in the opposite sex. She wasn't like other young girls who dreamed of meeting a boy and marrying. Instinctively, Kirsty knew that even though she felt undecided about what she wanted from life, she did not want that.

The sound of children's laughter outside floated up to her window, a reminder that her mother expected her to help. Kirsty sat up and swung her feet off the bed, walked to her bedroom door and locked it. Her mother could wait all evening for her to join in; she had no intention of budging from her room.

Ellen Campbell stared at the door through which her

daughter had stormed. What on earth had come over Kirsty? First, that scene this morning, which had left Ellen feeling useless, and now this. Meggie had been here to calm Kirsty after breakfast, but now the nursery maid had needed to take time off at short notice to tend to her unwell sister in Arbroath. What was Ellen to do?

She paced back and forth outside the door, torn between whether to return to the marquee or follow Kirsty and try to make her see reason. Robert wouldn't be home until later. He'd made the excuse this morning that he would have to stay late at the mill. Ellen knew perfectly well it was because he disliked parties and preferred the workplace. Resentment edged into her mind. He expected her to maintain a particular social image but did nothing to help her with it. He also had a responsibility to help her with any problems which arose, like the problem she now had with Kirsty. Why didn't he realise his place was by her side?

Music and laughter drifted over the lawn. She took two steps towards the marquee before changing her mind and, pushing open the back door, slipped into the house in search of her daughter. Inside, doors led off to the kitchen and scullery areas, while a flight of stone stairs led upwards. Ellen was unfamiliar with this part of the house, which was the servants' domain, but she guessed Kirsty must have used the stairs to get to her bedroom.

The hardness of the stone steps and the clack of her shoes echoing upwards unnerved her. She grasped the wooden bannister, making her way to the top and passing through the door to the safety of the main part of the house. She was more at home on the carpeted corridors at the top of the ornate stairway leading up from the rooms below.

Ellen's footsteps, now noiseless on the carpet, sped along the corridor to Kirsty's bedroom. She paused outside to allow a moment to control her breathing. It wouldn't do to let Kirsty know the effect her behaviour had on her mother. As soon as her composure returned, she tapped on the door, but there was no response.

'It's Mama, Kirsty,' Ellen called gently, waiting a

moment before trying the handle, but the door was locked. She felt a flicker of panic. 'Let me in, Kirsty. I only want to talk.'

Kirsty, behind the locked door, remained silent.

'Please, Kirsty. I'm worried.' She gasped; she hadn't meant to admit she was concerned.

'Go away and leave me alone.' The mumbled response was only just audible.

Ellen placed a hand on her chest to calm the fluttering sensation. What was she to do? And where was Robert when she needed him?

She stumbled downstairs and out of the front door. Far-off voices carried to her over the lawn. She would have to compose herself. She had a duty to entertain her guests and maintain the family's social standing in the community. Her distress at Kirsty's behaviour couldn't be allowed to jeopardise that. She forced a smile which didn't quite meet her eyes and walked across the lawn to the marquee.

Inside the big, striped tent, boys and girls clustered around a man in top hat and tailcoat who was performing magic tricks that made them gasp. Some children sat in front of him and others hopped up and down with excitement while their voices competed with the magician's patter. The children's nannies were fighting a losing battle to contain their charges, while mothers smiled indulgently as they nibbled dainties and sipped their drinks.

Bea Hunter sat among them chatting, diverting any attention which might be provoked by Ellen and Kirsty's absence. Her eyes narrowed when her sister re-entered the marquee. Something was up. She could tell, even though Ellen was doing her best to appear the perfect hostess. Her smile was too brittle and her body too stiff.

Bea rose from her chair and placed her glass of lemonade on the table. It only took a few moments to reach her sister's side. Close-up, she detected the glimmer of unshed tears in Ellen's eyes. It wouldn't take much to make them spill over.

She grasped Ellen's arm and steered her out of the marquee.

'You're upset,' she said, in hurried explanation. 'You don't want to give your guests any reason to gossip.'

Ellen tried to shake the hand from her arm, but Bea tightened her grip.

'Is it something to do with Kirsty? I notice she's not here.'

A tear trickled down Ellen's cheek.

Bea pulled Ellen into her arms.

'You can't keep it to yourself, so tell me all about it.'

'Oh, Bea,' Ellen wailed. 'I don't know what to do with Kirsty. She's changed so much and, now, I fear she's losing her mind.'

Ellen's tears soaked the shoulder of Bea's dress and she pulled her sister closer to console her.

'I've worried about Kirsty over the past three years. She was such a lively young girl and then, after Ailsa's birth, she lapsed into the doldrums. She wasn't the same girl. I've felt like shaking her sometimes.' Bea still blamed herself for not taking better care of Kirsty at that disastrous ball. But, at the time, she'd had no reason to believe that Kirsty wasn't safe with Johnnie Bogue. Yet it was that belief which had led to the dreadful events that followed.

She released Ellen from her embrace.

'Let's walk, and you can tell me what's happening. We don't want to be overheard.'

'You're right,' Ellen said as they walked. 'Kirsty's never been the same since Ailsa was born. The melancholy she developed after we brought the child home was so severe, the doctor advised she should be admitted to hospital.'

'You mean a lunatic asylum?' Bea gasped.

'We didn't entertain that idea,' Ellen said. 'Robert thought the disgrace would reflect on the family.'

They walked on in silence, listening to the night-time rustles in the shrubbery and the distant sounds emanating from the marquee.

'She's worse now,' Ellen continued. 'Hysteria seems to have claimed her. She's become difficult to handle. Too difficult.' She stopped and faced Bea. 'Do you know, she wrecked her room this morning, and sliced up some of her clothes with a pair of scissors? And after that, she attended a political meeting in Dundee, even though Robert had forbidden her from going. And now, she's locked herself in her bedroom and won't let me in.'

'It seems to me,' Bea said, 'that, perhaps, she's coming out of her melancholy. I can't think what else would cause her to act in this fashion.' She stared into her sister's eyes. 'Would you prefer her to suffer from melancholia for the rest of her life? Or would you like the old, spirited Kirsty back again?'

'I hadn't thought of it like that.' Ellen's brow furrowed. 'I suppose I expected her to rebel when I took over the care of her child and when she didn't, it made life easier.'

'Even though she was suffering from melancholia and her condition was such that a doctor felt she needed medical treatment?' Bea grasped her sister's arm. 'Did you and Robert give no consideration to the fact that Ailsa was her child? Recognise the wrench it must have been for Kirsty to give her up to you? She has had to live with her child without acknowledging her or having any part in her care. Of course, she's bound to have feelings about that and suffer pain.'

'There's nothing I can do about that,' Ellen said firmly, shaking off Bea's hand. 'If I'd allowed Kirsty to be a mother to Ailsa, it would have ruined both of them.'

'I'm not saying you made the wrong decision. What I *am* saying is that Kirsty must find the situation unbearable, and now that the melancholia is retreating, it seems, her despair is coming to the fore, resulting in this hysteria. If you want my opinion, the best thing for Kirsty is to live in a place where she'll not be tortured by it all every day.'

'You mean, leave home?' Ellen's voice sounded shocked. 'Her father would never allow it.'

17

Bea tapped at Kirsty's door.

'It's Aunt Bea, Kirsty. Can I come in?'

After a moment, the door opened, and after one glance at Kirsty's tear-stained face, Bea stepped into the room and enveloped her niece in her arms.

'What's wrong?'

'Oh, Aunt Bea, I can't bear it any longer. I have to live here, seeing Ailsa every day. Do you know what that feels like? She's so close, but I'm not allowed to care for her. She's Mama and Papa's child now, not mine. Even my room is the furthest one away from the nursery. It's as if they fear I'll take her from them.'

'It can't be easy, but I'm sure they thought they were doing it for the best.'

'It's not only that. They treat me like a child, but I'm growing up. I have all these feelings they never even acknowledge. It's impossible to move or do anything without their permission. I'm not alive in this house, Aunt Bea – I'm stifled. It's no way to live. I'd rather be dead because this isn't living. It's only existing.'

Misery surrounded Kirsty as she flung herself on to the bed and lapsed into a crying fit. Bea sat beside her. Not knowing what else to do, she laid her hand on the girl's shoulder to offer comfort and human connection. Eventually, as Bea made soothing noises, Kirsty's sobs subsided, and she raised her head again.

'I have no freedom. They won't let me out of their sight because they don't trust me. They blame me for bringing disgrace on the family. They think what happened to me that night was my fault when it wasn't. Why can't they understand I could never allow that to happen to me again?'

'I'm sorry, Kirsty. I should have taken better care of you.'

'I know whose fault it was, Aunt Bea. It wasn't your fault, nor was it mine. But try to get Mama and Papa to understand that? It's a hopeless task.'

Bea pulled Kirsty into her arms.

'The pain will lessen, Kirsty. You need to give it time.' Bea wasn't entirely convinced she was right. She'd never had a child, but she could imagine what it must feel like to give birth and then have your baby taken away. It must be worse than a bereavement, especially with a constant reminder.

'You know, Aunt Bea, while I was in Dundee this afternoon, I felt alive again. But that only made me realise how unhappy I've been. Watching Mama and Papa take over Ailsa's care since she was born . . . it's as if something died inside of me.'

'I can understand that. I can also understand you want to live again and to do that you feel the need to be away from Ailsa.'

'But that will never happen. They'll never allow me to leave home.'

'Leave it to me, Kirsty. I'm going to suggest to your parents that you come to visit me, and we can make sure the visit is an extended one.'

'You would do that for me?' Kirsty's face brightened.

'Of course. You're my favourite niece, after all.' Bea smiled as she patted Kirsty's hand. 'Now, you get some rest and I'll sort things out.'

The flicker of hope fluttering inside Kirsty at the thought she might live with Aunt Bea deserted her once her aunt left the room. While her mother might agree, persuading her father would be a nigh-on impossible task. Papa was set in his ways and intent on ensuring his daughter behaved in a way he felt was fitting to his status. He wouldn't want her to live anywhere away from his influence.

Kirsty's shoulders slumped. It was hopeless; he would never agree to Aunt Bea's proposal. She stared at the empty fireplace where no fire burned, and no vestige of ash remained. It seemed as dead as her heart.

Music drifted up to her window, reminding her she should be outside, mingling with her mother's guests, presenting herself as the perfect daughter in an idyllic family. No doubt her father would call her to task when he arrived home, but she didn't care. At least he wouldn't shout; that wasn't his style. He would be polite, perhaps sarcastic, but he would leave her in no doubt about his displeasure.

Kirsty sat still for a long time, staring into the fireplace, allowing her thoughts to drift and her resentment to increase. At some point, the music outside stopped and the voices died away, but she didn't notice. When the summons came, ordering her to come downstairs because her father desired her presence, she had no comprehension of the passage of time.

Refusal was the first thought that crossed her mind. Why should she do what her father demanded? But she had obeyed her father all her life, and the habit was difficult to shake. Besides, the request came from Aunt Bea, and she didn't want to disappoint her.

'I've talked to your father and mother.' Aunt Bea handed Kirsty a hairbrush. 'You might want to tidy your hair – it's all mussed.'

Kirsty rose and walked to the vanity dresser, peered into the mirror and brushed her hair back from her face.

'Will I do?' Anxiety overcame her. 'Is Papa very angry?'

'You look lovely.' Her aunt smiled, taking the hairbrush from Kirsty and replacing it on the dresser. 'The best way for you to respond to your father is to forget your resentment, be calm, and act like an adult. Show him you have a sense of responsibility.'

'Has he agreed?'

'Yes, Kirsty, he has agreed. Now you have to convince him he hasn't made a mistake.'

Bea took her niece's arm and they walked downstairs together.

Kirsty paused at the door of the lounge, taking a deep breath.

'Are you ready?' Bea nodded her approval and pushed open the door.

Kirsty's mother was seated in an armchair and her father stood in front of the fireplace, his hands clasped behind his back.

'Ah, there you are, Kirsty,' he said. 'I understand from your mother that you have been suffering from anxiety over the past few days. We have arranged for you to visit your aunt for a time, to allow you to rest and recover.'

Kirsty nodded, unable to speak.

'I am not too happy with this arrangement. But your mother and aunt think you need a holiday, and your aunt has kindly agreed to allow you to reside with her in Dundee until you are more rested. However, you are no longer a child and you will do nothing to bring shame or disgrace on this family. Do you understand, Kirsty? You will, at all times, act with propriety and you must remember your position in Dundee society as my daughter.'

'Yes, Papa.' Kirsty wondered if she should say more but decided against it. Far better to agree.

'I am putting my trust in you, Kirsty. I hope you will not disappoint me.'

'I won't. I promise, Papa.'

Her mother rose from her chair and wrapped her arms around Kirsty.

'I will miss you,' she said. 'But I hope this will give you a chance for your mind to recover. I hope you find peace.'

Tears pricked the back of Kirsty's eyelids. Her mother's arms around her made her feel safe and wanted. But this was no time to regret her decision to gain independence. She couldn't stay a child in her mother's arms forever.

18

Ethel tried to suppress her excitement as she and Martha hurried along the street to join the demonstration. Tuesday's gathering, listening to Christabel Pankhurst, had been inspirational. Tonight, though, was different. This was a political meeting for men only. Winston Churchill had been voted in as Dundee's parliamentary representative in May and he was here to address his constituency.

They joined a group of women standing in front of the Kinnaird Hall. Three stewards stood at the doors, trying to prevent them from entering. The women, not to be thwarted, pushed and jostled, forcing the stewards to spread their arms to form a barricade.

'I'm sorry, ladies. This meeting's for men only.'

'We're entitled to attend meetings.' One woman at the front squared her shoulders as if to prepare for a fight.

'That may be so,' the steward replied. 'But the ladies' meeting was this afternoon, so we haven't prevented you from hearing Mr Churchill speak.'

'Some of us couldn't attend this afternoon, and we wish to hear what our member of parliament has to say.'

'Makes no difference,' the steward in the middle said. 'You have to leave, otherwise, I'll be obliged to call our security guards and the police.'

A raucous laugh erupted from one woman. 'They'd like that, so they would. Give them a chance to rough us up again and put their hands where no respectable man would dare.'

Laughter echoed through the rest of the crowd, though several women looked a trifle embarrassed at the coarseness of the woman's speech.

Ethel tugged on Martha's arm.

'Will we force our way into the hall?'

'We could but what good would it do? They'd throw us out again. I've no doubt men with truncheons are waiting at the other side of the door, and they'd love to leave us with sore heads. And anyway, we wouldn't get much sympathy for the cause because they held a women's meeting this afternoon.'

'Were you there? At the meeting this afternoon?'

A rueful smile twitched at the corners of Martha's mouth.

'Oh, yes. I was there. Got thrown out within the first half-hour and they were none too gentle about it.'

'Were you hurt?' Ethel's eyes widened.

'No more than usual,' Martha replied. 'You get used to it.'

'What did you do to make them throw you out?'

'Asked a question. I wanted to know what Mr Churchill's plans were in relation to women's suffrage. They don't like that because we all know he is not in favour of women having the vote.'

'Do you think we'll ever get the vote?'

'If we do nothing, it'll never happen. Our job is to make ourselves visible, let the people in power know we won't give up. Most of all, we need to work on them to change their minds. Convince them that as women and taxpayers, we are entitled to vote and have issues affecting women discussed in parliament.'

Martha reached into the satchel hanging from her shoulder, pulled out a batch of leaflets, and thrust them into Ethel's hands.

'We make a start by giving everyone who attends the meeting one of these. Not everyone will want to take them, but if we can persuade even a few of the men who attend the meeting tonight, that will count as a success.'

More suffragettes arrived, some of them carrying banners, others handing out leaflets, and yet others haranguing the men arriving for the meeting. With a few exceptions, it was a good-natured demonstration, although many of the men aimed derogatory remarks in their direction.

Ethel continued to hand out leaflets although her arm ached, and she was sure a bruise was forming where the toff with the cane had landed a vicious blow.

'You're a disgrace to womanhood,' he'd snapped as he lashed out.

She'd wanted to give him the rough side of her tongue, but she'd smiled instead.

'And you, sir, are a credit to your station in life,' she'd responded, her voice dripping with sarcasm.

With a glare and a snort in her direction, he'd hurried into the hall. However, he'd been the exception. Most of the men had either accepted a leaflet or shaken their heads and she was pleased with her contribution to the suffrage cause.

After the last of the men entered the hall there was a lull; the women formed groups and chatted. But it wasn't long before the doors opened again, and the stewards hurled a woman out on to the street. She landed with a thump in the road and lay there for a moment before struggling to her feet.

Martha, followed by several of the women, rushed to her side and helped her up.

'Did they hurt you?'

'Ask a daft question,' the young woman said. 'What do you think?' She brushed at her skirt, but it remained soiled. 'Lost my best hat in there. Don't suppose I'll get it back.'

Martha laughed.

'I'm sure the funds will help you get another one. But never mind the hat. How did our plan work?'

Ethel hovered behind the group gathering around the woman. Was she the only one who didn't know what was going on?

'It worked beautifully, and I scattered leaflets throughout the hall as I lowered myself from the skylight. But as soon as I got within reach of the stewards, they grabbed me.'

A buzz rippled through the women. Some congratulated her and some expressed admiration. Several voices shot questions at her.

'Weren't you scared?'

'How did it feel dangling from a rope?'

'What if the rope broke?'

The questions and comments continued, but the young woman shrugged them off with a laugh.

Ethel pushed to the front of the group when Martha beckoned her.

'I want you to meet Gladys Burnett. She's just invaded the men's meeting by lowering herself on a rope from the skylight. I'm sure the *Dundee Courier* will give it prominent positioning in tomorrow's paper.'

Gladys turned to appraise Ethel. Her eyes were sharp but kind.

'New recruit, Martha?'

'Yes. Ethel's keen to support the cause. I believe she's capable of great things.'

Heat warmed Ethel's cheeks.

'Martha always has good judgement.' Gladys turned to Ethel and smiled. 'Welcome to the sisterhood.'

After a moment's hesitation, Ethel grasped the hand Gladys offered her. Few people wanted to shake a mill girl's hand, and she was still adjusting to these interactions with, as she considered them, her betters.

The meeting broke up an hour later and it gave them another chance to push leaflets into the hands of men emerging from the building. Apart from some ribald comments and pamphlets thrown back at them, it went without a hitch, although Ethel made certain she stayed well clear of the toff with the cane. One thump from that was enough for one night.

As the street quietened, the women dispersed. In small and larger groups, they left the front of the Kinnaird Hall to walk along the road. Excitement hung over them and Ethel could hear the buzz of voices as they left.

'We'll hang back and wait for Gladys,' Martha whispered to Ethel. 'She's talking to the reporter from the *Dundee Courier.*'

Ethel sneaked a glance at the man talking to Gladys. He was tall and good looking, and younger than she imagined a reporter should be. After a few moments, he shook Gladys's hand, tucked his notebook and pencil in his pocket, and lifted his hat in a farewell gesture.

'Did he say whether it will be in tomorrow's newspaper?' Martha asked when Gladys rejoined them.

'He's going to give it top billing.' Gladys grinned. 'Isn't that marvellous?'

'Come back to the house with us – you can tell me all about it. And I'm sure Ethel will be interested in your other exploits.'

It was midnight when Gladys eventually left.

'Don't be silly,' she said when Martha suggested they walk her home. 'It's only a few streets away and there won't be anyone around at this time of night.'

'If you're sure?' Martha's voice was hesitant.

'Of course, I'm sure. I can look after myself.'

'I don't doubt it,' Martha responded warmly and hugged Gladys. 'I'll see you on Sunday.'

Outside, the hollow sound of Gladys's footsteps broke the silence as they echoed along the deserted streets. Perhaps she should have accepted Martha's offer to accompany her home. But that was silly. She'd walked these streets at all times of the night and day before and thought nothing of it. Tonight, however, she couldn't shake off the feeling that all was not right.

The streetlight which lit the steps to her front door and allowed her to see the keyhole was in darkness. It was while she was fumbling with her key that the noose slipped around her neck.

'Thought you were clever tonight, didn't you?' The whisper sounded sibilant in the darkness.

Gladys dropped her key and tore at the scarf tightening around her neck.

'Not so clever now.' The sinister whisper was the last thing she heard as she slumped to the ground.

19

Martha hurried downstairs, eager to get to the WFL office so she could inspect the *Dundee Courier* for any mention of last night's meeting. The reporter had promised Gladys he would write an editorial on her invasion of the Kinnaird Hall and Martha was impatient to see it.

Lila Clunas and Florence Dakers were already in the office when she entered.

'I've brought the *Courier*.' She threw the newspaper on to the counter and spread it open. 'It's in the Stop Press bit – I suppose it went in too late for the main pages. See, here it is, *"Suffragette Invades Churchill's Meeting"*. He kept his promise,' she said. 'Gladys will be pleased.'

Lila rummaged in a drawer and brought out a pair of scissors.

'I'll pin it on the noticeboard so everyone can see it,' she said, brandishing the scissors. She snipped around the edges of the editorial and, following a further rummage in the cluttered drawer, she pinned it on the board with a brass tack. She stood back and admired it. 'We should applaud Gladys. This is bound to bring women's suffrage to the attention of more people.'

Martha nodded.

'I'll put the kettle on and make a pot of tea before we decide what to include in the next news-sheet. Gladys will take pride of place, of course.'

A room led off the main shop-front, and it was here that the women gathered to discuss their plans and share the latest news items. A sink filled the space in front of the rear window, which looked on to Martha's courtyard and the stairs to her house. A small gas hob sat at one side of the sink and a sideboard at the other. In the centre of the room was a large table and enough chairs to seat several women.

'Yes, we have a lot to discuss before Sunday's meeting.' Lila closed the paper and placed it on the top of the sideboard. 'Will your new recruit be attending?'

'Ethel moved into my house at the beginning of the week. I thought it for the best – her home life would have interfered with her wish to work for the cause. Her father, I believe, has a vicious temper.'

'Is that wise?' Florence struck a match and held it to the gas ring while Martha poured water into the kettle. Martha replaced the lid and set the kettle on top of the flame.

'I think so. I have more room in my house than is necessary for one person. Besides, she's keen and she'll be company for me.'

'You have a big heart.' Florence pulled a chair over to the table.

'I may have another recruit.' Martha poured boiling water on to tea leaves inside the teapot and set it aside to brew. 'I met this young girl, Kirsty Campbell, at the afternoon meeting. She expressed interest, so I've invited her to Sunday's meeting.'

Lila nodded her approval.

'The more people who show an interest in the cause, the better it will be. But, for now, it's time to catch up with the business and plan our next activity.'

Paul Anderson adjusted his tie and made sure his hat was straight. This morning's edition of the *Dundee Courier* was tucked under his arm. He rehearsed in his mind what he intended to say.

'Miss Burnett, thank you for speaking to me yesterday after your adventure in the Kinnaird Hall.' No, that wouldn't do. 'After you were thrown out of the Kinnaird Hall.' No, that wasn't right, either. He wanted to make a good impression so he could convince her to give him an exclusive on her life as a suffragette. Eventually, he settled on, 'Miss Burnett, thank you for talking to me yesterday. I've brought you a copy of the *Courier* and I was wondering if we could talk again.' Yes, that would do.

He raised his hand to knock on the door, but it swung open at his touch.

'Miss Burnett?' he called. There was no answer, so he raised his voice and called again. It echoed in the silence and there was no movement from within.

The entrance hall was gloomy but he could see a flight of stairs ahead to the left. To the right, at the end of the passage, a door stood ajar. His reporter's instincts drove him there, and it only took a moment for him to overcome his hesitation at entering a young lady's home uninvited. The sight that met his eyes was not what he expected. The woman lay sprawled in an armchair. Her head lolled at an unnatural angle and her arms hung limply over the arm of the chair, convincing him she wasn't asleep. The sash, draped across one shoulder, fell towards her lap in such a fashion that the words, *'Votes for Women'*, were to the fore.

He walked over to her and put hesitant fingers on her neck, afraid she might wake up and accuse him of assaulting her. But her cold skin and lack of a pulse convinced him she was dead. His first inclination was to leave and find a policeman. But the opportunity to look around for information to use as background for the story he intended to write was irresistible. It wouldn't take long and it would make no difference to Gladys Burnett, now she was dead.

He fished his notebook and pencil out of his pocket and mounted the stairs to inspect the rest of the house.

Paul hovered in the doorway of the police station. He had no great respect for policemen and the one behind the counter looked like a typical bobby with nothing between his ears but cotton-wool.

He let the door swing shut behind him, clearing his throat to draw the man's attention. After what seemed an age, the sergeant laid his pen on the counter and surveyed him with lugubrious eyes.

'Is there something you wanted, sir?' The man's walrus moustache wiggled as he spoke.

'I've come to report a death,' Paul said, glancing away from the policeman. If that moustache waggled any more, he wouldn't be able to suppress his laughter. He'd been feeling on the edge of hysteria ever since finding Gladys's body. He supposed it was a reaction to her death.

'Perhaps a doctor might be more appropriate, sir?'

'No, you don't understand. This is a suspicious death.' Paul could see the headline in the *Courier* – "*Reporter Finds Suffragette Dead*". The editor couldn't fail to be pleased that Paul had been on the very spot when the body was discovered.

'I see.' The moustache waggled. 'And what makes you think it's suspicious?'

Paul drew himself up to his full height, although the policeman was a good two inches taller than him.

'She was young and healthy. Young women don't just die.'

'You knew the young lady, sir?'

'Not really. I only met her yesterday.'

'Ah!'

Paul didn't like the tone of the man's voice.

'I'm a reporter. I interviewed her for the *Dundee Courier*. Look, see for yourself – there's the piece I wrote.' He slammed the newspaper on the counter and pointed to the Stop Press.

The policeman laid his pencil on the desk and inspected the newspaper.

'She be one of them suffragettes, I see.' Disapproval radiated from him. The pencil remained on the desk and he did not pick it up again.

'What's that got to do with anything? She's dead.' Paul struggled to suppress his irritation.

'Ah, well. Those suffragettes aren't natural women, are they? The things they get up to, I'm surprised more of them don't drop dead.'

'Does that mean you're not going to do anything?'

'I didn't say that, sir. I'll refer it to my boss, and I've no doubt he'll go up there and take a look. In the meantime, I'd be obliged if I can have your name and details for how to contact you, in case we can't find a relative or friend to take care of her.'

'And I, sir, will report the death and its outcome in tomorrow's *Courier*. If your boss is interested in updating the facts in my possession, I'll be happy to discuss with him what I intend to write.'

Unconvinced the police would do anything about the matter, Paul stamped out of the police station, slamming the door behind him. Head down, he barged past several constables coming through the archway into the quadrangle.

'Steady on, sir,' one of them said, but Paul glared at him and continued on his way.

Once he reached the street, he leaned against the wall and took several deep breaths until his anger abated. A reporter should always be objective and in control of his emotions. How many times had his previous editor said that to him? At last, his head cleared and he could think straight again. He would return to the locus of the death and wait for the police to arrive. If there was no police attendance, that would be included in tomorrow's editorial.

Three steps, bordered by a railing at each side, led up to Gladys's front door, and he sat on the top one, leaning his back against the iron bars. He pushed his hat to the back of his head and turned his face towards the sun, enjoying the warmth of the rays. The wait might be a long one, so he'd best make the most of the sunshine. It was better than being enclosed in a poky office, writing the next day's copy.

As it was, he didn't have long to wait before a police wagon rolled up to the kerb and a policeman dismounted, followed by a man in a shabby, black suit. The man consulted the sheet of paper he held before walking towards the house.

Paul grabbed the railing and hoisted himself to his feet. The man in the suit frowned.

'I presume you are the reporter Sergeant Edwards interviewed.'

'You mean the policeman to whom I reported Miss Burnett's death? I'd hardly call that an interview.'

'He claims you think the death is suspicious.' The man climbed the steps and stood in front of Paul.

'It certainly didn't look natural to me.' Paul moved aside to allow the man to enter the house. 'The door isn't locked. You'll find Miss Burnett in the room at the end of the passage.'

'You found her?' The man strode up the passage and into the room where Gladys lay in the armchair.

'I'm sorry, I didn't catch your name.' Paul trotted behind him.

'I didn't give it.'

'It would help to know who I'm talking to. You could be anybody,' Paul said. 'How do I know you're entitled to ask me questions?'

'Smart arse,' the man growled. 'I'm Inspector Hammond, and you'd do well not to annoy me.'

'Very well, Inspector Hammond. In answer to your question – yes, I was the one who found her.'

Hammond inspected the room.

'How long had you known Miss Burnett? And why were you here today?'

'I'm afraid I didn't know Miss Burnett all that well. I interviewed her yesterday evening, outside the Kinnaird Hall.'

'My understanding is that there were several suffragettes at that meeting. What was so interesting about this lady in particular? Or do you just like suffragettes?'

Paul ignored the disdainful tone of the man's voice and stared back at him, intent on not allowing the detective to undermine him.

'I found her interesting because she invaded Churchill's meeting by lowering herself with a rope from the rafters in the hall. I thought it must be someone exceptional who would do that, and that it would make good copy for the

Courier.'

Hammond bent over Gladys's body.

'Ah, I heard about that. These suffragettes will do anything to attract attention.' He raised Gladys's chin with one of his fingers and inspected the front of her neck. 'I reckon that would explain the marks on her neck. They must be rope burns from the rope she used.'

'Rope burns?' Paul spluttered. 'If she had rope burns from her descent, she would have hanged herself then, not wait until later to die.'

Hammond raised his eyebrows.

'I am sure the doctor who examines her at the mortuary will be able to identify the cause of death. In the meantime, we are finished here, but I may want to see you again after I receive his report.'

20

Paul pushed past the young policeman standing guard at the door and fumed all the way back to the *Courier* building. If Gladys had been anyone other than a suffragette, the police would have treated her death more seriously. It appeared to him they would prefer to brush it under the carpet, but he wasn't going to let them off with that. He determined to write an editorial which would force them to pay attention.

He was new to Dundee but keen to get ahead, and with suffragettes stirring things up, he was sure people would sit up and take notice of his editorials. Not that women's suffrage meant anything to him – it just made good copy.

'Anderson!' The summons came before he reached his desk.

Duncan Wallace, a burly figure who looked more like a navvy than an editor, strode into the pressroom with a glower on his face which boded no good for Paul. He came to a halt and stood, hands on hips and feet planted firmly on the floor.

Paul hadn't got his measure yet, and their paths hadn't crossed to any great extent since his interview with the *Courier*'s management. He'd got the impression then that they were pleased he was joining their ranks. But looking at the editor now, Paul reckoned he'd misjudged this man.

'My office. Now.' His voice brooked no argument.

Heat built below Paul's collar. The look on the editor's face was enough to tell him trouble was brewing. What had he done to incur his wrath?

His office was at the far end of the pressroom and Paul found it difficult to keep pace with Duncan's long strides. He was conscious of the other reporters and staff keeping their heads down in a semblance of work. It was as if a tornado was building and they wanted to stay out of the way.

Once inside the office, the editor slammed a copy of the day's newspaper on top of his desk.

'What is the meaning of this?' He pointed at the front page.

Paul swallowed. 'It's a stop press item that came in after the newspaper was ready to print.'

'You are aware that all editorial material is subject to my approval, are you not?'

'It was late and everyone, apart from the printing staff, had gone by the time I got back last night.' He tried to sound confident.

The editor's brows drew together in a frown.

'That's no excuse.'

Paul squirmed. Surely the man couldn't be such an ogre he required every word written to be passed by him before going to print? He resisted the urge to loosen his collar, which suddenly felt as if it was attempting to strangle him. Sweat trickled down his back; dampness soaked his armpits. He pressed his sweaty palms to his trouser legs, hoping the editor wouldn't notice.

'You're new here but there is something you need to understand.' The editor drew a breath and raised his voice. 'I will not have the *Dundee Courier* used to publicise suffragette antics. We are not in the business of promoting the suffrage cause. These women make a nuisance of themselves and our readers will not stand for it.'

'But you told me to report on Churchill's meeting, sir, and I still have to write the editorial on that.'

'Write your report but do not mention any of these women by name and turn them into heroic figures. The only newspaper space we will give them is to show they are troublemakers who gathered outside the hall, making a nuisance of themselves and bothering those attending the meeting.'

'Yes, sir,' Paul said. 'But there's been a development. Gladys Burnett has been found dead under suspicious circumstances.' He drew a breath. 'It's news, sir. We can't ignore it. Surely that warrants space in the newspaper.'

'Suspicious death, you say?' The editor stroked his chin as he thought for a moment. 'Have the police given you permission to use her name?'

'I didn't ask.'

'You should have. It is not this newspaper's policy to identify anyone in these circumstances until the family have been informed.'

'But, sir – we need to report the death. We can't ignore it.'

'Very well, but when you write your report, you will refrain from making any mention of her name or that she was a suffragette. We don't want to turn her into a martyr. As long as I am in charge of the news, the *Courier* will not be party to propaganda.'

'Blasted reporter, poking his nose in.' Hammond waited until the man was out of sight. 'If he comes back, make sure you keep him outside,' he said to the constable standing in the doorway. He stomped back into the house.

Now that he was alone, he sketched the crime scene in his notebook and re-examined the body. He was forced to admit that the reporter had a point; this death was suspicious. The silk sash draped over her shoulder obscured the extent of the bruising and he removed it to examine her neck. Creases in the sash convinced him it had been used as a garrotte to strangle her. He jotted a note alongside the sketch.

His search of the house revealed nothing of use to identify her next of kin, and it was obvious she lived alone. He tapped his pencil against his teeth and returned to the living-room, where the body lay. A further examination of the room provided little else of help apart from pamphlets produced by the Women's Freedom League. He thrust one of them into his pocket. Suffragettes annoyed him, creating trouble and unrest wherever they went. He would gladly see them in hell.

21

Inspector Hammond grabbed his hat from the top of the filing cabinet. All the preliminary work on the Gladys Burnett case had been completed, and the body removed to the mortuary. But he was no further forward with the investigation. The house search had revealed nothing of use, not even the hint of a clue on her relatives or friends apart from the Women's Freedom League pamphlet. It looked like he would be forced to visit the suffragette harridans in their lair; something he dreaded.

A fug of tobacco smoke in the corridor outside the constables' room indicated the recent presence of several of the men, but now only one constable remained, hunched over paperwork on his desk.

'With me, Buchan,' Hammond snapped.

The constable laid down his pencil and rose.

'Yes, sir.' He buttoned his jacket and reached for his helmet.

Hammond sighed. The young man's expression reminded him of a dog who wanted to please his master. Given the choice, he would have preferred one of the older, more experienced men. Men who could instil fear when interviewing witnesses and suspects. Not someone like Buchan, still wet behind the ears.

He strode up the corridor, through the charge-room and out into the quadrangle, Buchan at his heels.

'How long have you been with us now, Buchan?' Turning his back on the police wagon in the yard's corner, he walked through the archway to the street beyond.

'Three months, sir.'

'Hmm.' This constable would be as much use to him as a pencil with a broken point, although Hammond supposed he was better than nothing. The thought of interviewing women on his own always sent chills through the inspector. He was never at ease in the presence of women, and the suffragettes he was on his way to interview were a different breed again. Dominant and forceful, unafraid of men and with a tendency to aggression.

'When we reach our destination, I'll interview some women – *suffragettes* – and I want you to take notes.'

'Yes, sir.'

'These . . . suffragettes may prove difficult.' He grabbed the rim of his hat as a sudden breeze threatened to send it flying as they rounded the corner of Court House Square and Ward Road. 'Have you come across suffragettes during the course of your duties?'

'I was on plain clothes duty with Sergeant McKenzie in Albert Square on Tuesday, when Christabel Pankhurst was speaking.'

'Any trouble?'

'Apart from the usual hecklers, it was all right. These suffragette women weren't as fearsome as I'd expected.'

'Hmm.' Hammond remained unconvinced.

They walked on in silence until they arrived at the shop the Women's Freedom League used as their office. It looked no different from the shops on either side, apart from the posters calling for *Votes for Women* instead of the usual goods for sale.

Hammond rapped on the door and pushed it open, without waiting for a response.

The three women inside, two of them behind the counter and the third sitting in front of it, looked up in surprise. One of them rose to greet them.

'I'm Lila Clunas, can I help you?'

'Indeed, you can, ladies. I'm Inspector Hammond from Dundee City Police and I'm here to enquire about one of your members, Gladys Burnett.'

'Gladys has done nothing wrong.' Lila's tone hardened. 'It is not a crime to try to gain entry to a political meeting.'

'I am afraid you misunderstand me. I am not here to

arrest Gladys Burnett.' He smiled, taking a grim satisfaction from what he was about to say. 'I am here to interview you about your whereabouts yesterday evening and to acquire information on her relatives and next of kin.'

'Next of kin?' One of the other women rose, a look of alarm on her face. 'Has something happened to Gladys?'

'I am sorry to tell you we found her body this morning. The lady is deceased.'

'Dead! How can that be?' The woman clutched the end of the counter for support. 'How did she die?'

'I am not at liberty to tell you that. All I can say is, we found her body.'

The woman who had spoken sat down with a thump.

'It's my fault, I shouldn't have allowed her to walk home alone. I should have paid more heed to the letter.' She pulled a crumpled piece of paper from her pocket. 'I thought it was one of the usual hate-mail letters . . . we receive them all the time.'

Hammond lifted the paper, spreading out the creases until the words were legible. He read in silence and then stared at the speaker.

'This is a death threat,' he said, waving the letter under her nose. 'Why did you not bring this to the attention of the police?'

The woman straightened and glared at him.

'What good would that have done? You would have dismissed it, the same way you dismissed us when we reported one of our members missing.'

Hammond's mind flashed back to earlier in the week when he'd overheard two women in the office reporting a missing person. Victoria somebody or other; he couldn't remember the details.

'Well, I am not dismissing it now. I will keep this as evidence.' He folded the letter and placed it in his pocket. 'In the meantime, I need you to tell me everything you know about Gladys Burnett. After that, I will require you to give your names and addresses to the constable.'

Lila Clunas, who seemed to be the one in charge, rose to

address him.

'I am not sure how much help we can be. Gladys has been a member of the WFL for a few months. She was always keen to take part in demonstrations and to help us in any way she could. But she didn't talk about her private life much. I know she had a husband; I assumed they were separated because they didn't live together.'

'I see. This husband – would you happen to know his name and where I can find him?'

'I think his name is David Burnett, but I don't know where he lives. I'm sorry I can't help further than that.'

'That wasn't too bad,' Hammond said to Buchan after they left the office. 'All we have to do is find the husband. I want you to get on to that straight away. Check the electoral rolls and anything else you can think of. He is probably our prime suspect.'

'I wasn't aware Gladys had a husband,' Martha said after the police left. 'What about you, Florence, did you know?'

'She never mentioned it to me. But Gladys never discussed her private life.'

'She didn't talk about him,' Lila said. 'Which leads me to think they were no longer together as a married couple. She said he was a jute mill manager in India. Bengal, I believe.'

'You omitted to provide that information to the detective,' Martha said with a wry smile.

'I didn't think it relevant. The man's not even in this country, so he can't be the person responsible.'

'I suppose so,' Martha said. 'I wonder how long the police will look for him before they give up.'

22

Saturday, 27th June 1908

Martha ran to pick up the *Courier* when it thumped through the letterbox. Carrying it to the kitchen table, she spread it out. The front page, as usual, was filled with adverts and public notices; the only news that ever appeared here was the Stop Press, which was empty today. She leafed through the newspaper until she identified what she was looking for on page five. The entry was so small she almost missed it, and all it said was that a body had been discovered and police were investigating. There was no mention of a name or that Gladys was a suffragette.

'You're up early.' Ethel adjusted her shawl as she entered the kitchen. 'I'm off to work, but the tea in the pot should still be warm.'

'Thanks.' Martha blinked back a tear. 'I thought I'd check the *Courier* to see what they were reporting about Gladys.'

'What's it saying?'

'Nothing much. It doesn't even name her.'

Ethel peered over her shoulder.

'You'd think they might have included more, particularly when she made news the day before for invading Churchill's meeting.'

'Maybe the police haven't released the details.'

'I'll bet that reporter you met could find out what's going on.' Ethel fastened the front of her shawl with a safety-pin. 'I'd better go or I'll be late for work. I'll see you later.'

Saturday was a half-day in the mill, but by the time the long, mournful hoot of the mill's bummer signalled the end of work, Ethel was as tired as if she'd worked a full day's shift. She grabbed her shawl, waved goodbye to Maisie, and ran to the gates. If she hurried, she would have time to help out at the WFL shop. Other mill workers accompanied her part of the way, but when she turned the corner at the bottom of the road where East Henderson Street led to the West Port, she was alone.

The man waiting for her grabbed her roughly by the shoulder and spun her around to face him.

Ethel gasped. All week, she'd been expecting her da to search her out, but she hadn't expected him to be lying in wait for her on a Saturday in the middle of the day. She twisted her head from side to side, hoping to find someone to intervene, but this part of the street seemed deserted. Further up the West Port, several men clustered outside the Globe public house, while a carter watered his horse at the trough in front of it, but they were too far away to be of help. She could hear the clop of horses' hooves in the distance and trams rumbling along Tay Street, but the empty tram rails in the West Port glistened in the sun with no hint of a tram anywhere near.

'Hand it over,' he said, his voice full of menace.

Hughie's fingers dug into the flesh of Ethel's shoulder, and no matter how much she struggled, she couldn't escape his grasp. Her hand tightened around the pay packet in her pocket. She should have known he would come looking for money.

He pushed her against the wall.

'Thought ye could get away from me?' he hissed. 'Never forget, ye're my daughter and I own you.'

'You don't own me. I've left home and I'm not coming back.' Ethel kicked his shins and struggled to free herself, but his fingers dug deeper, making her wince with pain.

'Left home, have ye? We'll soon see about that.' He raised his fist and whacked her on the side of her jaw.

Pain sliced through Ethel's face and head. Tears spurted from her eyes and she slumped forward.

Hughie grabbed her hair and forced her head back. He

leaned his face so close to hers she could feel spittle on her cheeks when he growled.

'Ye're coming home with me now. It's where ye belong. And I'll have that pay packet, so hand it over.' He rummaged through Ethel's pockets until he found her the envelope. 'Thought ye could keep this from me, did you?' He shook her so hard her spine thudded off the wall at her back.

'That's enough of that.'

Ethel peered, through tear-filled eyes, to see where the voice came from, but the shape was a blur.

Hughie's hands released their grip on her shoulders and she slid to the ground.

The voices faded in and out of her consciousness as she attempted to sit up.

'I'm her da,' she heard Hughie say. 'I have a right.'

'You don't have the right to assault this girl even if you are her father. I've a good mind to arrest you.'

Ethel struggled to her feet. She wanted to be free of her da, but what good would it do if he was jailed? Her ma would feel the brunt of his anger and fists when he was released.

'Let him go,' she said. 'I just don't want him to come near me again.'

'Are you sure, miss?'

She nodded.

'Ye haven't heard the last of this,' her father muttered as he shuffled off along the street.

'I'd advise against that,' the constable said. 'I know who you are, and I know where to find you.'

Once Hughie was out of sight, the constable turned to Ethel.

'I think this is yours,' he said, handing her the pay packet he'd taken from her father.

'Thank you.' Ethel put it in her pocket and sneaked a glance at the bobby who'd come to her rescue. He was younger than most of the bobbies she'd seen on the streets of Dundee and he had kind eyes. 'I don't know what would have happened if you hadn't come along when you did.'

'You have the carter back there at the Globe to thank. He gave me a shout and told me there was a lassie in trouble down the road.'

'I didn't think they were bothering.' Ethel tucked a strand of hair behind her ear, though she wasn't sure why she bothered – she looked a sight in her mill clothes and her encounter with Hughie had left her even more dishevelled.

The constable frowned.

'What will happen when you go home? Will he be waiting for you?'

'You don't have to worry about that. I don't live at home. I've taken lodgings in the town.'

'In that case, Ethel, I'll accompany you to your lodgings in case he's waiting for you, thinking I've left.'

'How do you know my name?'

He returned her curious look with a smile.

'It was on your pay packet. I looked at it when I picked it up.'

23

Martha studied Ethel over the top of her teacup. The bruise on the girl's jaw had lost its angry, red colour and faded to blue, but it still looked painful. She laid her cup in the saucer and hesitated before she spoke, unsure whether Ethel would find her suggestion acceptable.

'I have been thinking,' she said, 'after your unfortunate experience, whether it is wise for you to return to your mill job.'

'But I have to work. I've no other way of earning my keep.'

Martha leaned forward and grasped Ethel's hand.

'I worry about you. Your father is a vicious man, and the next time he waylays you, it might be more serious than a few bruises.'

'Mill work's all I know. I don't have enough education to be a teacher or a shop assistant.'

'You are more intelligent than you give yourself credit for. I'm sure the league could find something for you to do.'

'I don't have any experience for that.' A wistful look crossed Ethel's face. 'I'm not able to stitch banners because I've never been taught how to sew, and I'd be no use typing the letters you send out. I can't imagine what I could do that would be useful. Besides, the league doesn't have enough resources for paid workers. It relies on volunteers.'

Martha laughed.

'If you have figured that out, you have more intelligence than you think. But I still believe you would be of more use to the cause than spending your time working in a mill. Give it some thought, at least.'

Ethel rose from the breakfast table and gathered the

plates and cups together.

'Best get yourself ready for this afternoon's meeting,' she said. 'I'll take care of these.'

Martha paused in the doorway.

'After you've tidied yourself, look into my room. I can help you cover that bruise with face powder.'

Ethel raised her hand and touched her face.

'I've never worn powder.' She turned away with a self-conscious smile and plopped the plates and cups into the bowl of hot water in the sink.

'There is a first time for everything,' Martha said.

Excitement fizzed in Kirsty all morning. This was the day she had been waiting for. She ate her breakfast in a trance without tasting the food, and didn't register the warmth of the sun on her face as she walked to church. The sermon made no sense because her thoughts were elsewhere. She sang hymns which, later, she could not have named.

This was Kirsty's third day with Aunt Bea, and she was finding it strange. Her heart ached for Ailsa, though the respite from her parents' demands and expectations brought relief. However, she was still testing out boundaries with her aunt, to see how amenable Bea might be to her plans. So far, all had gone well. Aunt Bea hadn't minded her forays out into the streets of Dundee, nor her visits to various department stores. But it was the Women's Freedom League meeting today, and she hadn't told her aunt where she intended to go.

After Kirsty left Reform Street and the High Street behind and turned into Union Street, her footsteps became faster as she neared her destination. But on arrival, her courage deserted her, and she hesitated on the bottom step leading up to the ornate entrance to the Mathers Hotel. It wasn't too late to turn back. But that was silly. What had happened to her resolution to be more independent? If she turned back, she would be running away. What was the point of that?

'Courage,' she muttered under her breath, staring up at the hotel in front of her. 'I've come this far; it would be foolish to turn back now.' Before she could change her mind, she mounted the three steps to the arched entrance, pushed through the glass doors, and followed the directions written in chalk on the board at the reception desk.

After the hush of the hotel's foyer and corridor, the impact of the combined voices in the salon was unnerving and Kirsty hesitated in the doorway. She'd expected a small gathering, similar to the tea parties she attended with her mother. But this was different. Women of all ages, and a few men, sat at tables or on the sofas along the wall or stood in groups, chatting and laughing.

Where were the suffragettes she had met on Thursday? Strong women, prepared to fight and stand up for their rights. Defying the men intent on circumventing their demands. These women in the salon were more genteel and ladylike. More like her mother and her society friends than their radical counterparts.

This was a mistake, she thought. She felt out of her depth here; she shouldn't have come. But she couldn't turn and leave so soon after her arrival, that would be impolite. So, pasting a smile on her face, she hovered at the edge of the gathering. Snippets of conversation came at her from all angles.

'Have you met Amelia? They say . . .'

Kirsty sauntered further into the room, wondering who Amelia was.

'I say, the London rally was spiffing.'

'Did you see Flora Drummond on her horse?'

'No, Archie, not a penny more. You've had . . .'

'What did you think of Churchill on Thursday?'

'Have you heard the latest . . .?'

The soft buzz of voices continued, mentioning people unknown to her, comparing fashions stocked by different shops, exchanging details of milliners who designed the best hats. Kirsty sidled towards the exit. She had nothing in common with the people here, who seemed to stand for everything she rejected. The sooner she made her escape, the better.

The door to the salon burst open before she reached it, and a group of women entered the room. Kirsty spotted several familiar faces among them, including Martha, the suffragette who had invited her to the meeting. She hesitated, unwilling to push herself into their company. What did people do in these situations? She was sure there must be some kind of protocol to follow in polite society, but she didn't know what it was.

The matter resolved when Martha looked up and saw her.

'You came!' Martha grasped her hand and drew her towards the group.

'Everyone – you must meet Kirsty Campbell. I met her at the Churchill meeting. She was kind enough to rescue my bonnet and parasol after they threw me out.'

Kirsty relaxed. There was no mistaking the warmth of Martha's welcome.

Martha continued to hold Kirsty's hand as she presented her to the women in the group.

'Lila Clunas, our organising secretary in Dundee. She founded the Dundee branch of the Women's Freedom League.'

'You're very welcome to join our branch, Kirsty. We are fighting for a worthy cause.'

Kirsty's brain was spinning by the time Martha had introduced her to several more members; she was sure she would never remember their names.

'And this is Ethel Stewart, who has only recently joined our ranks.' Martha slung her arm around the shoulders of the dark-haired girl who had given Kirsty a leaflet at the rally in the Albert Square. 'I'm sure you will find you have common interests. And now, I will leave Ethel to keep you company while I welcome our speaker and open the meeting.'

Ethel sensed Kirsty's nervousness.

'Shall we find a table before the meeting opens?'

Kirsty nodded.

'This is my first time here. I'm not sure what to expect.'

'I guessed as much.' Ethel smiled. 'It's bound to be overwhelming with so many people here. It's a pity your first meeting had to be one of the larger ones instead of an at-home afternoon.' Ethel led the way through the salon until she located a small table near the podium at the end of the room. 'This'll do,' she said. 'It's close enough to hear the speaker without having to strain our ears.'

'Will it be Christabel Pankhurst?'

'Good lord, no. Christabel will be back in London.' Ethel poured water from the jug on the table into two glasses. 'It's Constance Drysdale who's speaking today. Her talk is going to be about Women's Sunday in London last weekend. I hear tell there were thousands there and that the suffragettes wore white dresses and carried flowers. It must've been a sight to see.'

Ethel closed her eyes, visualising it. She'd never been to London, but in her imagination, she could hear the brass bands, watch the suffragettes march and listen to them sing.

The room fell quiet as Martha and a tall woman of imposing appearance mounted the small platform.

'I don't think Constance Drysdale needs much introduction,' Martha said. 'She is a staunch member of the Women's Freedom League and often attends rallies and demonstrations in London and elsewhere. She is here, today, to talk about Women's Sunday in London. This demonstration was one of the largest there has been this year. I give you, Constance Drysdale.'

Martha left the podium and joined Ethel and Kirsty.

'Well said.' The young man who approached their table tucked his cane under his arm and brought his hands together in silent applause.

'Do sit down, Archie. You look a trifle lost without Constance by your side.' Martha gestured to a chair. 'Archie is Constance's husband,' she said in an aside to Ethel and Kirsty.

'I would be at less of a loss if my wife would stay home

more often instead of traipsing away to London all the time.'

Martha put a finger to her lips.

'She's started to speak,' she whispered.

Constance made a commanding figure on the podium and Ethel listened in rapt silence to her speech. In her imagination, she was there with Constance, walking by her side in the parade. She yearned to take part in those events, but as long as she had to earn a living by working in the mill, there was little chance it would ever happen.

After the presentation, Martha returned to the stage and gave a short thank you speech before requesting the attention of all those present.

'You may have heard that we lost one of our members this week – Gladys Burnett. She was to have been a speaker here today, but the police have notified us they discovered her body, at her home, on Friday. The police have not informed us of the circumstances, but we will do our best to find out what happened.'

Unsettled murmurs echoed around the room.

'I have a request. Another our members, Victoria Allan, has been missing for five days, since early Tuesday morning, and we are becoming concerned. Her disappearance may be perfectly innocent, but it would set our minds at rest if we could locate her. If anyone has seen her or knows her whereabouts, could they let me know? Thank you.'

Martha led Constance over to the table.

'I must introduce you to our two newest recruits. Ethel is already a member of the WFL; Kirsty plans to join.'

Constance held her hand out, first to Ethel and then Kirsty.

'I'm pleased you've joined us. I'm sure you won't regret it.'

Embarrassment sent a rush of warmth to Ethel's face. Nobody shook hands where she came from and she hadn't yet become accustomed to handshakes from people she considered her betters. Uncertain whether to stand or remain sitting when Constance offered her hand, Ethel looked across to Martha and, noticing that her friend remained seated, she did the same and hoped she hadn't got it wrong.

'Spiffing speech, Constance. Makes me jealous I wasn't able to come to London with you.' Archie leaned back in his chair and smiled up at his wife, though Ethel noticed his eyes were appraising Kirsty.

'That's a nice thought, Archie, but you know I get on better at these marches without you. And I wouldn't want you wandering around London alone.'

Ethel's first impression of Archie was that he was a dapper young man with a roving eye. His wife was several years older, and she wondered if Constance didn't trust her husband. She pushed the thought away. The gentry weren't like the people she grew up with. They had a different set of rules and she'd noticed that fidelity wasn't something which appeared important in their world.

She turned her attention to Kirsty.

'Now that you've attended one of our meetings, do you think you'll want to join the Women's Freedom League?'

'I'd love to,' Kirsty replied. 'Though I don't think my parents would approve.'

'Do you need their approval?' Ethel hadn't sought permission for anything since she came of working age; she found the concept strange.

'I don't think they'd like the idea, and I haven't come of age yet. I don't think they can forbid me joining, though it would make life difficult.' Kirsty paused for a moment before continuing. 'Yes, I intend to join the Women's Freedom League.' Her voice was firmer than it had been a moment ago. 'I'll visit the office tomorrow to find out how to become a member.'

24

Paul Anderson arrived at the meeting after it started, but remained at the back of the room while Constance Drysdale regaled her audience with descriptions of the event in London. The talk was interesting, but that wasn't the reason he was here. Despite the editor's reaction to his recent editorial, his reporter's instinct told him there was a story to be had, and he meant to follow it up. He soon spotted one of the suffragettes he'd met on Thursday sitting at the front and he listened, with interest, when she asked for information on Victoria Allan. His instinct hadn't been wrong – there was a story here.

He edged between the tables towards the suffragette he recognised and arrived at the same time as a young lady. He stood aside and gestured for her to go ahead, though she didn't appear to notice.

'Martha, I may have seen Victoria on Tuesday when I was on my way to the rally.'

The suffragette he'd recognised turned to the speaker.

'Where was this, Amelia?'

'I was getting off the tram in Ward Road and I'm positive it was Victoria I saw going into the Howff.'

'The graveyard? What on earth would she be doing in there?'

'I don't know, but I'm certain it was her.'

'Thank you, Amelia. I will go along there now, though she will be long gone by this time.' She glanced at her companions. 'Anyone care to accompany me?'

'I'll come with you.' The dark-haired girl sitting at the table leaned forward. 'You mustn't go there alone.'

'I don't mind accompanying you.' The speaker was a soft-spoken, younger girl, whose auburn curls escaped from the confines of her bonnet to cascade down her back.

'Ladies.' Paul removed his hat and stepped forward as soon as Amelia left. 'I couldn't help overhearing, and I feel the Howff is perhaps not the best place for unaccompanied ladies. I would be honoured to accompany you there.'

'And you are, sir?' Martha didn't appear welcoming.

'We met on Thursday evening. I'm Paul Anderson, the *Courier* reporter.'

Martha looked him up and down with eyes so blue they did something strange to his insides.

'I remember,' she said. 'You are the one who mentioned Gladys in the Stop Press.' She narrowed her eyes. 'Did you know she died?'

'Yes. I'm afraid I found her body.'

'How did that happen?'

'She arranged for me to interview her at home, but when I got there, she was lifeless.'

'I see.' Martha leaned back in her chair. 'If you were the one who found her, I would have expected more of an editorial in the *Courier* instead of the few words they printed.'

Paul's hands tightened on the brim of his hat as his anger reignited and threatened to destroy his composure.

'My editor squashed my story.'

'In that case, perhaps you can enlighten us –' she gestured towards Ethel, Kirsty, Constance and Archie '– as to the full details of Gladys's untimely end.'

Paul related everything he knew, including the reaction of both the police and his editor to his opinions.

'I believe Gladys was murdered,' he finished. 'The marks on her throat could only have been caused by strangulation.'

'Do you think the police are covering this up?'

'I wouldn't go so far as to say that, but they certainly don't wish it made public.'

'The police refused to tell us how she died, but I knew it was suspicious.' Water splashed out of her glass on to the table, and Martha stared at the puddle, wondering how it got there.

Ethel reached over and grasped her hand.

'You're shaking. I should take you home.'

Martha pulled free and wiped a tear from her cheek.

'I can't return home until I satisfy myself about Victoria. Amelia said she saw her going into the Howff on Tuesday and we haven't seen her since.'

Thoughts whirled around in Martha's brain. Gladys was dead. Victoria was missing. What if Victoria was dead, as well? She clasped a hand to her head to stop the churning of her mind, but her thoughts always came back to the death threat letter.

No one else knew about that letter because she hadn't wanted to alarm anyone. But she couldn't help wondering if the lack of awareness had contributed to what happened to Gladys. The only consolation was that there had been no further letters, so maybe it was simply a more extreme example of the hate mail they received regularly.

Ethel placed a glass in her hand.

'Drink this, it'll calm you.'

Martha took a large gulp of the water before standing.

'I think it is time we visited the Howff. Amelia saw Victoria going in there and I won't be satisfied until we have checked.' She stood, picking her way through the tables, dodging people who were getting ready to leave. Kirsty, Ethel and Paul followed in her wake.

Archie made a move to go with them, but Constance laid a hand on his arm.

'I think they will be safe with the reporter escorting them. We need to return home – we are entertaining this evening, remember, dear.'

The warmth of the late afternoon sun revived Martha, and she strode along the street with purposeful steps, determined to find out what had happened to Victoria.

25

The screech of the gate's hinges set Martha's nerves jangling. Once inside the graveyard, she became calmer as the warm breeze wafted the scent of flowers towards them. Sun filtered between the overhanging trees, creating a feeling of peace as it dappled the ancient gravestones.

The place appeared innocent and pleasant, but she was glad she wasn't alone. Paul had insisted on accompanying her, and Ethel and Kirsty had followed. Archie Drysdale had also offered, but Constance had stopped him. Archie hadn't looked pleased, but he'd complied with her request.

Doubts filled her mind. It had been six days since Amelia saw Victoria entering the Howff. It was unlikely she would be here. But thoughts of what had happened to Gladys intervened. If Victoria was still here, then something must have occurred to prevent her from leaving.

'Which way?' Ethel's voice broke into her thoughts.

In front of them, several cobbled paths, bordered by flowering shrubs and bushes, wound in various directions. Martha had never been inside the graveyard before and didn't know where the paths led.

'Should we each take a different path?' Kirsty had spoken little since she'd joined their company and her voice was hesitant.

'That's not a good idea. I think we should stick together. But if Victoria is here, it's unlikely she would be in the part of the graveyard that borders on Barrack Street because she'd be visible from the road. I suggest we try the oldest part first. It's overgrown and there's more chance she'd remain hidden.'

Despite the warmth of the sun, a shiver crept up Martha's spine. Paul was talking as if he expected to find a body.

'I think you ladies should wait here while I investigate.'

'No, we will come with you.' Martha stiffened and took a step forward. No man was going to tell her what to do. She didn't need their protection.

Ethel and Kirsty murmured their agreement.

'As you wish.' Paul looked discomfited. 'We'll start here.'

Within a few moments, the foliage became denser and the shadows deepened. Bushes grew around and over the gravestones, giving the impression of neglect and decay. The only sounds were those of the birds in the trees, ominous rustles deep in the undergrowth, and the hushed clack of their feet on the mossy path.

The cobbles convinced Martha that fashionable shoes suitable for a hotel tea party were not the best choice for a walk here. As if to confirm her thoughts, one of her heels caught in the cobblestones.

'Do you want to turn back?' Ethel took her arm.

Despite her misgivings and an increasing sense of dread, Martha shook her head.

'I am all right. I snagged my heel and it threw me off balance.' She smiled at the girls but couldn't help noticing the worried look on Kirsty's face and the bravado on Ethel's. Maybe they were having second thoughts. 'You two can go back if you wish.'

'Where you go, we go.' Ethel's voice was stubborn, and Kirsty nodded her agreement. Paul had vanished out of sight around a turn in the path.

Silence hung over this part of the graveyard, and there was no birdsong. Martha suppressed an involuntary shiver and tried to gather her reserves of courage.

'We'd best catch up with Paul. If there is anything to be found, we need to be there.'

The smell, like nothing Martha had encountered before, assaulted her nostrils as soon as she turned the corner. She pulled a handkerchief from her reticule and held it over her nose.

'Stand back, ladies. You don't want to see this.' Paul

stood between two bushes, staring at something in the undergrowth.

Martha took several steps forward. A loud buzzing broke the former silence in the graveyard.

'What is that noise?'

'Bluebottles.' Paul looked at her. 'Please stay back. If this is Victoria, you won't want to see her like this.'

'But how will we know whether it *is* Victoria unless I look at her?' By this time, the stench was overpowering. Martha pressed the handkerchief even more firmly over her nose.

'You still wouldn't know, not seeing her like this.'

Paul backed out from between the bushes, clutching a handbag.

'I found this beside the body.' He brushed something white and wriggly from the surface before handing it to her. 'It may contain identification.'

Martha's stomach churned and bile rose in her throat, but she forced herself to open it and look inside.

'Yes, this is Victoria's handbag,' she said after a moment.

Paul put his arm around her shoulder. She wanted to push it away, but didn't. There was comfort in his grasp, and she was in sore need of it.

'We must inform the police,' he said.

'They've found her.' The two girls stood in a patch of sunlight at the bend in the path.

Ethel shaded her eyes with a hand and peered towards Paul and Martha. She'd identified the stench as soon as they reached the corner and held Kirsty back from going any further. It was the smell of death. She recalled the putrefying cat that had lain in the back green for weeks. It had stunk like that before someone took a shovel and threw it into one of the rubbish bins.

Her lips compressed as she watched Paul put his arm around Martha's shoulders and lead her along the path. When they drew nearer, Martha's shock was unmistakable.

Her eyes sunk into the pallor of her face, glittering with unshed tears, and the white bone of her knuckles highlighted the strength needed to hold a leather handbag in her shaking hands. Ethel pulled her into an embrace, forcing Paul to step back.

'Is it Victoria?' Ethel addressed Paul, who nodded in reply.

'What do we do now?'

'Report it to the police.'

Ethel snorted.

'They didn't bother too much about Gladys. What makes you think the bobbies will pay any more attention to this? They'll label it as good riddance and lose the file.' In Ethel's opinion, the bobbies were useless. She'd complained to them numerous times after her father had beaten lumps out of her mother.

'It's a domestic matter,' they had always responded. 'Nothing to do with us.'

As for suffragettes, they were only interested in harassing them and moving them on from rallies and meetings. Creating a disturbance, they called it.

'They can't ignore this death, nor can they overlook the fact that two suffragettes have died now – both in suspicious circumstances.'

'You're right, but that doesn't mean they'll do anything about it.'

26

By the time they reached the police station, Martha had regained her composure, but her resentment was growing. Paul's insistence that she shouldn't come close enough to see the body rankled. But if she was truthful with herself, viewing it might have been more than she could bear. Despite this, she couldn't stomach the idea that a man wanted to protect her from something he judged upsetting.

Two policemen, kneeling beside a bicycle at the far end of the police quadrangle, looked up, but Martha paid no heed to their curious glances.

'Ladies,' Paul said, holding the door of the charge-room open for them.

Martha ignored him but beckoned for Ethel and Kirsty to follow her into the police station. Her nose wrinkled as the warmth of the room increased the stench from the graveyard, which permeated their clothing. Her hand tightened on Victoria's handbag; maybe that was the source of the smell. She hoped so. Otherwise, she would have to discard the clothes she was wearing.

The sergeant behind the counter leaned forward.

'What can I do for you, ladies?'

His tone was gruff and his walrus moustache wobbled as he spoke.

Recognition was instantaneous. This was the policeman to whom Martha and Elizabeth Inglis had reported Victoria missing.

'We're here to report the death of a woman in suspicious circumstances.' Paul's voice sounded from behind her.

Martha gave a shrug of annoyance. Did he assume she was incapable of dealing with the policeman?

'Ah! It's Mr Anderson from the *Dundee Courier*. You do

seem to make a habit of finding bodies. What makes you think this one is suspicious, sir?'

Paul leaned his arms on the counter and stared the sergeant down.

'I think a body lying in the Howff graveyard for several days is a mite suspicious.'

'I reported Victoria Allan as a missing person to you on Wednesday,' Martha snapped, 'and it appears we have now found her.' She couldn't keep the bitterness out of her voice.

Sergeant Edwards turned to look at her.

'And how do you know this is the missing woman?'

'Because this handbag was beside her body.' Martha slammed it on to the counter.

'You should not have removed the bag until a policeman inspected it.' He leaned forward and scowled at her.

'And leave it there for anyone to remove? Far better to bring it here for evidence,' Martha snapped.

The sergeant sighed, lifted the flap at the end of the counter and opened the door to the quadrangle.

'Buchan. McDonald. You're needed.'

The two policemen left the bicycle they'd been attempting to repair and scurried over to him.

'McDonald, get yourself to the Howff and mount guard on the gate. Don't allow anyone to enter. Buchan, fetch Inspector Hammond. Off you go, then, the pair of you. At the double, no hanging about.' The sergeant returned to the charge-room. 'The inspector will want to interview you when he gets here, so I suggest you make yourselves comfortable.' He pointed to the wooden bench running the length of the room.

Martha glared at him, but she perched on the bench, thinking that she would never have described the seat as comfortable. Ethel and Kirsty, after sharing a glance, sat down beside her. Paul remained standing, one elbow leaning on the countertop.

It would probably be a long wait. Martha closed her eyes and tried to obliterate the picture her imagination was conjuring up of Victoria's body lying in the graveyard. She had no idea whether the image was worse or better than the reality.

Gran was in a foul mood. It had started at breakfast-time and all because he'd lain in his bed longer than usual.

'Lazy lie abed,' she'd said, dolloping a spoonful of porridge into his bowl.

'But I didn't get home until after midnight,' Hammond protested.

'That's another thing –' she slapped a second spoonful into the bowl '– stopping out until all hours of the night.'

'Saturday night's always busy. There's hardly one goes by without a riot in the Scouringburn.' He stirred the greyish mess in front of him. 'You know fine well it's my job.'

She snorted and banged the pot into the sink.

'Time you had a wife. I'm too old to be running around after you.'

Hammond concentrated on his porridge. Cold, tasteless and lumpy. Gran's cooking left a lot to be desired. As for finding a wife? Hammond had no intention of doing that. He hadn't met a woman yet who didn't strike fear into his heart. Why get tied to someone who would turn out to be just like his gran? He pushed the plate back and rose.

'I'm off to the office,' he said. 'I've reports to complete.' He didn't wait for her response.

It was the middle of the afternoon before he returned, and Gran was in an even worse mood. He was only two steps inside the door when she pounced on him.

'Why can you never be home on time? What time of day do you think this is to be served dinner? It's been ready since one o'clock.'

'Sorry, Gran, but I told you I had to finish reports.'

She snorted.

'I was tempted to let you go hungry, but I kept something back for you.'

'That was good of you.' He pulled out a chair and sat at the table.

Gran bent and drew a plate out of the oven. She slapped it in front of him, making the cutlery rattle and a cup teeter in its saucer.

'Don't say I'm not good to you.'

Hammond looked at it and swore under his breath. He wasn't having the best of days; Gran had taken care of that with her foul temper, and now this. He poked a sausage with his fork. Other folk got beef on a Sunday. But what did he get? Bloody sausage and mash, and burnt sausages, at that. He glowered at it and gave the sausage another poke.

His gran stood over him. 'Well, don't just look at it, get it down you.'

The clatter of boots on the path followed by a knock on the door sent his gran scurrying to answer it.

'It's one of your bobbies,' she said, returning to the kitchen. 'I suppose that means you'll be off out again.'

Hammond pushed his plate aside. A recall to the police station was preferable to eating the muck his gran cooked for him. He grabbed his jacket and, ignoring his gran's mutterings, rushed out the door.

'Sorry, sir,' Buchan said, 'but Sarge ordered me to come get you.'

'What's up?' Hammond reckoned it must be an emergency if the duty sergeant had sent for him.

'He didn't say, sir. But that reporter from the *Courier* turned up with three ladies. I reckon it must be something to do with them.'

Hammond suppressed a groan. He could do without having to deal with know-it-all reporters.

27

The edge of the wooden bench dug into the back of Ethel's legs. No matter how much she wriggled, she was unable to find a comfortable position. She wrinkled her nose. Maybe it was her imagination, but she was sure the smell of death hung over them.

Martha, slumped on her left, had lost her normal sparkle; Kirsty moved restlessly on the bench to her right.

Over by the door, Paul stood staring out into the courtyard, a cigarette between his fingers. Every few moments he puffed it, sending a cloud of smoke whirling around him.

Ethel reached out and gripped Kirsty's hand.

'Will we have to wait much longer?' Kirsty whispered.

Ethel shrugged.

'Depends how long it takes the inspector to get here, I suppose.'

'My aunt will wonder where I am.' Kirsty's eyebrows drew together in a worried frown.

'They're coming.' Paul nipped the glowing end of his cigarette between his finger and thumb and dropped the stub on the floor.

'It's about time,' Martha muttered. She stood up and faced the door.

The man who thrust his way into the room wore a black suit which reminded Ethel of the one her father had hanging in his wardrobe for special occasions. His eyes reflected a meanness of spirit and he didn't bother removing his bowler hat when he entered.

Ethel pursed her lips, unconvinced this man would waste any energy on finding Victoria's killer.

A policeman followed the inspector, and Ethel's eyes

widened as she recognised him. It was the constable who had rescued her from her father yesterday.

Hammond stamped into the charge-room, ignoring everyone apart from the duty sergeant.

'You sent for me, Sergeant Edwards?' He kept his voice abrupt. He liked to keep his officers in their place and knew the sergeant would recognise the implicit threat behind his question.

'Yes, sir. These women –' he looked at them with a contemptuous glance '– and this, here, reporter, reckon they've found the body of a woman in the Howff.'

'I would expect there to be bodies in a graveyard, sergeant.'

'Yes, sir. But they maintain this is foul play, sir, and I reckoned I should inform you.'

Hammond recognised the smaller blonde woman. She was one of those damned suffragettes. He'd seen her when he was investigating the death of that other woman. And now, here she was again. He supposed all three of them were suffragettes. Bad enough he had to interview the reporter, without having to deal with these harridans, as well. He glared at them for a moment before turning back to address the sergeant.

'Has anyone gone to check the Howff to determine if their claim has any substance?'

'I thought you'd want to do that yourself, sir. But I sent Constable McDonald to stand guard at the gate.'

'I see.' Hammond drummed his fingers on the countertop. He ignored the restless movements and muttering behind him. He'd talk to them when he was good and ready.

'Are we going to stay here forever, waiting for you to take our statements?'

Hammond's face tightened into a frown, his body stiffened, and he swivelled around to face the reporter

'Ah, Mr Anderson, I believe. You seem to have an

unfortunate habit of finding dead bodies.'

The reporter moved closer. Hammond stepped back to escape the smell of stale cigarettes on the man's breath.

'If you did your job better, then I wouldn't have to do it for you.' Annoyance radiated from the reporter's face and voice.

'Oh, for heaven's sake.' The blonde suffragette pushed the reporter out of the way. 'I informed you on Wednesday that Victoria was missing, and you did nothing. And all this time she's been lying in the Howff where her killer left her. If you had been doing your job, you would have found her instead of leaving it to us. And that's not all. She is the second suffragette to have been killed this week. You need to do something before there are more deaths.'

'Madam, I think I know how to do my job.' Hammond didn't bother to keep the annoyance from his tone.

The woman snorted with disgust, confirming Hammond's belief that suffragettes were harridans, not fit to be called women.

'Sit down,' he growled. 'When I want to talk to you, I will let you know.'

He turned to face the reporter.

'If you follow me, Mr Anderson, I will take your statement.' He led the way through a door to the inner corridor of the police station. 'You, too,' he called to Buchan. 'You can act as note-taker.'

'What a horrible man,' Martha said, as they left.

'I may wish to talk to you again,' Inspector Hammond had said, dismissing them after his interrogation.

'You certainly couldn't accuse him of being polite.' Paul stopped under the archway to light a cigarette. He threw the spent match on the ground and inhaled. 'I needed that.'

Martha smiled at him.

'Thank you for your support, but I think we can manage now.'

She was anxious for him to leave them because she

wanted to visit Victoria's sister, Elizabeth, and she didn't want a reporter present. The news about Victoria's death would be better to come from her than from the police.

'It's no trouble. I can accompany you as far as the *Courier* building – it's on my way.'

'That's very kind.' It was the opposite direction to the one in which Martha wanted to go, but she walked alongside him rather than risk him following her.

They parted company with Paul at the *Courier* building, and the three young women crossed the road to the top of Reform Street.

'I can see my aunt at the window.' Kirsty looked up to the first-floor window which curved around the corner of the building. 'I'd best leave you here.'

'I am so sorry we subjected you to such a distressing experience,' Martha said, grasping Kirsty's hand within her own. 'I hope it hasn't dissuaded you from joining the Women's Freedom League.'

'On the contrary, it's made me more determined. It's opened my eyes to how women are treated, and if I can help change that, I will.'

Martha reached into her reticule and drew out a calling card. She thrust it into Kirsty's hand.

'The address of the Women's Freedom League office is on the front and I have put my home address on the back. I hope we see you soon.'

'I'll call in tomorrow,' Kirsty said.

Once the door on the corner of the building closed behind Kirsty, the two women continued along the street.

'I'm going to visit Victoria's sister,' Martha said as they reached the end of the street. 'Someone needs to tell her what happened, and I don't trust the police to do it.'

'Would you like me to come with you?'

'I think it best if I go alone.'

After she left Ethel at the Nethergate, Martha's pace didn't slacken. Her task was not a pleasant one, but it had to be done.

28

The sculptures of literature and justice, carved into the stone above the arched doorway, stared down at Paul as he entered the *Courier* building by the staff entrance on Meadowside. With its russet-coloured stonework and arched windows, the impressive, five-storey structure looked more like a museum or fancy hotel than a newspaper office. He reckoned no other newspaper in Britain could boast an office equal to this. The building had been only been completed two years before and contained all the modern facilities it was possible to have. According to the other reporters, it was far superior to the old offices in North Lindsay Street.

The glass-panelled door swung closed behind him and he strode across the vestibule to the lift. Seconds later, he stepped out of it at the fourth-floor newsroom and hurried over to his desk. The desks were laid out in rows of two, so the reporters faced each other. It could be distracting but, if you were in luck, the reporter opposite might be out on a story. Paul was out of luck today. Old Angus – Paul had never heard him called anything else – looked up with a brief nod before returning his scrutiny to the copy in front of him, over which he made tutting noises as he scribbled corrections.

Paul slumped into his chair, grabbed a pencil and started to compose his copy for tomorrow's paper. He paid no attention when old Angus got up and padded off in the direction of the editor's office.

Several minutes later, the man returned waving his article.

'Duncan's in a good mood today. He gave the go-ahead, so it'll be in tomorrow.'

'Congratulations.' Paul suppressed his annoyance at the

interruption. 'Maybe he'll like mine for a change.'

Angus rolled the paper and stuffed it into a container for the pneumatic tube to whisk up to the case room on the fifth floor.

'I'm off now. Good luck.'

Five minutes later, Paul sat back, a satisfied smile on his face. This was one of the best news stories he'd worked on this year and he was sure he could expand on it. Tomorrow, he'd follow it up by interviewing the suffragettes.

He whistled under his breath as he sought out the editor. There was no way Duncan could refuse to print this.

Martha's footsteps slowed as she drew near Elizabeth's house on Perth Road. There was no easy way to inform her of Victoria's death. She hesitated on the doorstep for a moment before summoning the courage to knock. The door swung open so fast Martha suspected Elizabeth must have been hovering nearby, waiting for the delivery of bad news or for Victoria to return home.

'Have you found Victoria?' Elizabeth's eyes moved to look over Martha's shoulder as if she expected her sister to be behind her.

'I'm sorry,' Martha said. 'Can I come in?'

'Of course.' Elizabeth opened the door wider. 'Where are my manners?' She led the way up the corridor to the small living-room.

'Who is it, Lizzie?' The man sitting in the armchair looked up with an expectant look in his eyes. 'Oh,' he said. 'It's one of them. I suppose you've come to tell us that Victoria's off gallivanting in London. Damned suffragettes can't stay home for two minutes.' He spat in the empty fireplace.

'My husband, Davie. I don't think you've met him before. Pay no heed to him, he's got a bee in his bonnet about suffragettes. Him and Victoria used to have loads of arguments, but it made no difference to her beliefs.'

'Load of codswallop,' the man said, snorting.

'There's no need for that kind of talk, Davie.' Elizabeth scowled at him. 'Martha is as concerned as we are about Victoria.' She turned back to their guest. 'Have you found her?'

Martha's hand tightened on her reticule. This was more difficult than she had imagined. They were looking for good news and all she had to impart was bad.

'I'm sorry,' she said.

'She's dead.' The light faded from Elizabeth's eyes and her voice held no emotion.

'Yes.'

'How?'

'We found her body in the Howff. I don't know how she died, but someone killed her.'

Tears slipped down Elizabeth's cheeks and Martha grasped her hands.

'I expect the police will be along to visit you at some point, but I wanted you to hear it from me first.'

'Thank you,' Elizabeth mumbled.

'I always said no good would come from her mixing with suffragettes.'

'Oh, shut up, Davie! What do you know about it?'

A feeling of impotence crept through Martha. It was time to leave Elizabeth to her grief, though she wasn't sure Davie shared it.

'I'll leave now,' she said. 'If you need me, you know where to find me.'

Inspector Hammond paced back and forth on the cobbled path, waiting for the police doctor to finish his examination. His nose twitched, and he held a handkerchief to it in an effort to block out the stench. The smell of death was something he tolerated, but never got used to, and this one was fouler than usual.

Dr Jenkins emerged from the bushes at the side of the path.

'You don't need me to tell you she's dead,' he said.

'Been there several days, I'd say. They go off quick in this hot weather. She's not a pretty sight.'

'Can you identify how she died?' Hammond removed the handkerchief from his nose and tried not to breathe too deeply.

The doctor shrugged his shoulders.

'Not at this stage. I'll know more when I examine her.'

'I don't suppose it could be accidental?'

Jenkins laughed.

'Not a hope,' he said. 'By the way, she's wearing a suffragette sash, bit like the other one you put my way this week.'

'Damned suffragettes,' Hammond responded. 'If they would just stay at home where they should be, it would save us a lot of work.'

'Not much chance of that.' Jenkins laughed again and walked away from the inspector. 'I'll let Davvy know he can collect the body now – I see him waiting at the gate.'

Hammond grunted. He couldn't bring himself to thank the man.

Davvy trundled towards him, pushing the coffin-shaped barrow. The man never minded what condition a body was in when he removed it. Hammond reckoned he'd be lucky to get this one in the barrow in one piece.

The buzzing of the bluebottles increased and the stench intensified as Davvy got to work. Hammond clasped the handkerchief over his nose again. He'd be thankful when this was over.

After what seemed an age, Davvy closed the lid of the barrow and fastened the lock. With a grunt, he hoisted the shafts up and, grasping them, he set off for the mortuary. The wheels clattered over the cobbles and Hammond waited until the noise faded into the distance before calling to the constables standing guard at the gate.

'Buchan, McDonald – I want you to search the ground where the body was lying and the area surrounding it.'

'What are we looking for, Inspector?'

'Clues, man. Anything the killer may have left behind,

anything that might point to who he is.'

As Hammond left the graveyard, he chuckled to himself. The expression on the bobbies' faces had been priceless.

29

Monday, 29th June 1908

Martha's face was wet with tears when she woke to the clatter of horses' hooves in the Nethergate and the rattle of the milk cart. Her sleep had been fitful and filled with unpleasant dreams: Elizabeth sobbing and searching for her sister; the Howff, with its cobbled paths and crumbling gravestones; Inspector Hammond pointing an accusing finger at her; Paul restraining her and preventing her from seeing Victoria; and a faceless Victoria, rising from behind the bushes, covered in blood and gore. All of them pointing their fingers and saying, 'It's your fault.'

Was it her fault? If she'd told everyone about the death threat, would it have made any difference? And would Victoria still be alive? It was impossible to tell, and she couldn't change anything now. What was done was done.

She untangled the sheet from her legs and thrust them out of the bed. The blankets were bunched in an untidy mess and her pillow lay on the floor. Her dress was where she left it last night. When she'd returned home, Ethel had comforted her and tucked her up with a cup of cocoa.

'You'll feel better in the morning,' she'd said. But Ethel hadn't known Victoria, so her murder wouldn't have the same impact and she didn't know about the death threat.

Martha shivered. She would have to do something about that letter. At least, if the others knew, they would be on guard. Maybe it was a coincidence, as Inspector Hammond had stressed to her yesterday, but it was better to be safe than sorry.

Her lips tightened, and she frowned as she thought of the policeman. The man was a boor with no manners, and he'd treated her with contempt during her interview. At one point, she'd been tempted to walk out, but what good would that have done? Ethel was right, the police were useless and had no interest in protecting suffragettes from violence. She doubted if they would spend much time looking for the person who killed Victoria and Gladys. Apart from that, Inspector Hammond believed the two deaths were unconnected. Another coincidence according to him; but Martha was convinced it must be the same killer.

She forced herself to rise from where she sat on the edge of the bed, but she remained irate while she performed her ablutions and dressed. With no one to talk to, her anger simmered beneath the surface and she prepared and ate a breakfast that was tasteless in her mouth.

There was no point in leaving for the Women's Freedom League Office until ten o'clock, so she pottered about, keeping an eye on the clock even though the hands never seemed to move.

Eight o'clock chimed and then, after an eternity, nine o'clock. Martha stopped pacing and went to the window to stare outside at the long row of hansom cabs lined up in the church's shadow. Dundee High Street would be waking up, the shops and department stores unlocking their doors.

The thump of the door-knocker disturbed her ruminations, and she hurried along the hall to find out who was seeking her this early in the morning.

'I've brought you a copy of the *Courier*.' Paul Anderson held it out to her.

Martha caught her breath.

'How did you know where I lived?' She was certain she hadn't told him.

'I'm a reporter. It's my job to find things out.'

She took the newspaper from him.

'It's on page five,' he said. 'If you ask me in, I could show you.'

Martha narrowed her eyes. He had a cheek, thinking a woman on her own would allow a strange man to enter her house. But she was a modern woman, a suffragette, and she wasn't afraid for her reputation. In any case, Aggie, her daily maid of all work, would arrive soon. It would be a brave man who tried to get the better of this virago – she probably had more strength than any man in Dundee.

'I suppose you can come in.' She stood aside to allow him to enter.

'The editor made me remove "suffragette" and replace it with "woman".' He spread the paper out on the table.

Martha leaned forward to read the article.

'Do you think the police will investigate?'

'I reckon they'll have to, although I'm not sure how much effort they'll put in. But reporters are investigators, as well, and I thought I might make my own enquiries.'

'Where will you start?'

'I thought I might speak to the young lady who saw Victoria enter the Howff. There's a possibility she might have seen the killer.'

'Hmm.' Martha turned the idea over in her mind. 'You could be right.'

'I wondered if you would come with me. She's more likely to talk to me if you're present.'

'We should have her address on file. I'll get my jacket.' Martha's heart pounded with excitement. Gladys and Victoria's killer wasn't going to escape justice if she had anything to do with it.

Inspector Hammond chewed the stem of his pipe and scowled at the reports in front of him. Two women dead, and either there was a killer stalking women, or two murderers had struck within days of each other. Either way, it was a mess. The interviews yesterday had left him uneasy. He disliked interviewing women, and when they were suffragettes, that only made it worse.

The small one with the fair hair had been belligerent, and he'd lost his temper when she kept insisting on a connection between the deaths and the poison pen letter she'd received. It had made him more adamant there was no connection but, on reflection, she might have a point.

Footsteps thudded up the corridor and stopped at his door.

'Have you seen this, sir?' Sergeant Edwards placed a newspaper on the desk. 'It's on page five, sir. That reporter's wasted no time.'

Hammond waited until the sergeant left before opening the *Courier*. He groaned as he read the story. The Chief Constable was bound to be on his tail, wanting to know what he'd done about the murders.

He laid his pipe on the desk and strode along the corridor to the constables' room. A haze of smoke hung over the desks and several bobbies were trying their best to look busy.

'Buchan. My office, now,' he called, after considering the scene for a moment.

The young constable sprang to attention, but Hammond didn't miss the look of alarm in his eyes. He was probably wondering what he'd done wrong.

The corridor echoed with their booted footsteps as they returned to Hammond's office. Once there, the inspector slumped into his chair while Buchan stood in front of the desk.

'You will be attached to me while we investigate these murders. But don't think it is because you are a better bobby than the others, though you do write a good report. It's because you have been involved from the start, and the ladies seem to relax more when you are there. Not that I'm interested in pandering to them, you understand, but if they feel more relaxed, they will give us more information.'

'Yes, sir.'

'Now, your notes say it was a young lady –' Hammond scrolled his finger down the page '– Amelia Craig, who witnessed the victim entering the Howff. We need to interview her and find out what else she saw.'

'Yes, sir.'

'We don't have an address for her, so in the first instance we will call at the Women's Freedom League shop to enquire.' Hammond shuddered. That meant he'd have to deal with the suffragettes again. 'You can make the enquiry, but I will accompany you.'

'That's funny,' Martha said as they approached the shop. 'The door is open. It's too early for Lila or any of the others to be here.' She pushed the door and stepped inside. It took a moment for her eyes to adjust from the sunshine outside to the gloom. 'Is that you, Lila?' she asked as she focused on the figure sitting on a chair in front of the counter.

The woman's hat obscured her face, and she didn't move.

Martha frowned. The woman was too small to be Lila, but perhaps Lila had let her in to wait while she ran an errand.

'Something's wrong,' Paul muttered from behind her.

A chill that had nothing to do with the temperature in the room shivered through Martha. Paul was right. The lack of response from the woman was unnatural. She tiptoed towards her and put her hand on a shoulder.

'Are you . . .?' Before she could say another word, the woman slid sideways and her hat slipped from her head. Martha struggled to breathe. This couldn't be happening. Not again. Not here, where suffragettes should be safe.

Paul took hold of Martha's hand and removed it from the woman's shoulder.

'Who is she?' he asked in a soft voice.

The body slipped further to the side. One end of the silk scarf knotted around her neck dangled in front of her, revealing the motto, *'Votes for Women'*.

Martha shuddered.

'It's Amelia. She won't be able to tell us anything now.'

Hammond blew a cloud of pipe smoke into the air.

'You know what you have to do when we get there.'

'Yes, sir. I request information and the address of Amelia Craig.'

'Good lad. Don't let them fob you off. They're a tricky

lot, these suffragettes.'

'Yes, sir.'

When they reached the Women's Freedom League headquarters, Hammond clamped his teeth around the stem of his pipe and walked through the open door. Inside, a man and a woman stood over what looked like a body.

'Well, well, well. What have we here?' Hammond removed the pipe from his mouth.

'We have only been here a few minutes. She was like this when we arrived.' It was that infuriating blonde woman again, and her voice held a note of reproof.

'Likely story,' Hammond said. 'Strange that you are always on the spot when a body is found.'

He fixed his eyes on the reporter, but the man stared back with defiance.

'As Miss Fairweather has told you, we've only just arrived. We were on the point of sending for you.'

Hammond pulled his brows together in a frown. The man sounded convincing, but he had his doubts; there was something about him that didn't ring true. If the police doctor confirmed the death had been within the past hour, he would make sure the reporter spent time in the cells.

'Buchan, take statements from these two but do it outside while I investigate what has happened here. After that, run back to Bell Street and arrange for the police doctor to attend. You two,' he addressed Martha and Paul, 'wait outside until I've finished here.' Almost as an afterthought, he added, 'Who is she?'

'It's Amelia Craig, the woman who witnessed Victoria Allan going into the Howff.' The blonde woman glared at him. 'And there is no need to send this young man for the doctor; you may use our telephone.' She gestured to the instrument attached to the wall behind him before turning her back and flouncing out the door.

Hammond rammed his pipe into his mouth and clamped his teeth around the stem. Damn it, he thought; the killer had taken care of the only witness to the earlier murder.

30

Kirsty pushed the guilty feelings to the back of her mind as she clattered down the stairs. She didn't like being dishonest with Aunt Bea, but she dreaded her father turning up with a demand for her to return home. Besides, she wasn't really being dishonest. She'd told no lies. On the other hand, she hadn't told her aunt where she was going nor what she intended to do.

'I need fresh air and it's a lovely day,' she'd said after breakfast.

She knew there was no risk of her aunt offering to go with her because Kirsty had overheard her telling the maid to use the best china when her friends came to call later that morning.

Outside, the town was coming to life. Early morning shoppers barely looked at her as she sped along Reform Street. If only they knew she was on her way to commit herself to something destined to change her life. An action she intended to carry out in defiance of her father.

A few weeks earlier, she would have sought his approval, but now she didn't care.

Meeting and mixing with suffragettes had opened her eyes to the reality of being a woman in a man's society and the possibility of change, provided she was willing to fight for them.

Despite her rebellious thoughts, though, she was realistic enough to acknowledge her father's authority. If he demanded she return home, Kirsty would be powerless to resist.

The sixpence she clutched in her hand dug into her skin as her fingers tightened around it. This coin could open the door to her burgeoning independence. Once she handed over the sixpenny subscription fee, she would officially be a suffragette.

When she reached the end of Reform Street, Kirsty pushed her way through the crowds streaming into the Overgate to do their daily shopping. A brewer's cart pulled by a massive horse clattered past and she dodged behind it to cross the road.

Further up the Nethergate, Kirsty recognised Martha and Paul standing on the pavement. What puzzled her was the police constable talking to Paul and writing in his notebook. It was the same policeman who had been present yesterday when they were being interviewed at the station. What was he doing here? Maybe the police had found the killer. Or maybe they just wanted more information.

She quickened her step, eager to find out what was happening.

Martha looked up as she approached, and it surprised Kirsty to see tears in her eyes. Her breath caught in her throat.

'What's wrong?' Kirsty grasped the hand Martha held out to her.

'Ah, Kirsty, you have come to join us at the worst possible time.'

'What do you mean?'

Martha nodded her head towards the door, which hung ajar.

'There has been another death.'

'Another one?' It seemed the most inane thing to say, but Kirsty, caught unaware, could think of nothing else. She closed her eyes and tightened her grip on Martha's hand, feeling it tremble within her own. 'Is it . . . is it anyone I know?'

She searched her mind, trying to visualise the women she'd met yesterday, but the only face she could remember was Ethel's. Let it not be Ethel, she prayed inwardly.

'You met her yesterday.' Martha pulled free from Kirsty's grip. 'It's Amelia, the girl who told us she saw Victoria go into the Howff.'

Kirsty tried to conjure up Amelia's face but failed. She flushed as relief that it wasn't Ethel flooded, unbidden, through her.

Hammond laid the contents of the dead woman's handbag on the counter; a purse containing a few coins, lace handkerchief, mirror, perfume bottle, a few hairpins and what he presumed was a hairpin holder. He'd hoped to find a notebook or a diary, something to show whose company she had been in when she met her death. But there was nothing of assistance.

The door to the street crashed open, slamming into the wall behind it with a thud.

'This had better be necessary.' The man standing before him scowled. 'You've pulled me away from a consultation with a private patient and he was none too pleased at my departure.'

'Of course, it's necessary,' Hammond responded gruffly. 'I wouldn't have sent for you otherwise.'

'I suppose it's another dead body you've got for me, though why you think the dead are more important than the living is a mystery to me.'

Hammond bit back the retort hovering on his lips. Jenkins never failed to arouse his anger. The man was quick enough to accept the stipend attached to his position as police doctor, but he was less keen to turn out and do the job when the request was made.

Unable to keep silent any longer, Hammond pointed to the body.

'I am sure it will not take up too much of your time.' He stood back to give the doctor room for his examination.

'She's dead, all right. You didn't need me to tell you that. She's as stiff as a board.'

'I require the official declaration of death before I can move the body. You know that as well as I do,' he couldn't help adding.

'Well, you've got it. I'll be on my way, and good luck

removing her to the mortuary. Getting her into the barrow will be a challenge.' A faint smile twitched at the corners of his mouth.

'Before you go . . .'

Jenkins halted in the doorway.

'If you're going to ask me for a time of death, you needn't bother. I won't know that until the post-mortem.'

'Roughly?'

'Given the state of rigor, I'd say anything from eight to twenty-four hours.'

Hammond scowled, watching the door swing shut behind the doctor. His conviction the reporter and that brazen suffragette were involved didn't diminish although the woman had been dead long before they found her. In the meantime, he had insufficient reason to insist they accompany him to the police station. He'd have to let them go.

'Pardon me, ladies.' The portly man leaving the WFL premises lifted his homburg hat and nodded his head in their direction.

Martha stepped forward. 'Is the inspector finished?'

'Ah, now. That's something you'll have to ask him. If you'll excuse me, ladies, I must be on my way – my patients await.'

Kirsty watched him waddle off towards the High Street. She supposed he must be the doctor, though he was nothing like her own family physician. She turned her attention back to the group standing on the pavement. It had grown while they were waiting for Inspector Hammond to emerge. Lila Clunas, the WFL organiser for Dundee, had joined them several minutes ago, as well as Constance Drysdale. Despite having met both women the day before, she wasn't confident enough to address them and hovered in the background while they conversed.

Paul, who had been smoking furiously and pacing back and forth at the edge of the road, stopped to throw the butt of his cigarette into the gutter.

'I don't suppose you expected this kind of excitement when you chose to become a suffragette.'

'I wouldn't call it excitement,' she said, shrugging, her voice stiff with displeasure. She had no wish to make small talk with any man, and certainly not one who treated her with familiarity.

An amused look crossed the reporter's face but before he could answer her, Inspector Hammond appeared in the doorway. The police constable, who'd been lounging against the wall further along the street, sprang to attention and scurried to his side. Hammond glared at the assembled women.

'I won't be needing you to wait any longer. You may go.'

'When can we expect to gain entry?' Lila Clunas stepped forward. 'We have work to do.' Her annoyance sounded in her clipped tones.

'Not until we finish here and the body is removed.'

'How long will that take?'

'It could be an hour or two or it could be all day. There's no knowing at this stage.'

'I trust that when you depart, you will leave a guard on the door to prevent any ruffian from the streets from entering.'

'That won't be possible, madam.'

'In that case, I insist you lock the premises and deliver the key back to me.'

Hammond grasped the iron key, but Kirsty could see the displeasure on his face.

'You may collect the key from the Central Police Station.'

'That's not acceptable, particularly when you cannot give me a time-frame for your departure. I insist you deliver the key to me.' Lila's voice brooked no argument, and she stared at Hammond until he looked away.

'And where, may I ask, should I deliver the key?'

Martha's soft voice intervened.

'You can bring it to me at my house. It's the one in the

courtyard behind the shop.' She gestured to the close between the WFL shop and Peter Anderson's bakery.

'My constable can bring it.' A faint smile twitched at the corner of his lips. Kirsty hadn't seen him smile before and thought it made him seem less fierce.

'Come,' Martha said, 'shall we convene to my humble abode until the key arrives?' She looked at Hammond and smiled at him. 'I trust it won't be too long.'

Hammond didn't answer her. Instead, he turned to the constable.

'Run along, laddie, and get Davvy to bring the barrow to take the body to the mortuary.'

31

Sweat trickled down Ethel's back as she dashed backwards and forwards along the length of the spinning frame. Her hands were damp and slippery, and she feared she might lose her grip on the silvery flyers which stopped the spindles long enough for her to mend the broken ends of jute.

The heat in the spinning shed had reached an intolerable level; if it was like this midmorning, what would it be like later in the day? In the summer, she often wished she worked in one of the other departments, where it wouldn't matter if cool air from an open door blew through the room. The smallest breeze wafting between the frames here, though, meant far more broken ends as the jute flowed from the roves, between the rollers, to the bobbins below.

Time dragged. The hands of the clock above the door seemed motionless. But, at long last, the whistle which indicated the lunch-break shrieked and echoed through the room. Ethel wiped the sweat from her brow and, with a sigh of relief, switched the machine off and watched it power down.

A box at the end of her spinning frame held her shawl and packet of sandwiches. This was where she sat to eat during the colder weather but on fine, sunny days, like today, everyone headed outside to stand in groups in the courtyard.

Eager to find a shady spot outside, she grabbed her sandwiches and bottle of water and hurried for the door. She selected a place near to the room where the winders worked and waited for her ma to come out. She didn't have long to wait, and she stood to give her a hug.

'I've missed you, Ma.' The surge of emotion caught Ethel by surprise.

'Me, too.' Ma grasped her hands and looked at her with

tears in her eyes. 'But I've come to tell ye that ye need to go. Get out of here and don't come back.'

'Why?'

'It's Hughie. He's found out ye're a suffragette, and he's threatening to kill you. Says he won't stand for a suffragette in the family.'

'That's all talk and bluster. I can handle Da.' Ethel would have crossed her fingers if her mother hadn't had such a tight grip on her hands; she was holding so tightly Ethel's fingers ached.

'Not this time,' Margery said. 'He'll be waiting for ye when ye finish work tonight and he's got himself knuckle dusters. Says he won't stop until ye're dead.'

'But what about you?' Ethel's worries over leaving her mother increased. 'He'll take it out on you.'

'You can't protect me. Ye never could. I'm used to Hughie and I'm used to his fists. He might give me a hammering, but he won't kill me. He needs my wages.'

Ethel knew her mother spoke the truth, but that didn't dissipate her unease.

'I don't know how you've put up with it all these years.'

'Not much I can do about it. He's the man of the house and men do what they want. When was it ever any different?'

Ethel freed her hands from her mother's grasp and hugged her again.

'If women get the vote, we can make it different.'

'Ah, you and your vote. It'll never happen.'

'We'll make it happen.'

'Maybe. But if ye don't get out of here, ye won't live to see the day. Go, and don't come back, Ethel.'

'I can't leave you.' Despair clutched her. It was selfish to concentrate on pursuing her dreams when her mother would suffer.

'You have to go. Ye've no choice. I'd rather have a daughter I never see than a dead one.'

A tear slipped down Margery's cheek.

'Go. Go now. And watch out for your father!'

Ethel gathered her belongings together and left, making the excuse to the gatekeeper that she didn't feel well. She ran along the road without looking back, even though this would be the last time she saw the mill.

Ethel hesitated in the hallway. The murmur of voices from the drawing-room suggested Martha had visitors, and she wasn't keen for them to see her in her mill clothes. She crept past the door which hung ajar but had only reached the bottom step of the staircase before Martha came out of the room.

'I thought I heard you come in,' she said. 'Will you join us?'

'I can't, dressed like this.' Ethel gestured to her grubby skirt and blouse. 'I'll change first and have a quick wash. Will that be all right?'

'Of course. But be quick about it. There have been developments.'

Martha returned to the drawing-room, leaving Ethel wondering what could have happened.

By the time she finished her ablutions and changed from her grubby mill clothes into something cleaner, she felt more able to join the women congregated in the lounge, though she hadn't yet cast off the feeling they were her superiors. She turned back for a final look in the mirror before leaving her bedroom, adjusting the collar of her blouse with nervous fingers and pushing a strand of hair behind her ear. With a deep breath, she tried to calm her nerves, wondering why meeting other suffragettes, who were of a higher social standing, was scarier than facing a hectoring crowd as she dished out leaflets at rallies.

The sound of the doorbell echoed through the house as she closed her bedroom door. By the time she descended the stairs, Aggie was ushering a bobby along the hall.

Ethel's breath caught in her throat. It was the same one who had rescued her from her father and whom she'd seen yesterday at the police station. As she reached the bottom step, he turned.

'It's Miss Stewart, isn't it,' he said. 'I trust you've had no further trouble from your father?'

Heat crept from Ethel's neck to her cheeks.

'Thank you for your help yesterday. I'm hoping to stay out of my father's way, but I've heard he's making threats against me.'

Ethel avoided the bobby's eyes, feeling that, perhaps, she shouldn't have told him that.

'If I can be of any help . . .'

'This way, sir,' Aggie interrupted. 'I believe the ladies have been waiting for your arrival.'

Constable Buchan raised his eyebrows, offering Ethel an embarrassed grin before following the maid into the drawing-room.

Ethel entered behind him and surveyed the women congregated there.

Constance Drysdale sat, alone, on the velvet chaise longue to the left of the window. Two other suffragettes perched on chairs nearby, while Kirsty sat in an armchair at the opposite side of the room. Martha and Lila were engrossed in papers strewn on an occasional table, obscuring its walnut inset top. Apart from Kirsty, who looked up when the door opened, none of the others appeared to notice the policeman's entry.

He waited a moment before shuffling his feet and clearing his throat to draw their attention.

Constance removed her gaze from the window and raised her eyebrows. Martha and Lila looked up from the papers and Lila laid her pencil down. Ethel frowned. Why were they gathered here? And why did they show no surprise when the bobby entered the room? It was as though they were expecting him.

'Ladies,' he said. 'I've come to inform you that you are now free to return to your premises.' He produced a key from his pocket.

'Thank you.' Martha rose from her chair. 'I trust the inspector will keep us informed of developments.'

The policeman hesitated before replying.

'I'll inform him of your interest.'

As soon as he was out of earshot, Lila spoke.

'It is obvious the police won't keep us informed.'

'I'm sure you are right,' Martha agreed. 'But I intend to press for information at every opportunity.'

Lila dropped the key into her handbag.

'Florence and Helen are on this afternoon's rota for the shop, though we will remain closed today. It will give us time to set everything straight after what has happened.'

Martha nodded.

'Do you need me to help?' she asked.

'That won't be necessary, but we can discuss how best to handle this situation when you arrive tomorrow. Come, ladies, we have work to do.' Lila beckoned to the two women seated in the corner.

Ethel slipped further into the room and perched on the arm of Kirsty's chair.

'What's happened?' she whispered. 'What have I missed?'

Kirsty leaned closer to Ethel.

'There's been another murder, and they found her in the WFL office.'

'Who?' Ethel's breath caught in her throat.

'The woman who saw Victoria at the Howff. I think her name's Amelia.'

'How awful. Were you there when the body was found?'

'No, it was Martha and that reporter, Paul. I came along later.'

'They were together?'

Kirsty nodded.

'Where's Paul now?'

'He left us after the policeman said we could go. Something about needing to get back to the newspaper to lodge his copy, whatever that means.'

Ethel stared across the room at Martha, who was whispering to Constance and helping her adjust her feathered hat.

Things were happening that she didn't fully understand, and she wondered if they were being manipulated by Paul in his quest for headlines.

Constance was the last one to leave and Martha accompanied her to the door.

'I am sure Archie will recover soon,' she said, reassuring her friend.

She had been introduced to Constance on her arrival in Dundee, and they became firm friends because of their shared interest in the suffrage movement. Martha's commitment to it was unwavering, but no match for the level of Constance's involvement, especially in the more militant activities. Constance's only weakness was her husband, Archie, to whom she was devoted.

'The physician has prescribed complete bed-rest and a bland diet.' Constance caught her breath. 'He's convinced it must have been bad oysters he ate last night. I told him they were out of season, but he insisted on having them.'

'He's young, he'll soon recover.'

A wry smile tugged at the corner of Constance's lips.

'I am sure you're right.' She descended the stone steps to the courtyard and hurried through the narrow close leading to the main street.

Martha pondered the couple's relationship as she returned upstairs. Constance was older than Archie, but they appeared to be happy, even though Archie had a roving eye at times.

Ethel and Kirsty were whispering together when Martha entered the drawing-room. Despite the differences in their backgrounds the two girls had become friends.

Kirsty rose from her chair.

'I must take my leave. I fear I may have overstayed . . .'

'Nonsense. You're welcome to stay.' Martha gestured to the chair Kirsty had vacated and crossed the room to sit beside her. 'I worry that Ethel doesn't have anyone nearer her age to talk to about the things that interest young girls.'

'You mean things like fashion and boyfriends? I'm not

interested in any of that.' Ethel frowned.

'Nor am I.' Kirsty's voice was quieter but no less firm.

'That may be the case, but I am ten years older than you and it's beneficial to have a friend your own age.' Martha watched the two girls exchange glances. She wasn't wrong. Her two protégés: Ethel, a mill worker, and the more refined Kirsty, had grown close in the short time they'd known each other.

'I take it you are aware of why we were gathered here today?' she asked.

'Kirsty told me about Amelia's death.' Ethel shuddered. 'That makes three now. Do you think someone is targeting suffragettes?'

'It's possible. You missed the meeting, so won't know that the outcome is we intend to restrict our activities on the streets for the time being and to alert as many of our members as we can. WSPU and NUWSS members will need to be made aware, so Lila is arranging for this to happen. We will also issue a warning during our meeting next week in the Kinnaird Hall. In the meantime, I want you both to be careful when you are out and about. Try not to be alone on the streets in the evenings.'

'I'm not sure the bobbies are treating this seriously.' Ethel drummed her fingers on the arm of the chair. 'Shouldn't we be doing more than just alerting folks to be on guard?'

'I must admit I find the inspector rude and dismissive, but surely his job is to find the killer.'

'You haven't had much experience dealing with bobbies.' Ethel laughed mirthlessly.

'And you have?' Martha's eyebrows rose. Ethel's outlook on life continued to astonish her.

'Not personally.' Ethel shrugged. 'But we used to see a lot of them where I lived before. They didn't need an excuse to arrest the young lads, even if they hadn't done anything, and they liked to wallop heads with their batons. When the posh boys came and caused trouble, though, that was a different matter.'

Martha leaned back in her chair with a smile on her face.

'I believe you are cynical, Ethel.'

'With good reason. But don't you see? It's because the murdered women were suffragettes. The bobbies look on them as nuisances and are glad to be rid of a few, so they won't do anything.'

'You might have a point. What do you think, Kirsty?'

'I have little experience with the police. But I think Ethel's right. I saw the way the inspector looked at us. We were like the dirt under his fingernails. I didn't like his attitude.'

'Where I come from, we deal with things ourselves,' Ethel stated. 'Leave it to the bobbies and they've got you over a barrel. They'll fiddle with the evidence and make it fit so they can say they've done their job. Doesn't matter to them whether they get the right person or not.'

'Are you saying they falsify evidence?' Martha couldn't keep the shock from her voice.

'I've seen it happen. There's more than one lad locked up for something he didn't do, just because it suits the bobbies.' Ethel clenched her fists. 'My da should be in prison for beating on my ma. He broke her jaw once, and she's had broken arms and more bruises than you can count. But do they come for him? No, because they know he's tough and gives as good as he gets. Besides, he's a man, and a man's allowed to beat his wife.'

'Oh, Ethel, I am so sorry.' Martha wanted to throw her arms around the younger woman, but she didn't think the girl would welcome the embrace.

'And now, he's threatened to kill me because I'm a suffragette. I've had to leave my job so he can't find me.' Ethel's voice was muffled, indicating the shame she felt with this admission.

Kirsty leaned over and took hold of Ethel's hands.

'That's terrible, but you'll always have friends willing to help.' She looked at Martha, a question in her eyes.

'Of course,' Martha responded. 'Your home is here now, and we will make sure you stay safe.'

'That's easier said than done. And now, because of him, I've no job and no way of supporting myself.'

'That is not something you need to worry about.' Martha's voice brooked no argument. 'The women who belong to our cause have always looked after each other. If your father finds you and becomes more of a problem, I can arrange for you to help the cause elsewhere.'

'You mean leave Dundee?'

'If it becomes necessary, yes.'

'Would you come with me?'

'I don't think that would be possible, because my work with the league is here in Dundee. But we could stay in touch.'

'Then I'm not going. I'll take my chances here.'

Martha was unsure whether it was fear or defiance she detected in Ethel's eyes, but she had no intention of arguing with the girl.

'As you wish.'

'Besides, if the police aren't prepared to do their job, we'll have to do it for them.'

'You mean, we should look for the killer ourselves?' Kirsty looked at Ethel with awe. 'But wouldn't that be dangerous?'

'Not any more dangerous than sitting back and waiting for him to claim his next victim, which could be you or me.'

A smile tugged at the corner of Martha's mouth.

'That is perhaps a trifle extreme, Ethel, although I admire your keenness. But we are not the police. They might look on it as interference.'

'I couldn't care tuppence what they think.' Ethel scowled.

'Maybe we can tackle it in a different way. Make discreet enquiries and feed our findings to the police.'

'I can't see that inspector paying attention to anything we say.'

'There is more than one way to skin a cat,' Martha murmured. 'That constable who accompanies him seems to have taken a shine to you, Ethel. Perhaps you could give him a little encouragement and we could impart our findings that way.'

Kirsty gasped, but Ethel nodded her head vigorously.

'I can manage that.' Ethel turned to Kirsty and patted her hand. 'Don't worry. I know how to handle men – I won't come to any harm.'

'In that case, I suggest we make some initial enquiries,' Martha said.

32

Kirsty tapped the top of her boiled egg and peeled the shell away. Her thoughts were on the events of yesterday. She'd never been involved with anything of this nature before and, though it sent shivers up her spine, it was strangely exciting. Murder! Up to the present, it had been a word with which she was unfamiliar but now, within the space of a few days, the bodies of three women had been found in circumstances that indicated they had been murdered.

On top of that, there was Ethel's problem with her father. Kirsty couldn't imagine a father inflicting violence on his daughter, but Ethel came from a background very different from her own.

'You are up bright and early.' Aunt Bea bustled into the room. 'Have you something planned for today?'

'I'm seeing my friends, Martha and Ethel. We thought we might partake of tea at a hotel.'

Kirsty concentrated on her egg rather than meet her aunt's eyes. She didn't think her aunt would approve of a meeting at the WFL headquarters, nor its purpose.

Aunt Bea pulled the bell-cord hanging at the side of the fireplace and crossed to sit at the table.

'I'll have scrambled egg and toast,' she said when the maid entered the room, 'and bring fresh tea.'

'I haven't had the pleasure of being introduced to your new friends. In her last letter, your mother was wondering how you were spending your time.'

'She still doesn't trust me.' Kirsty's voice shook with the effort of disguising her resentment.

'It is natural for a mother to be concerned about her child.'

'But I'm not a child any more. I'm eighteen. I'll be nineteen in August.'

'That might be so, but you are under the age of consent, so your parents have a responsibility for you.'

'Would that be in the same way they have a responsibility for Ailsa?' Kirsty couldn't disguise the bitterness in her voice. 'Did they mention Ailsa?'

'I'm afraid not. Perhaps they think it better not to remind you.'

Kirsty stared at her aunt in dismay. Aunt Bea was usually understanding, but all of a sudden, she appeared to be siding with Kirsty's parents. The sense of suffocation she thought she'd thrown off reappeared and Kirsty had trouble breathing. She rose from the table and crossed to the window to hide her distress. Would she ever escape the expectations of her family?

Outside, the town was coming to life. A carter struggled to calm his horse after a tram car clanked past. A convoy of hansom cabs making for the cab rank in the Nethergate bowled along the street in single file. Two young women, their faces obscured by hats, passed below the window. The feathers in their bonnets danced in the breeze as a man doffed his cap to them. Kirsty imagined them giggling as they continued on their way, and she envied their freedom.

Several deep breaths later, once her composure returned, Kirsty came back to the table. Her aunt raised her eyebrows, questioning silently.

'I'm sorry if I've disappointed you, but I don't want to be dependent on my parents for the rest of my life. As long as they treat me like a child, that will never change.'

Her aunt leaned over and patted her hand.

'I understand, Kirsty, really I do. But it would be common courtesy if I met your friends.'

'Of course. I'll mention it to them. I'm sure I can arrange something.'

'I am free this afternoon if you wish to invite them to take tea with me.' It was more a command than a statement.

Kirsty left the breakfast-room, wondering how to manage

this. She couldn't imagine Martha indulging in polite chitchat without mentioning her belief in women's rights or the necessity of women acquiring the vote. Neither could Kirsty suggest these topics didn't arise. She had been accepted into the league and didn't want to lose face by making any such request.

She adjusted her bonnet, anchored it to her hair with a hat pin, and left the house. It was time to meet Martha and Ethel and follow through with their plan.

Ethel stood at her bedroom window, scanning the street outside. Her da never ventured to the city centre, but he was a fearsome man when roused and there was no knowing how he might react when he couldn't track her. By this time, he'd probably have taken his anger out on her ma. Guilt swept through her and she shivered. But she'd never been able to protect Ma from his fists, so it made no difference whether or not she was at home.

Tears formed in her eyes and she shook her head in despair. There was nothing she could do to change things in the past. She would have to learn to accept that and concentrate on her new life. A life where she had purpose and could fight for the cause of women, freedom from male subjection and a right to have a say in the laws of the land.

A door slammed downstairs, indicating the arrival of Martha's maid. Ethel pushed her distressing thoughts into the recesses of her mind. It was later than she thought. She raised her hand to the roll of hair nestling on her neck, checking for any stray wisps before hurrying to join Martha.

'Miss Fairweather is waiting for you in the drawing-room,' Aggie said, passing her on the stairs.

'Thank you.' Ethel ran down the last few steps. She never knew how to respond to Aggie. Despite wanting to be friendly, there were no maids where Ethel came from and she wasn't sure how to react when they met.

She was out of breath as she swung the drawing-room door open. The scene before her eyes wasn't what she had expected: Martha sat by the window, studying a newspaper spread out on the occasional table in front of her. Early morning sun glinted through the windows, colouring her cheeks and making her blonde curls look more golden than usual. The reporter stood beside her, leaning over to point to something on the page. Even from where Ethel stood, she could see his admiration for her friend.

For a moment, Ethel experienced an unexpected pang of jealousy, which she quickly suppressed. She had no right to feel that way.

'Come, Ethel.' Martha held out a hand towards her. 'Paul has brought today's newspaper. It has an article about Amelia. It doesn't mention she was a suffragette, but it does say she was found at our headquarters.'

'There was more detail in the piece I wrote,' Paul said. 'But my editor cut it.'

'At least he included the story,' Martha responded. 'And if the deaths are being reported in the newspapers, then the police will have to take the matter seriously.'

Ethel raised her eyebrows but made no comment. Martha had more faith in the bobbies than she did.

'I thought we were ready to leave?' Ethel said, after studying the newspaper for a moment.

Martha reached for her hat on the chair next to her.

'You're right. It is time we left. Kirsty will be there before we arrive.' She perched the hat on top of her curls and rose. 'Paul will accompany us. He has offered to help.'

'Is that necessary?' Ethel's voice sounded curter than she intended.

'I'm a reporter,' he said with a note of amusement. 'I can often access information that others might find difficult.'

Ethel's cheeks burned. He was right; he could be useful.

Kirsty's mind churned as she thought about the events of yesterday. She tried to visualise Amelia, but her memory of her was fleeting. All she could remember was a young girl, not much older than herself, and her excited manner as she'd talked to Martha.

'I don't think they open until ten o'clock.'

Kirsty, jolted from her thoughts, nodded her thanks to the elderly woman. She watched her hurry across the street toward the Overgate.

She turned back to the entrance to the WFL headquarters and tried the doorknob again. If it was locked now, it must have been locked on Sunday night, when Amelia was killed. Questions rumbled around Kirsty's mind. How could the body have been left here if the place was locked? According to Martha, there was no sign of forced entry when she and Paul arrived yesterday, though the shop door was hanging open. Did the killer have a key? Did Amelia have a key? Perhaps she knew her killer and let him in. Was it a tryst gone wrong?

So many questions and no answers. Kirsty paced while she tried to calm her mind. After a time, she stopped to peer through a gap between the posters in the window, but it was too dark inside to see anything.

Where were Martha and Ethel? They'd said they would be here at nine o'clock, and it was now well past that. Should she call at Martha's house, or would that be an impertinence?

Despite the earliness of the morning, the street was busy. Women, shopping baskets clutched in their grasp and intent looks on their faces, were heading for the shops and markets. Some of them headed along Whitehall Street on their way to the Green Market, where the best vegetables were to be found. Others sped towards the Overgate and the shops that lined this narrow thoroughfare.

At last, she heard footsteps in the close at the side of the shop, but when Martha and Ethel emerged, they weren't alone. A frown creased Kirsty's brow as she took in the reporter's form. What did he want?

'I'm so sorry we are late,' Martha apologised. 'I have no excuse other than that Paul brought us the early edition of the *Courier*. There is a small piece about Amelia in it. Have you seen it?'

'No, I'm afraid I haven't,' Kirsty said.

Martha produced a key from her handbag and, unlocking the shop door, she ushered them inside.

'I was wondering,' Kirsty said, 'whether Amelia had a key?'

'No,' Martha said, her voice thoughtful. 'Amelia was a member, but she wasn't part of the organisational team.'

'It's just . . .' Kirsty hesitated while she wondered if she was being too forward. 'It's just that . . . whoever killed her must have had a key.'

Silence descended on the group as the implications of Kirsty's statement sank in.

33

Hammond scowled at the files on his desk, one for each of the victims. Why couldn't the damned women stay at home where they should be, instead of roaming the streets and getting themselves killed?

It was all that suffrage stuff, filling their heads with nonsense about votes for women. If he had his way, he'd stamp it out, just as the London police did. They didn't stand for it down there. The least little thing and they hauled the suffragettes to court and locked them up in Holloway. Pity the Scottish police didn't do the same, but their instructions were to maintain order and send them home with a flea in their ear if they were misbehaving. Mark my words, Hammond thought, it won't be long before they get up to their militant tactics here and when that time comes, he vowed to himself, he would run them in the same as he would do with any criminal.

He opened the file on the first victim, Victoria Allan, although her body wasn't found until after the murder of the second woman. The autopsy report made grim reading. Statements from her brother-in-law and sister were brief, and he wondered if he should have pressed them for more information. He had to admit to himself that he hadn't given the investigation any priority. In the scheme of things, a dead suffragette was not as important as other investigations awaiting his attention.

Gladys Burnett's file was just as sparse. Death by strangulation. He'd sent Constable Buchan to do a door-to-door enquiry, but that had produced nothing. No one had seen or heard anything. They hadn't been able to trace her husband and, as far as he knew, Gladys had no other relatives, though he hadn't wasted time trying to find any.

The third file, on Amelia Craig, was similar. If he transposed the information to either of the other two, they would read the same. He could no longer ignore the similarities between the deaths. There was a killer on the loose in the streets of Dundee.

He closed Amelia's file and placed it on top of the other two, letting his hand rest on it for a moment while he thought of how little information he'd gained. He'd been too quick to disperse the witnesses yesterday so he could concentrate on the body and the crime scene. Not that either of those had told him very much. A return visit to the WFL shop was in order.

With a sigh, he levered himself out of his chair and stomped down the corridor to the constables' room. The clamour of voices died to a murmur and cigarettes were hastily dropped to the floor to be stood on and extinguished. Smoke nipped his eyes, but he narrowed them to slits to peer through the haze until he spotted Buchan hunched over a desk at the back of the room.

'Constable Buchan,' he roared. 'This way. We have work to do.'

The constable grabbed his helmet.

'Yes, sir,' he said, adjusting the strap under his chin.

Martha pulled a file from the wooden cabinet in the corner.

'I'm sure there will be information about Amelia in here.' She riffled through the contents. 'We always document our members' details when they join.'

Ethel and Kirsty hovered behind her while Paul wandered around, examining posters and literature.

'I don't see anything, but I have found Gladys's registration form.' Martha laid a sheet of paper on the counter.

Paul turned around, but Ethel grabbed it before he picked it up.

'This is private information.' She glared at him.

A smile tugged at the corners of his mouth.

'And here are Victoria's details.' Martha kept on sorting through the papers. 'Amelia's must be here, somewhere.'

The door swung open and Lila entered the room.

'You are early today,' she said, divesting herself of her jacket and hat.

'I thought I might pay Amelia's parents a visit, and I was looking for the address and any other details, but they seem to be missing.' Martha closed the file and turned back to the cabinet. 'I'm not even sure if anyone has informed them of Amelia's death.'

'I visited yesterday evening.' Lila hung her hat from one of the elaborately carved hooks on the coat stand. 'They were distraught. I came away thinking I hadn't provided them with any solace.'

'All the more reason for me to visit and extend my condolences.'

Lila rummaged in the recesses of a writing bureau. Finding what she was looking for, she handed it to Martha.

'I was in too much of a hurry to replace this yesterday. File it away once you have what you need.'

Martha selected three notebooks from the top of the cabinet.

'You don't mind if we take these, do you? They'll come in handy to write our notes if we find information that might be helpful to the investigation.'

'You don't need to ask,' Lila said. 'You know you are welcome to anything.'

Martha smiled her thanks and ran her finger over the embossed WFL logo on the cover of the notebook before opening it. The information on the forms was scant, but she copied everything, giving a separate page to each of the murdered suffragettes. Once she had finished, she handed a spare notebook to Ethel and the other to Kirsty.

'Amelia worked as a dressmaker at Draffen and Jarvie,' she said to Ethel. 'Could you and Kirsty call there and find out what you can about her? Who her friends were, if she had any admirers, that kind of thing. Make sure to detail anything you find out in these notebooks. While you do that,

I will visit her parents to offer my condolences.'

'You will need pencils,' Lila said, handing one each to Ethel and Kirsty. 'Good luck!'

Martha drew Kirsty to one side.

'I have an account there,' she whispered, 'so take the opportunity to buy some new clothes for Ethel. Perhaps a skirt and blouse and some undergarments. If necessary, explain to her it is normal practice to help our volunteers to present a professional appearance and it is not charity. Don't listen to any objections.'

'Leave it to me.' Kirsty smiled.

After Ethel and Kirsty left, Martha turned to Lila.

'Those two young women will be a credit to our organisation. We need to encourage them as much as we can.'

'Had you anything in mind?'

'Ethel has lost her job in the mill. It would be helpful if we could employ her officially. Use her as someone who can talk to working women. A little encouragement and she could be a good speaker for the cause.'

'I am sure we can arrange something for her to do in the shop,' Lila said. 'And I can send her out as a support to our regular speakers to start her training.'

Martha tucked the notebook into her handbag.

'I will let you know how Amelia's parents are coping.'

Paul, who had followed Ethel and Kirsty outside, was waiting for Martha.

'You're still here,' she said.

'Yes, I waited to go with you to Amelia's parents.'

'I don't think that would be a good idea. They might find a reporter intrusive.'

'Well, at least let me escort you there.' He shrugged. 'I could stay outside.'

'Why would you do that?'

'That's obvious. It isn't safe for any suffragette to be on their own with this killer on the loose. I wouldn't like you to come to harm.'

'But it is morning and broad daylight. What harm could

come to me?'

'Don't forget, the first victim was killed in the middle of the day.'

Martha failed to be convinced there was any risk involved in her visit, but it was easier not to argue.

'Very well. But you must promise to stay outside and not make yourself known to Mr and Mrs Craig.'

'On my honour,' he said.

34

The sun was high in the sky and shoppers crowded the streets. Ethel linked her arm through Kirsty's and the two of them threaded their way through the throng as they headed for Draffen and Jarvie's.

Sunlight glinted off the glass doors inset into the impressive façade of the department store. This place was too grand for the likes of her, Ethel thought. She was accustomed to shopping at the market barrows and small shops in the Overgate. Her footsteps slowed, and she came to a stop.

'I'm not sure about this,' she said.

'Neither am I, but Martha's counting on us.'

'I suppose.'

'Is something else bothering you?' A frown creased Kirsty's forehead.

Ethel shuffled her feet.

'This shop's too posh for me. I'd be out of place.' She wanted to curl up and disappear.

'Nonsense.' Kirsty grasped one of Ethel's hands. 'You're as good as anyone else. All you have to do is keep your head up and smile. And remember, I'm right beside you.'

Kirsty's grip on her hand was so tight that Ethel had no option but to follow her into the store. Her eyes widened when she saw the interior. Crystal chandeliers dangled from the ceiling and glass counters displayed all sorts of luxuries she could only dream of. Perfumes, jewellery, lace goods, embroideries, silk scarves and parasols, all laid out in tempting displays. An abundance of supercilious young women attended to the needs of customers. Ethel shrivelled inside but, remembering Kirsty's advice, she held her head high, gritted her teeth, and smiled as they strolled among the throng of ladies testing the latest fragrance, admiring necklaces and rings, and chattering among themselves about colours and fashions.

'Over here.' Kirsty grasped Ethel's hand and drew her between the counters to an ornate staircase. 'Ladies' dresses and lingerie are on the next floor.'

Marble stairs, bordered with black and gold balustrades and handrails, led up to a half-landing before turning right and ending up in another massive room furnished with glass-fronted cabinets and rows of drapery drawers. Here and there, mannequins wearing the latest fashions stared with sightless eyes and waxy smiles.

The floor manager approached them.

'Good morning, ladies. What can I help you with today?'

'My friend,' Kirsty said, 'is looking for a skirt and blouse ensemble. Something smart but not too ostentatious.'

Ethel squirmed. What was Kirsty playing at? She couldn't afford a skirt and blouse.

'Certainly, madam.' The floor manager smiled. He clicked his fingers and beckoned to an assistant. 'Madam wishes a skirt and blouse ensemble.'

'Yes, sir.' She turned to Ethel and Kirsty. 'If you'd like to follow me.'

Ethel was sure contempt flickered in the woman's eyes as she looked at them. Despite wanting the floor to open up and swallow her, she kept the smile pasted on her lips and tried to look as confident as Kirsty.

'What are you doing?' Ethel whispered to Kirsty. 'I've no money to buy a skirt and blouse.'

'Bear with me,' Kirsty said. 'We need an excuse to be here if we want to get information.'

The saleswoman halted in front of a display cabinet that stretched part of the way along one wall. She indicated two chairs upholstered in gold damask.

'If you care to be seated, I can show you a selection of ready-to-wear skirts.' She slid the glass doors open. 'Or we can arrange for a skirt to be made to your measure.'

'We'll have a look at your ready-to-wear ones first.

Perhaps something in a dark or navy blue, smart but not ostentatious.' Kirsty sat and patted the adjacent seat for Ethel.

'This style is popular this year.' The woman removed a garment from the display rack inside the cabinet. 'As you can see, it falls in soft folds from the waist and flares out nearer the hemline. It combines a smart look with comfort for walking.'

Kirsty fingered the fabric. 'It feels nice. What do you think, Ethel?'

Ethel had never possessed a skirt as stylish as this one and she could only nod her approval.

'Madam mentioned blouses. Would you care to see our range?'

'Certainly,' Kirsty said. 'Would something in white with a high neck suit you, Ethel?'

Ethel nodded again. Her discomfiture grew, and she wriggled on her seat. Kirsty seemed a different person here, authoritative and confident, while Ethel was the opposite. She wondered how they would get themselves out of this situation without committing themselves to buying something. She only had a few pennies in her purse, and she was sure Kirsty didn't have much more.

The saleswoman returned with several blouses in her arms. She laid them on a low table in front of them.

'This one is popular, madam.' She lifted an ornate lace blouse with several pleats and voluminous sleeves.

'I'm afraid that's too fancy for our needs,' Kirsty said. 'What about this one?' She selected a front-buttoned, white blouse. The high neck was trimmed with lace, while the fluted yoke and lace panels below were enough to provide an attractive look without being too fussy.

The saleswoman nodded her approval and, ignoring Ethel, she addressed Kirsty. 'We have a fitting-room if you would care to try them on for size.'

Ethel's self-esteem plummeted, but she stiffened and hoped her smile hadn't turned into a grimace.

Amusement flickered over Kirsty's face.

'The skirt is for my friend. Perhaps you could escort her to the fitting-room.'

'Certainly, madam.' The woman's eyes flicked over to Ethel. 'This way.' She didn't wait for Ethel to rise from her chair before walking towards the back of the shop.

'Come with me,' Ethel whispered to Kirsty, a touch of panic in her eyes. 'If I'm left alone with that bitch, I'll strangle her.'

'I really believe you would.'

'When are we going to ask her about Amelia?' Ethel had been so caught up in her feelings of worthlessness that she'd almost forgotten why they were here.

'I'll engage her in conversation while you try on the clothes,' Kirsty said, 'although she doesn't look the type of person who would consort with dressmakers.'

Ethel didn't have a chance to reply before the saleswoman ushered her into the fitting-room.

The woman laid the skirt and blouse on a chaise longue that matched the chairs on the sales floor.

'I'll be outside, should you require any help.'

Ethel waited until the door clicked shut before she started to unbutton her blouse, though why she should try the garments on was beyond her. It was a waste of time because she wouldn't be able to buy them. However, she thought she had better go through the motions.

The voices mumbling outside the fitting-room were too indistinct for her to make out, even when she put her ear to the door. She tried to hurry so she could join Kirsty in the enquiries they'd been entrusted to carry out, but her fingers fumbled with the buttons. Eventually, she was clothed in the new blouse and skirt. She inspected herself in the free-standing mirror and had to admit they were smart. The outfit put her own shabby clothes to shame. She pushed the thought away. It wouldn't do to become dissatisfied with her lot now.

She opened the fitting-room door.

'I'm not sure.' She looked at Kirsty with a mute plea in her eyes. Kirsty would know how to escape from the store without having to buy the garments.

'The blouse is perfect,' Kirsty said. 'It suits you. But the skirt's too long. It may need a hem taken up.' Kirsty turned to the saleswoman. 'Can one of your dressmakers do the necessary?'

'I'll see to that right away, madam.'

'Perhaps you can ask for Amelia?' Kirsty turned back to Ethel.

'Miss Simpson doesn't know Amelia, but I'm sure she can arrange for her to make the adjustments to the skirt.'

A few minutes later the saleswoman returned, accompanied by a young girl.

'I couldn't locate Amelia. I trust Sarah will do.'

Kirsty followed Ethel and the dressmaker into the fitting-room.

'I'm sure you'll appreciate a second opinion,' she said to Ethel, closing the door before the saleswoman could follow.

The dressmaker sank to her knees on the floor and withdrew pins from the pincushion hanging from her waist.

'It won't need much,' she said. 'Two inches should do it.'

Kirsty perched on the end of the chaise longue.

'I had been enquiring about an acquaintance, Amelia Craig, but Miss Simpson doesn't appear to know her.'

'Miss Simpson doesn't really associate with any of us.' Sarah removed a pin from her mouth and stuck it in the skirt's hem.

Ethel noticed the touch of bitterness in Sarah's voice.

'Not good enough for her, are you?'

'I didn't say that.' The girl looked startled.

'You didn't need to.'

'But you must know Amelia if you work in the same department,' Kirsty chimed in.

'Yes, miss. But Amelia didn't turn up for work today and Miss Morgan isn't pleased.'

'Miss Morgan?'

'She's in charge of dressmaking and tailoring.' Sarah pinned more of the hem.

'Is that usual?'

'Oh, no, miss. Amelia's never late, she's one of our best workers. Something must have stopped her coming to work.'

'Maybe she has a man friend?'

'She did have, but they broke up when she became one of them suffragettes.'

'I see. Would you perchance have a name for him?'

'Billy, she used to call him. She let slip once that he was Irish, and I think she said his second name was Murphy. I don't think her dad liked him.'

'Do you know where he works or lives?'

'No, miss. We don't have much chance to talk in the workroom and Amelia was always in a hurry to go home after she finished.'

'And there's no one in the store who's taken a shine to her?'

'No, miss. The men and the women don't mix. The bosses don't approve of us talking to each other inside the store.'

Sarah placed the last pin and stood.

'Does that meet with your approval?' She regarded them with anxious eyes.

'That's admirable,' Kirsty said. 'What do you think, Ethel?'

Ethel nodded, wondering how on earth she would evade the haughty saleswoman and leave the store without committing herself to the sale.

'I'll leave you to get changed to your own clothes, Ethel. Just leave the skirt and blouse here, in the fitting-room, while I have another chat with Miss Simpson.'

Ethel changed hurriedly into her own clothes and spread the skirt and blouse on the chaise longue. She gave them a regretful glance as she left the fitting-room and joined Kirsty, who was deep in conversation with the saleswoman.

'Thank you for your custom,' the saleswoman said as they left.

Ethel was so desperate to leave the shop she paid no heed to the comment.

35

The house was a cottage in a lane which led off Constitution Road. Well-kept grass bordered the path leading to the front door, though a few daisies had been left to grow. The doorstep was spotless, and the windows gleamed in the sunlight. A curtain twitched, and Martha knew her approach had been witnessed. She rang the bell and, moments later, a woman whose face reflected her grief opened the door.

'I'm sorry to intrude, but I'm Martha Fairweather, a friend of Amelia's. I wanted to offer my condolences.' From the corner of her eye, she spotted Paul lingering at the junction with Constitution Road. She hoped he would keep his promise to stay outside.

'That's kind of you,' the woman said. 'Please, come in. I'm Ina Craig, Amelia's mother.'

Martha followed her into a small vestibule and, from there, a compact living-room. The man, slumped in the armchair by the side of the empty fireplace, did not look up.

'Callum,' Ina said, 'Miss Fairweather is here to pay her respects.'

The man looked up and grunted.

'I suppose you'll be one of them suffragettes she was taking up with. A lot of good that did her.'

'Now, now, Callum. Miss Fairweather's a friend. There's no need to be rude to her.'

'That's all right,' Martha said. 'It's a sad time for both of you and I can't imagine what it must feel like to lose a daughter.'

'Will you sit, Miss Fairweather?' Ina Craig gestured towards the armchair at the other side of the fireplace.

'Thank you, but one of the other chairs will do nicely. I wouldn't wish to deprive you of your seat.'

Ina pulled a dining table chair to the middle of the room.

'I'll make tea. Do you take milk and sugar?'

'There's no need,' Martha said. 'I don't want you to go to any trouble on my behalf.'

'It's no trouble. I'm glad of something to do to keep me busy.' She turned to leave when there was a thunderous knocking at the front door. She scurried out of the room with a look of alarm on her face.

Martha pressed her lips together. She had told Paul to stay outside, but what else could she expect from a reporter.

'It's the police,' Ina said when she returned.

'Damned bobbies,' Callum said. 'What do they want?'

Hammond strode in behind Amelia's mother. He glared at Martha.

'Why are you here?' Without stopping for a reply, he continued. 'I must ask you to leave while I talk to Mr and Mrs Craig.'

Ina Craig placed a restraining hand on Martha's shoulder.

'Stay.' She turned to Hammond. 'What right have you to order anyone from my house?'

Hammond scowled and his face reddened.

'This is police business. I have the authority to say who should be present.'

Martha revised her opinion of Amelia's mother. She had appeared weak and worn down with misery when Martha entered the house but now, stiff with anger, she appeared much more formidable.

'And this is my house,' Ina repeated. 'Miss Fairweather was a good friend to Amelia and I say she stays. Aren't you going to say something, Callum?'

Callum looked up and grunted.

'Very well, if that is your decision.' Hammond's voice was as stiff as Ina's. He stood with legs apart, clasping his hands behind his back.

It was obvious Ina Craig was not going to invite him to sit, and Martha took pleasure from the inspector's discomfiture.

'Constable,' Hammond said, 'take notes.'

'Yes, sir.' Constable Buchan suppressed a smile and pulled a notebook from his pocket.

'When did you last see your daughter, Mrs Craig?'

The man could be polite, at least. There was no need for his bullying tone. Martha clenched her hands and, though she was tempted to remonstrate, she held her tongue.

'Sunday evening. After she came home from the Mathers Hotel, she had her tea and then helped me tidy up. She's a good girl, Amelia, and even when she was tired after her work she always helped in the house.' Ina stopped talking to wipe a tear from her eye. 'She went out again at nine o'clock. Said she was meeting someone and wouldn't stay out late, but she never came home.'

'Who was she meeting?' Hammond appeared oblivious to Ina's distress.

'Do you think I wouldn't tell you if I knew?' Ina glared at Hammond. 'Amelia was a grown woman, and we trusted her. Why would we question her about her friends?'

Hammond ignored her outburst. 'You mentioned her work. Draffen and Jarvie, I presume?'

'Yes, she was a dressmaker.'

'Did she mention anyone she might be seeing from work?'

'No. She always came straight home after she finished for the day.'

'Any boyfriends?'

'Not since she broke up with Billy.'

'How long ago was that?'

'She hasn't been seeing him since she became a suffragette, oh, three months ago. He didn't approve.'

'I'll need his details.'

'Billy Murphy. I'm not sure of his address, but he always referred to living in Little Tipperary so I reckon it must be somewhere in Lochee.'

'He's one of the Irish lot, then.' Hammond's voice was scathing.

Ina glared at him.

'Just because his parents came over from Ireland doesn't

mean he isn't Scottish. He was born here and is as Scottish as I am.'

Hammond tightened his lips and scowled.

'Is he in employment?'

'He's a clerk at Cox's jute mill.'

'Anything else we should know about him?'

'He's a nice lad,' Ina said. 'I was sorry when they split up, but he didn't like Amelia being a suffragette and she wouldn't give it up. I'm sure he cared for her and he said he just wanted her to come to her senses. But if you think he would harm her, you're mistaken.' She drew a breath and glared at the inspector again. 'Now, if you're finished, we all have work to be getting on with.'

'That'll be all for now, but if I need further information, I'll be back.' He turned to leave the room. 'Come on, Constable. We're done here.'

'What an abominable man,' Ina said after the door closed behind the two policemen.

Martha nodded her agreement.

'Shall I help you make that tea? It will help you recover.'

An hour later, when she was standing on the doorstep saying her goodbyes, Ina Craig pushed a parcel into her hands.

'It's a banner Amelia was sewing for the league. It would be a shame for it to be wasted even though it's not finished.'

Martha sensed the reluctance behind the gift and saw the tears in the woman's eyes. She couldn't imagine how hard it must be for Mrs Craig to give away something her daughter had worked on with so much dedication.

'Thank you,' she said. 'It will be truly valued and will ensure Amelia's memory is preserved.'

Her own tears were not far away as she walked along the lane and left the cottage behind her.

'Well. What did they tell you?' Paul demanded as Martha rejoined him at the corner of Constitution Road.

Martha's lips twitched. She could sense the man's

impatience for a news story, but she hadn't discovered anything she would be reluctant to share with him.

'Amelia's parents are distressed and they cannot understand why anyone would want to kill their daughter.'

'I saw the police go in. It's a wonder they let you stay.'

'They didn't have a choice, Ina Craig insisted on it. Did they see you lurking here?'

'I tried to keep out of sight, but I wasn't successful. The constable gave me a nod. The inspector ignored me. If they question me later, I'll say I had intended to interview Amelia's parents but changed my mind, so I didn't get in their way.'

'Do you think they will believe you?'

'Whether or not they do is immaterial.' Paul shrugged and they continued to walk towards the city centre. 'You haven't told me what you found out.'

'Not much. Although the information I got was thanks to the police.'

'Go on.'

'Amelia was walking out with a young man until three months ago when she joined the Women's Freedom League.'

'Is Inspector Hammond considering him a suspect?'

'Hard to tell. But Ina was adamant he'd never harm Amelia.'

'The police are a suspicious lot – they're not going to believe that. I hope, for his sake, the young man has an alibi. But, more to the point, do you think he might have something to do with her death?'

'Anything is possible. I'd like to know whether it was Amelia or Billy who ended the relationship, and how he feels about it all now.'

'Did Amelia's mother say why they broke up?'

'He disliked her involvement with the suffrage cause.'

'So, he could have an aversion to suffragettes. That could be a motive for the killings.'

'I never considered that.' Martha turned the thought over in her head. It made sense.

'Give me his name and address. I'll check up on him. It wouldn't be safe for you.' Paul hauled his reporter's notebook from his pocket.

'I don't have an address for him apart from the Lochee district. But his name is Billy Murphy and he works as a clerk for Cox's jute mill.'

Paul scribbled the details in his notebook and returned it to his pocket.

'I'll keep you informed.'

Had she done the right thing by allowing Paul to become involved? Martha wasn't sure, and doubts crowded her mind as they continued to walk to the city centre.

Draffen and Jarvie's glass doors swished closed as they left the store and Ethel released her grip of Kirsty's hand.

'Sorry,' she mumbled, 'but I'm not used to posh places like that.'

'You have as much right to shop there as anyone else.'

'The problem is, we weren't shopping and I'm sure that stuck-up bitch knew we didn't have any money.'

'That stuck-up bitch, as you call her, is no better than you are. She's having to work for her living, the same way you had to.'

Ethel wasn't convinced. She was sure shop assistants looked down their noses at mill workers, even unemployed ones. But she pushed the negative thoughts to the back of her mind, determined not to let her experiences in Draffen and Jarvie erode her confidence. As a suffragette and a woman fighting for the rights of all women, she was worth something. Kirsty was right, she was as good as any of them.

With a fresh spring in her step, she headed back towards the WFL shop with Kirsty at her side.

As they walked, Kirsty and Ethel discussed their findings, which didn't amount to much. Amelia was a good worker, she kept to herself and didn't have friends in the store. She had broken up with her boyfriend when she became a suffragette.

'Do you think the boyfriend might be a suspect?'

'Could be. But I'm not sure how we find him.'

'Martha will come up with something. She's determined to find the person responsible.'

'Did you note his name?'

'I didn't want to write it down in front of the store staff, but I've memorised it. I'll record it as soon as we get back.'

The bell above the door tinkled as they stepped from the heat of the street into the cool interior of the shop.

'Thank goodness you are here,' Lila Clunas said.

She finished rearranging leaflets in the window before dusting her hands on her skirt and removing her hat from the coat stand.

'I have an urgent appointment but was reluctant to close the shop. Can you hold the fort until I return?'

'Of course,' Ethel said. 'Is there anything special we should know?'

'Membership forms and cards are in the top drawer of the cabinet. Pamphlets, badges and other paraphernalia are priced. Any money goes in the till.' Lila pulled the handle attached to the drawer of the oblong wooden box on the counter. It opened with a ping. 'The only thing you have to do is note the sale on the till roll.' She pointed to an aperture on top of the box through which the paper till roll could be seen. 'Not that there is ever much money in it. But one can hope.' With one hand, she placed her hat on her head and with the other, she grabbed her bag. 'I'll get back as soon as I can.'

'Do you think we should have mentioned her hat was on squint?'

'It's obvious you don't know Lila,' Ethel replied, laughing. 'I don't think she would give two hoots about that.'

The next hour sped past. Ethel dealt with three women seeking information, and Kirsty sat in the corner studying the pamphlets and reading some of the articles which were on sale.

The tinkle of the bell over the shop door heralded Lila's

return, some time later.

'Any problems?' she asked, removing her jacket and hat.

'I sold one article and enrolled a new member. I've noted her details on a form.' Ethel picked up a sheet of paper. 'I wasn't sure what to do with it after that.'

Lila lifted the counter hatch and joined Ethel at the other side.

'That's a good start,' she said. 'Now you enter the details into the membership ledger.' She produced a book from beneath the counter and opened it to the last entry. 'The name and date go here. After you've done that, we file the form under the surname initial. It is a simple system; you shouldn't have any trouble grasping it.' After Ethel finished doing the paperwork, Lila continued. 'Martha is aware I have been struggling to cope with the shop now that I no longer have Gladys to help. We do have other volunteers, but their attendance is spasmodic. She told me you had left your employment and suggested you might be available to assist me on a more regular basis.'

'Do you mean, be a shop assistant?'

'Yes, that's exactly what it means.' Lila smiled in amusement at Ethel's reaction. 'However, as an organisation, we can't afford to pay a high wage, but you will be remunerated.'

Excitement bubbled up inside Ethel. The amount she would be paid didn't matter to her. It was nothing compared to her new status as a shop assistant, a step up from being a mill worker.

'Does it matter that I don't have any experience?'

'Not at all, you will soon pick it up and then we can go from there.'

Ethel wondered what she meant, but as elation mixed with trepidation consumed her about the task ahead, she gave it no more thought.

36

The steeple clock chimed two o'clock and Martha was surprised at how much time had passed since she set out that morning. Hunger pangs niggled her stomach and she headed for home rather than returning to the WFL shop.

Aggie, her maid, busy polishing the mahogany furniture in the dining-room, looked up when Martha entered.

'Have ye eaten?'

Her tone was disapproving, but Martha didn't mind; Aggie had been with her ever since she had arrived in Dundee. She was used to the woman's dourness and direct speech.

'Not yet,' she said.

'Ye don't eat near enough if ye ask me.' Aggie laid her duster on the sideboard. 'I'll leave this and make something for ye.'

'I was thinking a sandwich would do me fine. Do we have any of that nice ham left?'

'It's a meal ye need, not a sandwich.' Aggie snorted.

Martha followed her to the kitchen.

'Sorry, I don't have time to wait for you to prepare something. I'll eat properly later. Now, about that sandwich.'

Muttering under her breath, Aggie thumped a loaf on to the breadboard and attacked it with a bread knife.

'Make enough for Kirsty and Ethel, too,' Martha said. 'I don't suppose they've eaten. Wrap them in paper and I'll get them after I've performed my ablutions.'

'You want pickle with the ham? I've a fresh jar of Hayward's Military Pickle in the press.'

Martha stopped in the doorway to consider.

'Better not,' she responded after a moment. 'I'm not sure whether Kirsty and Ethel like pickles.'

Fifteen minutes later, she collected the wrapped sandwiches. She noticed Aggie was still scowling.

'You can prepare something and leave it in the oven,' she offered as a compromise. 'Ethel and I will have it later.' Hoping she had mollified her maid, Martha clattered down the stairs and out the front door.

'How exciting,' Kirsty exclaimed. 'I'm sure you'll make an excellent shop assistant.'

'I hope so.' Ethel looked up from the ledger she was studying. 'It's a lot different from working in the mill.'

A tinge of envy tempered Kirsty's pleasure at Ethel's job offer and she realised she had led a cosseted life. She had never needed to worry about money or where her next meal was coming from. Everything had been provided for her, and the only training she had ever received was in how to be a lady.

She had no desire to be a lady, nor to fulfil her family's expectations to marry.

The thought filled her with horror, but the alternative was to remain a spinster and rely on her family to support her for the rest of her life. A life of torment. Faced daily with a daughter she could not acknowledge and an ache in her heart that would never heal. Kirsty realised that cutting the ties with Ailsa would be beneficial for both of them, in the long run.

Yet, despair filled her. She so wanted to be the same as Ethel, self-supporting, making her own way in the world. But how could she do that? She didn't know what it was like to work or to have a job. If she left her family, she would have nothing. Anger replaced despair. What was to prevent her from learning to be more self-sufficient?

The tinkle of the bell above the door interrupted her thoughts.

'Ah, there you are, Martha,' Lila said. 'Are Mr and Mrs Craig coping with their loss any better?'

'As to be expected, they are still distraught.'

Kirsty laid down the article she had stopped reading when her thoughts overtook her. Ethel snapped the ledger shut.

'What about you two?' Martha asked, addressing Kirsty and Ethel. 'Did you find anything out at Draffen and Jarvie?'

'Not much,' Kirsty said. 'She didn't have close connections with any of the department store employees. They're not aware of her death. One thing we discovered is that she had a man friend, but they broke up when she became a suffragette. The dressmaker thought his name might be Billy Murphy, but that was all she knew.'

'That ties up with what Mrs Craig told me. She also said it was unlikely he would harm Amelia, though I am not sure the police inspector shares that view. He visited while I was there and questioned Mr and Mrs Craig in quite an aggressive manner.'

'Should we talk to this Billy Murphy?'

'Paul offered to find out what he can about him. He has promised to keep us informed.'

'Is that wise?' Ethel frowned. 'What do we know about this reporter, except that he's always hovering around when anything happens?'

'I agreed because the only thing we know is the man's name and that he might live somewhere in Lochee.'

Kirsty shared Ethel's reservations and noted that while Martha sounded confident, her eyes looked troubled.

'We can do no more until we have information on Billy Murphy,' Martha continued, 'and I am sure you must be starving, so I've brought sandwiches with me.' She laid the parcels she was carrying on the counter. 'Oh, I almost forgot. Mrs Craig gave me something Amelia was working on. She never got the chance to finish it.' She unwrapped the largest parcel, revealing the banner.

'It's beautiful,' Kirsty said, running her fingers over the silky material. 'What a shame Amelia couldn't complete it.' She picked it up to examine the stitching. 'I could finish it for you. My parents made me learn embroidery . . . I'm sure I could make a good job of it. The stitches are quite simple.'

'That would be marvellous,' Martha said. 'And once it is finished, we could hang it on the wall to remind us of Amelia.'

Embroidery had never been a favourite pastime of Kirsty's, but it pleased her she could contribute something to the cause. She vowed to make sure her stitching was perfect. It was the least she could do.

37

'It's natural for your aunt to want to meet me,' Martha said as they walked up Reform Street an hour later.

Kirsty smiled and tried to ignore the fluttering in her stomach. It had taken all her courage to issue the invitation, but Martha had agreed without hesitation. However, it didn't quell her nerves.

Ruthie must have been listening for their footsteps on the stairs because she came scurrying from the direction of the kitchen as soon as Kirsty opened the door. The girl, the daughter of Aunt Bea's cook, was younger than Kirsty and had been part of her aunt's household from the day she was born. It was natural that she became a maid when she was old enough. Kirsty had her doubts whether anyone else would have employed her because she lacked all her faculties. She was what most people described as 'simple'.

'Your aunt's in the drawing-room, Miss Kirsty. She said for you and your friend to join her there when you arrived.' She glanced at Martha and then looked away. Kirsty sensed her curiosity and wondered what the girl might have overheard about this afternoon's visitor.

'May I introduce Miss Martha Fairweather,' Kirsty said as she entered the drawing-room.

'It is a pleasure to meet you.' Bea Hunter rose from her seat by the window. 'Please sit. The window overlooks Albert Square and there's a fine view of the Albert Institute from here.'

Martha settled herself on the chair at the opposite side of a small table set into the window recess.

'It is indeed a fine view. You are to be envied in your choice of home.'

'I have instructed tea to be brought. I trust you like tea?'

'It is my favourite beverage.' Martha smiled warmly.

'Now, if Kirsty will pull the bell-rope to let cook know we are ready, it will give us more time to chat.'

Kirsty groaned inwardly as she walked over to the fireplace. It would be so embarrassing if Aunt Bea cross-examined Martha. She tugged the velvet pull which dangled beside the mantelpiece and, though she heard nothing, she knew it would jangle in the kitchen. Returning to the window, she pulled up a chair.

'What a coincidence,' she heard Aunt Bea say. 'My husband was a solicitor. He owned most of the buildings on this side of Reform Street and had his office in one of them. That is why we came to live here when we were newly married. I do miss him.' Bea Hunter sighed and gazed out of the window, appearing lost in memories. After a few moments, Bea turned her attention back to their visitor. 'Your father, Miss Fairweather – does he have his own law practice?'

'He is a full partner in the practice my grandfather established. My brother is also a lawyer, though he is currently concentrating on his political ambitions.'

Ruthie interrupted them, arriving with a tray laden with dainty cucumber sandwiches, Dundee cake, sponge fingers and shortbread. Mrs Paton, the cook, followed behind, bearing the crockery and teapot.

'Thank you,' Bea said. 'I will ring if we need anything else.'

Kirsty picked up a napkin to protect her hand from the heat in the silver teapot's handle and poured tea into the three cups.

'Please, help yourself to whatever you fancy, Miss Fairweather. We mustn't disappoint cook when she's gone to so much trouble.' Bea Hunter picked up the silver tongs and plopped two sugar lumps into her cup.

'You are very kind, Mrs Hunter. But, please, call me Martha. Miss Fairweather makes me sound like a schoolmistress.'

'And you must call me Bea.'

Kirsty sipped her tea. So far, the meeting was going well. The similarities between Aunt Bea and Martha's family backgrounds had been fortunate, but Kirsty wasn't so sure her aunt would approve of Martha's suffragette activities.

'You say your brother is interested in politics.' Bea replaced her cup in its saucer.

'Yes. He intends to stand as Glasgow's parliamentary member in the next by-election. He stood in the Dundee one earlier this year but was unsuccessful when Churchill was elected.'

'He is not a member of the Liberal party, then.'

'I am afraid he is not.' Martha smiled. 'He is a member of the ILP.'

Bea looked slightly taken aback.

'The Labour party do not have much of a foothold in government.'

'I think that may change.'

'You have political views?' Bea did not have to add how unusual that was for a woman; her surprise was obvious.

'I am afraid I come from a progressive family. Discussion of politics over the breakfast table was common, and it didn't matter whether you were male or female. Everyone had a right to their own view.'

'How interesting,' Bea said.

Kirsty wondered whether her aunt meant 'how strange,' and she held her breath, wondering where the conversation was heading. After a few moments, Bea continued.

'I had noticed Kirsty was taking an interest in politics. Her attendance at the recent Winston Churchill meeting annoyed her father. He is traditional. He doesn't think women should be interested in such things.' Aunt Bea sounded sympathetic. Kirsty let her breath out.

'It is a sad fact that many men hold these views. That is why I support the cause of women having the vote. Why should we not have a say in things that affect us? Why should we always have to be dependent on the male members of our families?'

'Your enthusiasm does you proud.' Bea swirled the dregs

of her tea around in her cup and studied the pattern of tea leaves in the bottom. It was obvious she was contemplating Martha's outburst.

Silence gathered in the room and Martha glanced at Kirsty with an apologetic look on her face.

At last, Bea responded.

'I have not depended on a man for a long time, and I must admit I enjoy making my own decisions. However, I am not sure I am in accord with the notion that women should have a vote. I cannot see how that could make any difference in my life.'

'Then you are fortunate,' Martha said. 'Many women do not have that level of independence.'

'My father doesn't allow me to have any opinions,' Kirsty cut in. 'And he's never allowed me to make any decisions about my life.' Kirsty found it hard to keep the bitterness out of her voice.

The atmosphere within the room changed from welcoming and conversational to chilly in a moment.

'You must forgive Kirsty,' Bea said to Martha. 'There has been a disagreement within the family, but I am sure it will resolve itself.' Bea fell silent again, and Kirsty knew by the look on her aunt's face that she was deep in thought. She feared there were more questions to come.

After several moments, Bea addressed Martha in a voice that was apologetic yet firm.

'I trust you do not find my questions offensive, but you have to understand that I am responsible for Kirsty's safety while she is in my care.'

Martha took a sip of her tea and the blue of her eyes deepened as she studied Bea with gravity.

'I don't mind at all,' she replied.

Bea hesitated for a moment.

'You are a single lady, and from what I have seen and heard, you have a comfortable lifestyle. That makes me curious as to how you have the means to live independently in Dundee when you have no husband.'

Kirsty detected reluctance in her aunt's voice and realised

it was difficult for her to ask such a personal question.

A smile crinkled the edge of Martha's eyes.

'You have every right to be suspicious; it is not normal for a woman to live by herself with no visible means of support. But I assure you, I am completely respectable. I am in a similar position to yourself and have private means.' There could have been a sting in her answer, but there was none.

A flush rose to Bea's cheeks. 'My husband left me a wealthy woman.'

'As did my grandfather. The family business at Speyside, a long-established whisky distillery, is profitable even though run by managers. My great-grandfather would have liked his son to run the business, but he was more interested in a legal career. At the time of my grandfather's death, he was a High Court judge, and he left equal shares of the business and his estate to his children and grandchildren.'

'Even the women in the family?'

'Yes, even the women. As I said, my family has a progressive outlook.'

'That is unusual, indeed.' Bea's eyes widened in astonishment.

'I can see you still have concerns about Kirsty's welfare and the company she is keeping, and I would like to set your mind at rest. The ladies in the Women's Freedom League take turns to host an at-home meeting and this week it is my turn. You are welcome to come along this Sunday afternoon. I am sure you will find no harridans or ogres in our midst, and we are perfectly normal people.'

Bea nodded her acceptance. 'That is most kind of you.'

Martha folded her napkin, placed it on the table and rose from her chair.

'This has been lovely, but I must take my leave. I have taken up too much of your time. Thank you for the refreshments.'

'It has been my pleasure,' Bea said. 'Kirsty will ring for Ruthie to show you out.'

'No need,' Kirsty said. 'I'll accompany Martha to the

door.'

Downstairs, at the door leading to the street, Martha leaned towards Kirsty.

'I suspect your aunt may have thought I was a woman of ill-repute. I hope I have set her mind at rest.'

Kirsty wasn't sure what a woman of ill repute was but didn't want to display her ignorance by asking. Instead, she nodded, smiling her farewell to Martha. On her return to the drawing-room, Bea beckoned to her.

'Come sit beside me. I am assuming Martha is a suffragette,' Bea said.

'Yes.' Kirsty's voice was barely audible.

'And what about you, Kirsty? Has she indoctrinated you with her ideas?'

'I needed no indoctrination.' Kirsty stiffened. 'I met Martha at a political meeting when Mr Churchill was in Dundee, and it was a revelation that women could do things I had wanted to do for such a long time.'

Bea sighed. 'Then you are a suffragette.'

'Yes. Will you tell father?'

'I don't know, Kirsty. For what it is worth, I did like Miss Fairweather and I admire her for standing up for what she believes in.' Bea paused. 'But that doesn't mean I approve of your decision to become a suffragette. And, I can tell you now, your father will never sanction it.'

Before finishing her daily work at six o'clock, Aggie had prepared a beef stew, which she left in the oven for Martha and Ethel's evening meal. The food Aggie cooked never differentiated between the seasons, and she did not approve of the reduction in Martha's appetite during the present heatwave.

'You don't eat enough to keep a bird alive,' she retorted if Martha tried to suggest something different.

The heat didn't affect Ethel, who ate everything placed in front of her. Martha supposed that might be due to the restricted diet of the working class. Ethel had once admitted that meat was a rarity for her at home, though she hadn't elaborated any further.

Seven o'clock chimed on the steeple clock as Martha pushed her plate aside. The modicum of guilt she felt by not eating everything didn't last long, and she ignored Ethel's raised eyebrows.

Ethel gathered up the plates and carried them to the sink.

'I'll take care of these,' she said. 'You finish drinking your tea.'

Unlike most ladies of quality, Martha did not object to dining in the kitchen and tending to the tidying up after Aggie, her daily maid, left for the day, but Ethel had assumed most of these tasks after she came to stay.

One thing Martha loved was tea with the merest drop of milk and plenty of sugar, so she didn't argue. As she sipped the hot drink, she watched Ethel lift the copper kettle from the hob and pour boiling water into a basin which nestled in the sink. The girl was a treasure. Helpful and intelligent, despite her mill-worker background. Martha knew many workers were illiterate, but Ethel had applied herself to the part-time schooling she had received in the same way she was applying herself to learning how to manage the WFL shop.

Several knocks on the door resounded up the stairs and into the kitchen. Ethel withdrew her hands from the soapy water, but Martha placed her cup on the table and stood.

'That will be Paul,' she said. 'You finish up here and then join us in the drawing-room.'

Martha ushered Paul upstairs and, a few minutes later, Ethel joined them.

'Did you manage to speak to Amelia's boyfriend?'

'I didn't get there in time. Inspector Hammond has arrested him.'

'Amelia's parents were convinced he could never harm her.' Martha frowned. 'Besides, there were other murders. What reason would he have to kill Victoria or Gladys?'

'The police must have their reasons.' Paul shrugged. 'I talked to his mother and some clerks he worked alongside at

Cox's Mill. They all say the same thing – he's a pleasant, mild-mannered young man. He's never shown anger or aggression, even when provoked.'

Ethel remained silent until after Paul left.

'Seems to me the police have found a likely scapegoat. Anyone who lives in the Little Tipperary tenements and works in a mill is fair game for our bobbies.'

'I think you may have a point,' Martha agreed, 'but what can we do?'

'Wait until the killer strikes again.' Ethel drew her brows together. 'I feel so helpless, but I know one thing . . . If he starts on me, he'll get more than he's bargained for.'

38

Wednesday, 1st July 1908

'Please be careful,' Bea warned as Kirsty left the house the following morning.

Kirsty wasn't usually demonstrative, but she kissed her aunt on the forehead.

'I will, I promise, though I doubt there's much risk at this time of day. And Martha and Ethel always escort me home.'

The sun dazzled her as she stepped outside and she pulled the brim of her hat forward to shade her face before joining the throng of shoppers heading for the High Street and the Overgate. The WFL shop was still closed, and she stood in the doorway until Martha appeared, brandishing the key.

'Lila not here yet?' She pushed the door open and ushered Kirsty inside. 'How was your aunt after I left yesterday? Does she approve of me?'

'She approves of you but not the suffrage cause.' Kirsty shrugged. She couldn't fathom her aunt's thoughts; part of her wondered if Aunt Bea was as disapproving of suffragettes as she claimed.

'As long as she doesn't forbid you to come here. It can create difficulties when there is a conflict of interest.'

Ethel barged through the door.

'Sorry I'm late, I had to redo my hair. I was trying to shape it into a French roll, but it wouldn't behave and I ended up tying it back.'

'A French roll?' Kirsty was unfamiliar with modern hairstyles. Her mother wore her hair in a bun, while Kirsty's own hair flowed in waves to her shoulders.

'Yes, you comb it, secure it with hairpins, then roll it between your fingers so it sits above your shoulders like a sausage, which you have to pin into place. Christabel

Pankhurst wears her hair that way.' Ethel laughed. 'It's not as easy as it looks. I gave up.'

'Hand me some pamphlets, Ethel. I will try distributing them in the Overgate today instead of standing in front of the Pillars. There was a council meeting yesterday, and I got glares from the town councillors going inside. I'll be back here for one o'clock, in time to go to the house and we can catch up on everything. See if you can find large sheets of paper somewhere – I'm sure we have some for making posters.'

'Won't that leave the shop with no one to tend to it?' Ethel handed her a pile of leaflets.

'We close at one every Wednesday. You won't find any shop open this afternoon – it's Dundee's half-day.'

'We didn't get half-days in the mill during the week,' Ethel said after Martha left. 'How was I supposed to know?'

It was mid-afternoon by the time Martha spread three large sheets of paper on the dining-room table.

'I don't know about you two,' she said, 'but I am worried we are getting nowhere in trying to find this killer. The police are no better, though they have arrested Amelia's boyfriend.'

'Do you think he killed her?' Ethel's voice held a note of doubt.

'It is possible, I suppose. But why kill the other two? That is what I can't understand. Anyway, I thought we could make notes and see if we find any crossovers. One sheet for each victim.'

Eight chairs were arranged around the table. Martha pulled one out, picked up a pencil, and sat. Kirsty leaned on another chair, at her right, while Ethel hovered on her left. Martha selected a sheet of paper and, after nibbling the end of the pencil, she started to write.

Victoria Allan, she wrote on the first sheet. *Body found on Sunday, 29th June, but thought to have been murdered on Saturday, 23rd June. Relatives, Elizabeth Inglis, sister.*

Davie Inglis, brother-in-law.

Both girls leaned forward to watch.

'That doesn't leave us much.' Martha gestured at the paper. 'I suppose we could put Davie down as a potential suspect.'

'Are we only looking at men as suspects?' Kirsty asked.

Martha looked up.

'I had only been thinking about men. But you are right, it could have been a woman. Anti-suffragist women can be more vicious than men.' Under suspects, she added Elizabeth's name.

'That only gives us two suspects for Victoria.' She tapped the pencil against her teeth. 'Unless she had an admirer we don't know about.' She added a question mark under *Suspects.*

'What about motive?' Kirsty asked.

'Davie didn't approve of her suffragette activities, and although Elizabeth was noncommittal, she has expressed no interest in the cause.' Martha added this under *Motive.*

'Now for Gladys.'

Martha wrote *Gladys Burnett* on the second sheet of paper. *Body found on Friday, 26th June; murdered the evening before. Strangled with her sash. Relatives, none known apart from her estranged husband, David Burnett. Husband thought to be working in India, therefore, opportunity not present.*

On the third sheet of paper, she wrote *Amelia Craig. Body found on Monday, 30th June; murdered the previous evening. Relatives, Callum Craig, father. Ina Craig, mother. Potential suspects. Father, he disapproved of Amelia's suffragette activities. Billy Murphy, boyfriend, currently under arrest. Motives similar, disapproval of suffragette activities.*

'We don't have much information,' Kirsty said. 'Do you think the police have more than we do?'

'The bobbies aren't going to tell us anything.' Ethel glared at the sheets of paper. 'Look at the way they treat us when we have something to report. Face it, they see us as a nuisance. All they're interested in is pinning it on some poor sap like Billy Murphy so they can say they've found the killer.'

'I am in no doubt you are right, Ethel.' Martha drummed her fingers on the table. 'Perhaps Billy is the person responsible, but if he's not, then we still have a killer roaming the streets of Dundee.'

Kirsty had been studying the details on each sheet of paper while they spoke.

'I can't see a connection between the victims apart from being members of the WFL. There doesn't seem to be any other crossover, although there's someone else linked to every murder.'

'Is there?' Martha's interest was piqued.

'Yes. Paul, the reporter. He's been present when each of the bodies was found. He was with us at the Howff and knew which path to take to find Victoria's body. He found Gladys's body when he went to interview her – at least, that's the reason he gave. And he was with you, Martha, when Amelia's body was discovered.'

'Surely, that must be a coincidence. A reporter is always on the hunt for news stories.'

'I am not sure I believe in coincidences,' Kirsty said. 'And you've missed out a possible motive for Amelia.'

'Have I?' Martha scrutinised her notes.

'We considered, at the time, that Amelia's murder might have been connected to her having seen Victoria entering the Howff to meet her killer.' Kirsty directed an apologetic look towards Martha. 'And Paul was present when she told us that.'

Martha opened her mouth and closed it again. Kirsty was right. Paul had been there when Amelia made her statement.

She wrote Paul's name on all three sheets of paper and included the additional motive on Amelia's one.

'We are making suppositions but, to be on the safe side, I suggest we make sure we are never on our own in Paul's company from now on.'

A shiver ran through her as she thought of the number of

times she had already been alone with him.

The next three days passed with no further information coming to light, and Martha became restless. She read her notes over and over again but could add nothing to them. In the house, she prowled from room to room and when she went out, she darted in and out of the WFL shop, stopping only long enough to arm herself with leaflets to hand out.

Neither of the policemen returned during this time, which made her think they were certain they'd found the killer. Paul was conspicuous by his absence, for which she was grateful, because she wasn't sure whether she should regard him as a suspect. She was convinced her reactions in his presence would betray her suspicions.

Martha had never been afraid during her forays on behalf of the cause. Not even on the few occasions when she'd travelled to London to join protests. But now, flickers of fear shivered through her when she found herself alone. It was as if a dark cloud hung over her, and she wondered whether it was a warning. A premonition.

Several times, she caught Kirsty and Ethel looking at her with concern in their eyes, and she resolved to ignore her misgivings. She had no time for such foolishness.

39

Over the next few days, Kirsty spent several hours working on Amelia's banner while Ethel continued to learn how to manage the shop.

'Martha thinks I might have the makings of an organiser,' she confided in Kirsty. 'Fancy that! Me, an organiser.' She was wearing her new skirt and blouse, although Kirsty knew Ethel had been embarrassed by the gift.

'You can't refuse to accept them,' she'd told Ethel. 'You'll offend Martha if you do. Think of it this way. Martha is grooming you to become an organiser, and that means you need to look smart.'

Once Ethel accepted that she took pride in wearing her new clothes.

At home, Aunt Bea remained quiet and thoughtful. Kirsty couldn't fathom whether this signified disapproval of her continued interest in the suffrage cause. She felt she was waiting, anxiously, for the time when her aunt would share those concerns with Kirsty's parents.

'I worry when you leave the house,' she told Kirsty.

'There's nothing to worry about. All I do when I go out is meet my friends. Besides, I thought you liked Martha.'

'That is true, but I noticed in the newspaper that a third woman had been found dead in suspicious circumstances. According to the talk on the streets, they were all suffragettes. I would not like to think you were at risk when you leave this house.'

'I'm no more at risk than any other woman in Dundee, and I don't wear the colours or a sash, so my interest in the cause isn't obvious.'

Kirsty shrugged off the pang of guilt she felt. She wasn't

as brave as Ethel or Martha, who were open about their commitment.

'It doesn't stop me worrying.'

'In that case, I'll restrict my visits to the daytime and spend the evenings with you.' Kirsty hoped that would mollify her aunt, though she had no intention of staying away from Tuesday's suffragette meeting in the Kinnaird Hall.

Sunday dawned bright and sunny, and the dark cloud lifted from Martha.

She loved the special at-home meetings, and she bustled about the house preparing for the afternoon. Aggie didn't work on a Sunday, but Martha enjoyed the domesticity of providing for her guests.

'Let me help,' Ethel said as they finished breakfast.

'Aggie baked scones yesterday and she's left a Victoria sponge and a Dundee cake.'

'I can make sandwiches if you like?'

'That would be lovely. I think we have ham, and there is always cucumber. The ladies do love a cucumber sandwich.'

The morning passed in a haze of activity and Martha cast her eye over the refreshments. The sandwiches were not as dainty as Martha was accustomed to, but she said nothing to Ethel. The girl had been so keen to help, and Martha recognised someone trying to fit into a world she didn't feel entirely comfortable in yet. Ethel was learning fast but had not yet acquired the social skills to feel at ease in society gatherings.

Lila was first to arrive, followed closely by several others. They gathered in the drawing-room, seating themselves on sofas and chairs.

Martha surveyed the room and was pleased Ethel had shown the foresight to bring the dining-room chairs through to increase the number of seating options.

The only people missing were Kirsty and her aunt. Martha wondered whether Bea Hunter had decided to ignore her invitation. If she had, it was likely she thought it not in Kirsty's interests to attend.

Kirsty hoped her aunt couldn't hear her heart thumping as she walked, arm-in-arm with her, through the close into the courtyard. Aunt Bea's acceptance of Martha's invitation had seemed a good idea at the time but now, Kirsty didn't feel so sure. She took a deep breath to calm her nerves, trying to bolster her courage before climbing the small flight of steps curving upwards to Martha's front door, which swung open before Kirsty reached for the knocker.

'I was watching from the window and saw you coming.' Ethel's eyes moved to the woman standing behind Kirsty. 'You must be Kirsty's aunt. It's so nice to meet you at last.'

Kirsty hid a smile as she watched a bemused expression cross her aunt's face when she heard Ethel's Dundonian accent.

'You must be Ethel.' Bea held out a white-gloved hand.

Ethel, after a moment's hesitation, shook it with more energy than normal. It was obvious she was unused to shaking hands, and Kirsty saw her aunt flinch slightly and try to hide her reaction from the younger woman. It was enough to change Kirsty's amusement to worry, making her lag behind as they climbed the internal stairs. Would Aunt Bea think Ethel wasn't suitable to be her friend? Would this be another concern to be added to the ones she already had about her niece's involvement with suffragettes?

Kirsty shivered. If her father found out, he would whisk her home without a moment's delay. Doing her best to blank the worries from her mind, she fixed a smile on her face before they reached the drawing-room.

Martha broke off her conversation with Lila and hurried across to greet them.

'How good of you to come. Let me introduce you to our ladies.' She led Bea across the room and, after the introductions, she offered her a seat beside the window. 'I kept this chair for you – I thought you might want to chat to

Constance. She's been involved with the cause for longer than most of us.'

Bea settled herself in the chair and removed her white, cotton gloves before spreading and smoothing her skirts. There was deliberation to her movements, which Kirsty recognised as subtle clues she was not at ease.

'Come,' Martha said to Kirsty. 'I think Ethel might appreciate your assistance in handing around the refreshments.' As soon as they were out of Bea's hearing, Martha whispered, 'Constance will put your aunt at ease.'

Kirsty nodded, but as she handed out plates of sandwiches and cakes, she couldn't avoid glancing at her aunt and Constance. She only relaxed when she observed her aunt laughing at something Constance had said.

40

Tuesday, 7th July 1908

The speeches were over and the audience was becoming restive inside the Kinnaird Hall, where the heat was suffocating. The questions directed at the speakers focused more on the recent murders and whether a killer might still be stalking the streets of Dundee rather than on the scheduled activities.

'Be careful at all times,' Lila Clunas told them. 'However, we need to continue our endeavours to bring our cause to the attention of those who matter. Until we are certain the police have caught this man, make sure you are never alone during the evening.'

Ethel shared a smile with Martha. It had not escaped their notice that Kirsty had barely been able to sit still while the speakers were on stage and her enthusiasm was contagious, affecting them both.

Martha rose from her seat and placed a hand on Kirsty's shoulder.

'I am pleased you enjoyed the meeting.'

'Was it that obvious?' Kirsty followed Ethel and Martha out of the building.

'You will make a good advocate for the suffrage cause.'

'I hope so.'

'Go on ahead, girls. I want to have a word with Constance.'

Ethel and Kirsty joined hands and descended the steps.

'There ye are, ye wee bitch.' Hughie pushed Kirsty out of the way, grabbed Ethel by the shoulders, and rammed her against the wall. 'Thought ye could get away from me, did ye?'

His whisky-laden breath made Ethel gag as she struggled

to free herself from his grip, but his hands were like vices and he shook her so hard her teeth rattled.

Kirsty grabbed his arm, but he shoved her aside and punched her in the stomach before turning his attention back to Ethel.

'Ye'll give up this suffragette nonsense or ye'll never see the light of day again,' he growled before his hands closed around her throat. The last thing Ethel saw before everything went dark was the mad gleam in her father's eyes.

Kirsty landed on the steps in front of the hall. She grasped her midriff and shook her head to get rid of the ringing in her ears. The madman had Ethel by the throat! Kirsty struggled to her feet. She had to help Ethel – but how? The man was too strong for her. She launched herself at him, catching him by surprise. He glared at her, eyes wild with fury. He removed one hand from Ethel's throat and lashed out. Kirsty, unable to stop him, screamed. If she couldn't fight him, she could make enough noise to attract attention.

The sound of running feet echoed up the street as women turned back. Kirsty drew in a ragged breath. Help was coming.

'Get off me, ye bloody witches.' The man staggered under the onslaught of several suffragettes.

One of them thumped him repeatedly until her parasol broke.

'I won't be forgetting you,' he snarled, glaring at her, before striding off along the street.

Ethel lay in a heap on the pavement in front of the Kinnaird Hall. Kirsty knelt beside her, cradling her in her arms. She'd never experienced such violence before. She feared Ethel might be dead.

'Is she all right?' Martha's voice sounded anxious above her.

'I'm not sure.'

As Kirsty spoke, Ethel's eyes fluttered open, and she moaned.

'Thank goodness,' Martha said, bending over her. 'We must get you home and have a doctor examine you.'

'I'll be fine, I'm just sore.' Ethel struggled to her feet. 'Nothing that won't mend.'

'I'm sorry, Constance,' Martha said to the woman holding the broken parasol. 'We won't be able to walk home with you, after all.'

'Not to worry. Archie, bless him, instructed me to make sure I came home in a hansom cab, and that nice reporter offered to go to the cab rank to arrange for one to collect me here. I'll be safe enough.' She threw the parasol into the gutter. 'This will be of no further use.'

Kirsty's stomach ached from the punch she'd received, while her head felt as if it would burst; a result of the fall on the steps. She dreaded to think what effect this encounter, and the bumps and bruises she wouldn't be able to hide, would have on her aunt.

Ethel swayed and Kirsty grabbed her arm to prevent her from falling.

'Who was that man?' The memory of the madness in his eyes sent a shiver coursing through her body.

'My da.' Ethel's voice sounded resigned and bitter. 'My ma told me he wanted to kill me for becoming a suffragette, but I didn't think he'd find me.' She looked over to Constance. 'Thank you for coming to my rescue. I'm sorry about your parasol.'

'I have other parasols.' Constance shrugged. 'The main thing is that you are safe and that he doesn't attack you again.'

The clop of a horse's hooves resounded along the street.

'Ah! If I'm not mistaken, this must be my cab now.'

Martha pulled Constance into her arms in a quick embrace.

'I'll see you tomorrow. Give my regards to Archie when you get home.'

'I am sure he will appreciate that, provided he can raise his head from the pillow.' Constance placed her foot on the step and unlatched the cab door. 'Although I fail to understand why men always feel they are dying whenever the least little thing is wrong with them.' She completed her manoeuvre and slid into the cab, pausing for a moment to nod her farewell to them before closing the door.

Kirsty, who had only met Constance on Sunday, wasn't sure what to say. She settled for an embarrassed smile. Once the cab vanished out of sight at the turn in the road, Kirsty turned to Martha and Ethel.

'I've enjoyed tonight. Well, not this bit, but the meeting. Now, I must get back to my aunt's house, I don't want her to worry.'

'I haven't thanked you for coming to my rescue,' Ethel said. 'How are you going to explain the bruise and the state of your dress?'

Kirsty raised a hand to her cheek.

'Ouch,' she said, touching it. 'I'm not sure how I'll explain it. I'll have to think of something that won't alarm my aunt.' She ran her tongue around inside her mouth. 'At least my teeth are intact. Thank goodness for that.' She smiled at her friend.

Constance tutted as she climbed into the cab. She could remember a time when cabbies descended from their perches and assisted their passengers, but this man, oblivious to her displeasure, stared straight ahead. The horse pawed the ground while she settled into the seat, before moving off in response to the cabby's click of his tongue and pull on the reins.

The motion of the cab, along with the rhythmic clopping of the horse's hooves, was soothing after the excitement of the evening and she closed her eyes. She opened them again when it jerked to a halt, but instead of the familiar sight of her own front door, there was nothing around but trees.

The evening light slanted through the leaves and branches overhanging the narrow road in front of the cab. She looked up to peer through the small window in the compartment's roof, but there was no sign of the cabby. The horse whinnied and pawed the ground, tossing its head in a restless motion.

Constance waited a moment, her hand resting on the cab door. Perhaps the cabby had gone into the trees to relieve himself. But that didn't answer the questions at the forefront of her mind. Where was she? And why here? Her breathing grew shallow and nerves fluttered in her stomach.

This was ridiculous, she thought. She had battled London police, been incarcerated in Holloway more than once and fought prison guards. She was damned if she would allow a mere man to frighten her. She unclipped the door latch and stepped out of the cab, ready to confront the cabby. But her first impression was correct – he wasn't on his perch behind the cab's compartment, nor was he anywhere to be seen.

A slight movement between the trees caught her eye, but it wasn't repeated, and she decided it must have been the wind or a passing animal. Her sense of foreboding increased, and she gathered her skirts in her hands in readiness to mount the steps to the cabby's perch. If she could get hold of the reins before he returned, she'd be off and out of his reach.

A hard punch in the middle of her back knocked her off balance before her foot reached the step. She toppled sideways and slumped to the ground. Darkness swallowed her in its embrace.

41

Despite her show of bravado, Ethel had trouble quelling the fear that her father might return when the suffragettes dispersed. Martha and Kirsty sensed her anxiety, and each grasped one of her hands, Kirsty on the left and Martha to her right, as they left the Kinnaird Hall and strode along Bank Street.

When they reached the end where it intersected with Reform Street, Kirsty squeezed her hand. For a moment, Ethel thought the girl intended to hug her. After a slight moment of embarrassment, Kirsty spoke.

'I have to leave you here. I'm late and my aunt will be worrying.'

'We can accompany you to your door.' Martha took a step forward.

'No need,' Kirsty said. 'I can see the house from here, and it'll take you out of your way.'

'In that case, we will stay here until we see you get inside.'

'That's kind of you. I'm sure I'll be perfectly safe.'

Kirsty stopped outside the corner door to her aunt's house at the top end of Reform Street and waved to them before entering.

Turning to the right, Ethel and Martha walked along the lower section of the road. Apart from a few stragglers from the meeting the street was quiet until they reached the opening to the Overgate. At this time of night, the Overgate teemed with people. Ethel scanned the crowds, fearful her father might be lying in wait for them, but there were too many people everywhere for her to be sure he wasn't amongst them.

'I think we should hurry,' Martha said.

Ethel nodded and the two women quickened their pace until they turned the corner into the Nethergate. Crossing the road before they reached the line of hansom cabs in front of the Steeple Church they soon arrived at the close leading to Martha's house. It was not yet dusk, but the shops at either side were in darkness and no light penetrated the narrow opening through the building.

It struck Ethel suddenly that she didn't know whether her father had discovered where she was living. What if he was lying in wait for her? She stiffened her spine and straightened her shoulders. If she remained afraid of him, he had won, and she wasn't fit to call herself a suffragette. Her decision made and determination bolstered, she strode into the close ahead of Martha. Emerging into the courtyard at the other end, she was relieved to find no one lurking in the shadows.

Kirsty eased the door shut behind her and tiptoed up the stairs. She crept past the open drawing-room door, sighing in relief when she noted her aunt's attention was focused on a book. With luck, she would reach her bedroom before her aunt noticed the disarray of her clothing and bruised face.

Halfway up the second set of stairs, which led to the bedrooms, a stair creaked under her foot. Aunt Bea's hearing was sharp. The sound was bound to have alerted her to Kirsty's return. She scurried up the remaining steps.

Her aunt emerged from the drawing-room before she reached the top.

'Is that you, Kirsty?'

'Yes, Aunt Bea. I thought I would go straight to bed, and I didn't want to disturb you.'

The gaslight in the upper corridor flickered, and Kirsty hoped it was dim enough to mask her dishevelled state.

'I see.'

Her aunt was silent for a moment, allowing time for Kirsty's guilt to resurface. She was tempted to confide in her. Aunt Bea was open-minded and – so far – she hadn't disapproved of her involvement with suffragettes. Her father was a different matter. He would definitely disapprove, and she knew Aunt Bea would be honour-bound to tell him. Once again, she pushed her guilty feelings away. She couldn't risk it.

'You had a good evening with your friends?'

'Yes, Aunt Bea. It was pleasurable.'

Kirsty waited until her aunt returned to the drawing-room before continuing upwards.

Wind sighed through the trees bordering the narrow road, as if expressing grief, but he was oblivious to everything except for Constance lying beside the rear wheel of the hansom cab. His breath caught in his throat and he fought against the familiar feeling of remorse at the waste of another life. He had thought the first killing would be the worst and it would become easier with the following ones. But it didn't get easier, and he had to steel himself to finish the task he'd set himself.

He wiped the slim blade of the rapier on the grass and replaced it in its wooden sheath. It had served its purpose, for the time being. Placing the cane on the cab's elevated seat only took a moment. It wouldn't do to leave it behind.

Constance stirred and moaned. His task was not complete. He leaned over her and plucked the suffragette sash from her body before wrapping it around her neck and pulling hard. Regret swept through him. Constance was a good woman, but her death was necessary.

He sat back on his heels and leaned against the wheel to catch his breath. It was done. And now, he must leave her where she could be found. Her body was heavier than he expected, but after a struggle, he propped her on the seat inside the cab. He arranged her dress and the scarf around her neck so that the ends fluttered free, exposing the motto, *'Votes for Women'*. Satisfied, he closed the door, but it was too early to return to the city. He preferred darkness cloaking his actions.

Turning his back on the cab and its cargo, he strolled through the wood, listening to the leaves rustling in the breeze and the movements of unseen animals. He sighed with pleasure. If only life was as simple as this, there would have been no need to do the things he had done. But now, his plans were coming to fruition and soon he could leave Dundee, knowing that he had completed his task.

Beyond the fringes of the wood, cottages clustered at the far end of a field. He leaned against a tree and, making sure he was hidden from view, lit a cigarette. Drawing smoke deep into his lungs, he closed his eyes and relaxed. When he opened them again, streaks of orange and gold from the dying sun glimmered through the slate-grey cloud-bank. Shadows gathered among the trees. Soon, it would be dark enough to return to the city.

He stubbed his cigarette against the tree trunk, watching sparks flicker to the ground. It was time. Turning, he retraced his steps through the wood and mounted the rear perch of the cab. Shaking the reins and clicking his tongue, he steered the horse out of the wood.

The cab rank in front of the Steeple Church was full, and he guided the horse into position behind the last one at the foot of South Lindsay Street. The horse was well-trained and accustomed to waiting in line at the rank, so it would be some time before Constance's body was discovered. He secured the reins then jumped down and hurried along the street. He would get rid of the cabby's coat, muffler and cap in Mid Kirk Wynd, and then merge with the crowds in the Overgate. It was unlikely anyone would recognise him or notice his passage through their midst.

42

'What the buggery have you called me out for this time?' Hammond made no attempt to soften his voice as he glowered at the duty sergeant.

'It's another body, sir. A cabby reported it to the beat bobby. Said he went to check when the cab in front of his didn't move up the rank, he intended giving the other cabby a piece of his mind, but he wasn't there. He'd left his cab unattended on the rank. That's when he found the body. Inside the cab, it was.'

'Where is the cabby?'

'He wouldn't leave his cab, sir. Said he'd done his duty and now it was up to the bobbies.'

'We'll see about that. Which bobby took the report?'

'It was Constable Fraser, sir. He was patrolling with Constable McDonald when the cabby called him over.'

'Get Fraser. I want to hear what he has to say.'

'I'm sorry, sir, but Constable Fraser returned to the rank to mount guard on the cab.'

Exasperated, Hammond shook his head.

'I'm assuming Fraser left McDonald guarding the cab while he came here to report?'

'Yes, sir.'

'Then why, tell me, does it take two of them to guard it?'

The sergeant shuffled his feet and flushed with embarrassment.

'He thought that was what you'd want, sir.'

'What I want –' Hammond glared at the sergeant '– is a constable to take notes while I question the cabby and other witnesses.'

'I thought you might. So, I took the liberty of calling out

Constable Buchan to assist you. I hope I did right.'

'Where is he?' Hammond's voice rose several decibels.

'I'm here, Inspector Hammond.'

Hammond whirled around and glared at the young constable, standing in the doorway to the inner office.

'Well, don't just stand there. We have work to do.' He turned and slammed out of the door without waiting to see if Buchan followed him.

Darkness clothed the streets and buildings. Nothing stirred the silence apart from the constable's footsteps pattering behind him. Hammond bit on the mouthpiece of his pipe. He didn't mind the quiet, though his pace quickened as he walked along Barrack Street where the wall of the Howff bordered the road.

When he reached the end of this street and entered the Overgate, it seemed like a different world. This was where the drunks and the doxies gathered. Petty thieves and pickpockets roamed among them, looking for easy pickings. He pushed his way through a bunch of men arguing over a bottle and crossed to the other side of the thoroughfare before hurrying along Tally Street to the cab rank in the Nethergate.

By this time, his temper had increased, and he glowered along the line of cabs until he found the two constables standing guard. He marched over, removed the pipe from his mouth, and glared at them.

'Which of you is Fraser?'

'That's me, sir.' The man who stepped forward was the older of the two. He stamped his feet together and saluted.

'Well, don't just stand there. Where is the cabby who found the body?'

'He's sitting on the perch of his cab, sir.'

'I would like to interrogate him.' Hammond enunciated the words, annoyed because he was having to spell out what he wanted. If the constable had any gumption, he would have realised that without having to be told.

'Yes, sir.' Fraser scurried to the cab behind the one he'd been guarding. 'Inspector would like a word,' he shouted to the man sitting on the high perch behind the cab's compartment.

The cabby secured the horse's reins, slotted his whip into its holder, and climbed down, a scowl on his face.

'I'm losing customers,' he grumbled. 'Those bobbies won't let me get on with my work.'

Hammond studied him with narrowed eyes. The man wore the typical cabby's uniform – tight trousers, a high-necked jacket with military-style brass buttons, and a bowler hat. His rigid stance emphasised the outrage which shone from his eyes, but the inspector had met his type before. Taking his time, Hammond tapped the bowl of his pipe on the low wall surrounding the church. Satisfied he'd emptied the ash, he thrust the pipe into his pocket.

'That's too bad.' He returned the man's scowl. 'I need you to answer my questions before we can let you go.'

'Let me go? I'm not being arrested, am I?'

'Not at the moment.' Hammond watched the man squirm.

'I've told the bobbies everything I know.' The cabby's voice was sullen.

'Well, now I need you to tell me. Start at the beginning, when you found the body.'

'I parked my cab in behind this one, but it didn't move on when the cabs in front were hired. We have to wait our turn, you see. I thought the cabby might be asleep, so I went to give him a poke and tell him to move up to the next space. He wasn't on his perch, so I looked into the cab, thinking he might be inside.' The cabby took a deep breath. 'That's when I saw the lady. I thought she was sleeping, even though that seemed strange. Then I saw that thing around her neck and her face looked all peculiar. I didn't know whether she was dead or maybe had a funny turn. So I ran up Tally Lane looking for a bobby. I knew I'd find one in the Overgate.' The man stared at Hammond with an anxious look in his eyes. 'That's all I know, sir. I swear it.'

Hammond waited until Constable Buchan stopped writing in his notebook before continuing.

'What time did this take place?'

'Midnight was striking on the steeple clock when the rest of the cabs moved up the line, so it must have been a few minutes after that.'

'What about the driver of this cab? Did you see him when you parked behind?'

The cabby shook his head.

'The cab was here when I arrived and I didn't see anyone. Maybe one of the cabbies in front might have seen something.'

Hammond turned to the two constables guarding the cab.

'Did either of you question any of the cabbies further up the line?'

'No, sir.' Fraser shuffled his feet.

'Well, what are you waiting for? Get on and do it.'

'Yes, sir.' Fraser beckoned to McDonald, and they headed for the cabs further along the rank.

'Right, you.' Hammond turned back to the cabby. 'Give your name and address to my constable here and then you can get on with your work. But no funny business, mind. I can easily track you down.'

The cab containing the woman's body was no different from any of the others in the rank. The horse stood patiently, held by its reins secured to the narrow iron rail on top of the cab, while the perch sat empty. Hammond reckoned that any cabby who took a tumble from there would be in danger of breaking their neck. The passenger compartment was flanked by two large wheels at either side, which raised the cab high off the ground.

Hammond grabbed the wheel when the cab swayed as he placed his foot on the iron step. Pausing for a moment to regain his balance, he hoisted himself upwards to the higher step running the length of the compartment. He peered over the wooden, folding doors; it was as the cabby described. The woman sat with her head resting against the back of the seat as if she were asleep. The ends of her silk scarf dangled in front of her, and although Hammond couldn't decipher the words in the gloom, he knew they said '*Votes for Women*'. It was another one of those damned suffragettes.

He opened the half doors to examine the body. He searched her dress for pockets and looked for a reticule or handbag. The only thing he found was a handkerchief with the initials *CD*. Closing the doors again, he clambered down from the cab.

'I told the cabby he could get on with his work and he's moved up the rank. I hope I did right, sir.'

'Yes, yes. You got his name and address first?'

'Yes, sir.'

'Fraser and McDonald? Have they reported yet?'

'They're on their way back, sir.'

Buchan's constant use of 'sir' grated on him, but he'd no intention of telling him to stop. The young bobbies needed to show respect to their elders.

'Well,' he snapped as the two bobbies reached him. 'Did any of the others see anything?'

'No, sir.' It was Fraser speaking again. Hammond wondered whether McDonald had a tongue, or if he was in the habit of following Fraser's lead.

'What about the cab? Did they have any information on the driver?'

'No, sir. But they said there should be registration details on a plate or card either inside or outside the cab. It's the licensing law, sir.'

'Good lad. We'll have a look for that when we get the cab back to police headquarters.'

Buchan looked startled.

'Can we do that, sir?'

'It's better than trying to remove the body here. It would help if we could identify her first.' Hammond stared across the street to the houses opposite. 'As I recall,' he said, 'two suffragettes live around here. They might be able to identify her.'

'At this time of night, sir?'

Hammond ignored the comment.

'You know the address and you've been there before, so you can lead the way.'

Buchan shuffled his feet, his reluctance obvious.

'Snap to it, Constable. Why are you waiting?'

'But they're ladies, sir, and they could be alarmed if we rouse them in the middle of the night.'

'Ladies?' Hammond spluttered. 'They are suffragettes, lad, and they get up to all sorts, doesn't matter if it's night or day.'

'Yes, sir.'

'In the meantime –' Hammond addressed Fraser and McDonald '– you two remain on guard here until we get the body identified. After that, one of you will get the job of driving the cab to headquarters.' He turned back to Buchan. 'Come on, Constable. Let's rouse the ladies from their beds and get this over.'

43

The sound of someone thumping on the door echoed through the slumbering house. Ethel's eyes shot open and she stared into the gloom, her heart pounding. She wanted to pull the covers over her head and hide. Da had found her.

The thumping sounded again, louder this time, and she heard Martha emerge from her bedroom. Throwing the sheet aside, she jumped out of bed and ran to the door. Her da had a violent streak. She must warn Martha.

'Wait! You're no match for him.'

'What do you mean?' Martha paused in front of Ethel.

'It's my da. He's found out where I'm living, and he never thinks twice about using his fists.'

'You can't be sure it's him and we won't know unless we go downstairs.'

Ethel shuddered.

'I'm coming with you.' She darted into her room, rammed her feet into her shoes and grabbed her shawl from the peg on the back of her bedroom door. Her da would have to come through her first before she'd let him touch Martha.

'I promise not to open the door until I confirm who is on the other side,' Martha reassured her as Ethel re-joined her.

Martha tightened the tie-belt on her robe as they reached the door.

'Who's there?'

Ethel held her breath, waiting for the explosion of foul language that peppered her da's speech.

'Inspector Hammond, Dundee City Police.'

Ethel exhaled and relief surged through her body, though this was quickly replaced by feelings of unease. It wasn't normal for the bobbies to come knocking on respectable folks' doors in the middle of the night.

'What on earth do you want?' Martha fingered the key in the lock but did not turn it.

'Open up. That's an order.'

Martha stiffened at the gruff sound of the inspector's voice, but she turned the key and opened the door.

'What is the meaning of this? What right have you to come disturbing us at this time of night?'

'There has been another death, and it is my belief you may know the victim.'

Martha's eyes widened, but her sharp inhalation of breath was only audible to Ethel, standing next to her.

'I don't suppose it occurred to you that you could have waited until morning before informing me of this?'

'The body requires identification before we move it to the mortuary. As she appears to be a member of your organisation, I must insist you come with us and do the needful.' Hammond's voice brooked no argument.

'Like this?' Martha pointed to her robe. 'I can't leave my house unless I am properly attired.'

Hammond reddened and the constable behind him seemed to be having difficulty keeping a straight face.

'Very well. But be quick about it,' Hammond responded gruffly.

Martha closed the door, leaving the policemen standing outside.

Ethel raised her eyebrows.

'Should you have done that? Might it not have been more polite to ask him to wait inside?'

'He's an obnoxious man. He can wait there while we get dressed.'

By the time Martha opened the door again, half an hour later, Hammond was pacing back and forth, and obviously in a foul mood.

'This way.' He glared at them.

Ethel suppressed a smile and noticed Martha doing the same. They followed the inspector across the road until he came to a halt beside a hansom cab.

'The body's in there.' He pointed. 'You'll have to climb

up to the running board to see it.'

Martha grasped the cab's wheel, lifted her skirt, placed a foot on the steep step and hoisted herself up to the running board in front of the cab's passenger compartment.

Constable Buchan crossed to Ethel's side.

'I'm so sorry we had to disturb you tonight, Miss Stewart. But the inspector insisted.'

She glanced at him. He was nicer than his boss and she liked him.

'That's all right,' she said.

'Well?' Hammond demanded. 'Can you identify her?'

Martha remained perched on the running board, staring into the cab, seemingly oblivious to everything around her. Fear clutched Ethel's heart. Something was wrong.

Hammond bit on the mouthpiece of his pipe and stamped to the back of the cab to prevent himself from shouting to the woman to get on with it. How long did it take to identify someone? He shuffled his feet and glared at Buchan and the girl. Damned young bobbies were all the same when they saw a pretty girl. Thank goodness he wasn't afflicted that way. In any case, they didn't stay pretty forever; they grew into women like his gran.

At first. he thought the woman was ignoring him when he asked if she could identify the body, but after a moment, she looked down to him and nodded her head.

Tears slipped down her cheeks and she turned to look over to the girl standing beside Constable Buchan.

'It's Constance,' she said. Her voice trembled and she stifled a sob.

Buchan darted to the side of the hansom and held his hand out to aid the woman as she descended from the running board. Hammond scowled, making a mental note to tell the young constable to keep his distance from suffragettes. Getting too close to them could only mean trouble.

'Well?' Hammond demanded as soon as Martha stepped

on to the pavement. 'I am waiting for the identification.' He towered over her, forcing her to step back a pace. Heat built in his neck and face as he waited while she smoothed her skirts. The woman was deliberately provoking him. 'Well?' he demanded again.

'Yes, I can identify her.'

He had never struck a woman in his life, but he was tempted now.

'Buchan!' he shouted. 'Bring your notebook and get the identification details from this . . . woman.' He turned away, but not before he saw her smile of satisfaction. Damned woman was enjoying his discomfiture. Hammond stamped off in search of someone to drive the cab back to the police station.

Martha struggled to control her feelings and forced a smile. Nothing would please the inspector more than if she were to display her distress in front of him, but she was determined not to break down in front of this obnoxious man.

He beckoned to the constable, glared at Martha, and marched off.

'I'm sorry to trouble you at a time like this,' the young constable said, 'but the inspector does need to know who the victim is.'

Victim. The word sounded alien when applied to Constance, one of the most active members of the league. It was Constance who took part in the London demonstrations. She'd broken windows and battled with the police along with the best of them. Imprisonment, hunger strikes and forced feeding were sacrifices she had made for the cause. It didn't make sense for her to become a victim in Dundee, far away from the trouble and violence of a suffragette's life.

'Lady Constance Drysdale.' Martha tried hard to keep the wobble out of her voice.

Constable Buchan wrote the name in his notebook.

'She's a Lady? The inspector's not going to like that.'

'Constance hasn't been in the habit of using her title since she remarried after the death of her first husband.'

Martha wasn't even sure Constance was still allowed to use the title, but she thought that if the inspector was aware of it then it might have some influence on the investigation. It would force him to treat her death more seriously than the others.

Her lips tightened as she stared at the inspector, who stood gesticulating to a cabby further along the rank. She couldn't understand why he hadn't treated the earlier deaths with the thoroughness they deserved. Was it simply that he didn't like suffragettes? Or did he have a hidden agenda of his own?

The constable cleared his throat and Martha forced her attention back to him.

'I'm sorry,' she whispered, 'but Constance's death has shocked me. It is only a few hours since we parted company outside the Kinnaird Hall. We never, for a moment, considered her to be in any danger because she was returning home in a hansom cab.'

'You must have been one of the last people to see her.' The constable stopped writing, regarding her with interest. 'What can you tell me about the cab she left in?'

'It was just a cab, like any other. What do you want to know?'

'Can you describe the cabby?'

Martha shrugged.

'One doesn't take much notice of cabbies. I did think he was a bit muffled up considering the evening was still somewhat warm.'

'In what way?'

'Well, he was wearing an overcoat, although that is not unusual. But he also wore a white muffler which covered the lower part of his face so you could only see his eyes below his bowler hat.'

'And that didn't make you suspicious?'

'Why should it? He was only a cabby and you see them all the time. They are part of the Dundee landscape.'

Buchan tapped his teeth with his pencil while he thought.

At last, he spoke.

'Where did Lady Constance get the cab? Did she come here, to the rank?'

'It was a lovely evening, and we had planned to walk here, but Paul said he would send one to collect her.'

'Paul?'

'Paul Anderson, the *Courier* reporter. He was covering the meeting for his newspaper.'

'I see. So that means Lady Constance was still at the Kinnaird Hall when the cab arrived.'

'That is correct.' Martha observed the frown on the constable's face and, not for the first time, she wondered about Paul Anderson. Was he as helpful as he purported to be? Or did he have an ulterior motive? She pushed the thought away and vowed to stop suspecting every male with whom she had contact.

'Lady Constance's husband,' the constable continued. 'I presume he does not attend these meetings with her?'

'On the contrary. Archie usually accompanies her. But he wasn't here today – he has been suffering from food poisoning after eating out-of-season oysters.'

'I don't appear to have a note of her husband's full name or their address,' Buchan said.

'Archibald Drysdale. I'm not in a position to know whether he has any middle names,' Martha said. 'We just know him as Archie. They are currently living in their townhouse in the west end of the city, although the family estate is north of Aberdeen and they spend much of their time at their London home in Belgravia.' She watched as he wrote the address she gave him in his notebook.

'They're not short of a bob or two, then.'

'I am sure I don't know what you mean.' Martha regretted her tart reply as soon as she said it. Constable Buchan had been kind and pleasant during his questioning and didn't deserve it.

Buchan closed his notebook.

'I think I've got everything I need for the time being,' he said. 'Though if Inspector Hammond requires further details,

I'll have to speak to you again.'

Martha nodded her head in acquiescence.

'You took your time.' Hammond's eyes itched from the lack of sleep. He'd given up hope of returning to his bed in the foreseeable future.

'It is the middle of the night, you know,' Dr Jenkins snapped. He mounted the step of the hansom cab, which now sat in the police courtyard. Several minutes later, he dismounted. 'I'm sure you had no trouble noticing she was dead. You didn't need to call me out, it could have waited until a more civilised hour of the day.'

'Are you suggesting we should leave her where she is until morning so you can get your beauty sleep? Have some respect, man. The poor woman needs to be transported to the mortuary, and until she is officially declared dead, that can't be done.'

Hammond snapped his fingers and beckoned to the man leaning on the coffin-shaped barrow in the corner of the yard.

'In any case,' he continued, 'that is what the police department pay you for.'

The doctor snorted.

'The pittance they pay me doesn't cover the number of times I've been called out.'

'In that case, you won't mind if I recommend using a different doctor when your contract comes up for renewal.'

Jenkins pulled himself erect, glaring at the inspector for a moment before stomping out of the courtyard.

'I will expect you to supply the cause of death to me before lunchtime,' Hammond called after him.

The wooden wheels of the barrow clattered over the cobbles. 'How does we get her out of there, sir?' Davvy balanced the barrow on its shafts alongside the cab.

'Buchan will help you get her down.'

'Aye, sir, but it won't be easy.'

Hammond stood back and watched Buchan and Davvy

manoeuvre the body from the interior of the cab.

'She be pretty stiff, sir.' Davvy descended to the ground and waited for Buchan to lower the body. Buchan clambered down as soon as Davvy grasped it and, between them, they carried Constance's lifeless form to the barrow. A frown creased Davvy's face.

'I didnae open the lid,' he said. 'D'ye think ye could dae it for me?'

Hammond sighed and raised the lid, closing it again after Davvy and Buchan deposited Constance inside the box. Davvy fastened the latch before positioning himself between the shafts and lifting them to waist height. With a nod to the policemen, he trundled the barrow across the cobbles.

'Sir,' Buchan said, 'I thought Lady Drysdale had been strangled, but when I lifted her body, I noticed there was blood on her back.'

'Why didn't you tell me before we let Davvy leave?'

'I thought you knew.'

'Well, I didn't know, and now you will have to run after Davvy and stop him so I can check.'

A wry smile twisted the corner of Hammond's mouth as he sauntered after the constable's running form. Served him right for not speaking sooner, Hammond thought.

'Your bobby says you be wanting another look at the lady before I takes her to the mortuary.' Davvy still stood between the shafts of the barrow; Buchan leaned against the wall, trying to catch his breath.

'That's right, but you will need to pull the barrow a wee bit further along so it is under the streetlamp.'

Davvy adjusted his hands on the shafts and pulled the barrow underneath the gas lamp.

'Be there enough light here?' He lowered the shafts to rest on the ground and rubbed his hands together.

'That will have to do.' Hammond stared at the box and steeled himself to examine the body again.

'Will you be wanting me to open the lid?'

'You stay where you are, Buchan can open it.' He glared at the constable. 'Well, get on with it. We don't have all night.'

'Yes, sir.' Buchan's fingers scrabbled with the latch until he prised it free and opened the lid. He hesitated as if waiting for further instructions.

Hammond shook his head. If the man had any common sense, he would know what was required without having to be told.

'Turn her over so I can see this blood you were telling me about,' he snapped.

The constable's eyes widened; his reluctance obvious by the hesitancy with which he reached into the box.

'She won't bite you. She's dead.'

Hammond leaned over to inspect the woman's back as Buchan rolled her on to her side. Damn, the constable was right. There was a bloodstain. He pulled the dress down from her shoulders, exposing her flesh, noticing as he did so that the constable averted his eyes. The puncture wound was small, and he had to peer to see it. Not a knife, then. Something slimmer, but not as slim as a needle. This complicated things. It made this death different from the others and yet, the manner in which she had been left, with the sash knotted around her neck, was the same. Why was nothing ever straightforward?

'All right, constable. Close the box and let Davvy be on his way.'

He clamped his teeth on his cold pipe and strode back to the office without waiting for Buchan. He had a lot to think about.

44

Martha cradled the cup in her hands as she stared, unseeingly, out of the window. She hadn't slept since identifying Constance's body. She wondered how Ethel had fared.

A board creaked in the room above, followed by the sound of footsteps descending the stairs.

'I couldn't face breakfast this morning,' she said when Ethel appeared, 'but there's tea in the pot.' She gestured to the silver tea service.

Ethel came over and stood at her side.

'I'm sorry about Constance. I know you were close.'

'Yes.' Martha blinked, fighting gathering tears. One escaped and rolled down her cheek. 'We both supported the cause from its earliest days, though Constance was more militant than I ever was.' Silence fell over the two young women.

'It looks so normal in the street. It's as if last night never happened.' Ethel's voice was strained, little more than a murmur.

Martha turned away from the window. She couldn't bear to see the line-up of hansom cabs in front of the church. She laid her cup on the table and smoothed the wrinkles from her dress.

'I must visit Archie. I'm not sure he'll know . . .' Her voice faltered. She couldn't say the words 'Constance' and 'death' in the same sentence. 'How on earth am I going to tell him?' She dashed another tear from her eye.

'I'll come with you. We can do it together. Lila won't mind if I take the morning off. I'll let her know before we leave.'

'We can't exclude Kirsty. She has been part of our

murder investigation since the beginning.' Martha stepped away from the window and placed her cup in its saucer. 'I have sent Aggie to her aunt's house with a note.' She could see Ethel thinking and wondered what was going through her mind. At last, the girl spoke.

'Do you think her husband had anything to do with Constance's death?'

'Archie?' Martha couldn't keep the surprise out of her voice. 'I hadn't given that any thought, but I suppose we shouldn't rule it out. However, I was thinking he might know if anyone had been following Constance or held a grudge against her. In any case, the poor man has been somewhat debilitated since he ate those bad oysters.'

Laughter and raucous voices mingled with the sound of doors banging and feet thumping in the corridor, announced the arrival of the early shift.

Hammond groaned. His eyes felt glued together and his joints ached. The hard wood of the canteen bench he'd fallen asleep on hadn't helped his back any; he groaned again as he tried to move. He struggled into a sitting position and rescued his hat from the floor. He was getting too old for the hassle his work entailed, though being in the job protected him from his gran's company. She must be as old as Methuselah, and he was fed up waiting for her to kick the bucket.

By the time he massaged feeling into his limbs, the worst of the noise had died away. Faint commands echoed from outside, indicating the bobbies had gathered in the courtyard on morning parade.

The sink in the corner of the canteen was full of dirty mugs, but he splashed cold water over his face before wandering up the corridor to his office. He wanted to check whether Constable Buchan had carried out his order to write a report on the evening's events.

The room was in its usual state of disarray. Papers and files littered every available surface and most of the floor.

Buchan's report lay in a cleared space on the desk, pinned down by a brass ashtray. He slumped into his chair to study it, but the further he read, the more depressed he became. It wasn't Buchan's fault. The lad could write a damned good report, even if he wasn't much use at anything else. It was these damned suffragettes who kept getting themselves killed.

Footsteps clomped up the corridor and Buchan appeared in the doorway.

'Thought you might want a cup of tea,' he said, pushing papers aside and placing a mug on the desk.

Hammond swallowed a mouthful. The tea was so strong he had to stop himself from gagging. But that was the way bobbies liked it; brewed until it resembled tar.

'I've examined the hansom cab and noted the details of the cabby it belongs to.'

Buchan's expression was similar to that of a puppy looking for praise and Hammond suppressed a groan. What right did the constable have for being so bright after the night they'd put in?

'Good lad,' he said, though he wanted to kick him into submission. 'We will follow that up after we've visited the victim's husband.'

With a shower of sparks and the grinding of wheels on iron rails, the tram clanked to a halt. On a normal day and in a normal situation, Martha would have hired a cab, but after the discovery of Constance's body during the early hours of the morning, she'd shuddered at the very thought. It had been Ethel's suggestion they travel by tram car and, although the journey had been less comfortable, it had eased Martha's distress.

Kirsty, Ethel and Martha waited on the kerb for a bicycle and then a horse and cart to pass before crossing to the other side of Perth Road. Springfield was a cul-de-sac of Regency, terraced houses, bordered by waist-high walls topped with iron railings. Doric pillars at the entrances and ornamental balustrades on the edge of each roof indicated the occupants were wealthier than their Perth Road neighbours.

Martha counted the numbers until she came to the house halfway along the east side of the street. She turned into the entrance, followed by Kirsty and Ethel, but before she could announce their presence, the door flew open and Inspector Hammond strode out. Constable Buchan followed in his wake. Hammond stopped when he saw Martha.

'I might have known you lot would tramp all over my investigation. What are you doing here?'

'I've come to pay my respects,' she snapped, stiffening. 'There's nothing wrong with that.'

'If you lot weren't out roaming the streets all the time, you wouldn't be getting yourselves killed.'

'Lock us in the house. Tie us to the kitchen sink. Is that how men think they should treat women? Well, sorry to disappoint you, but there are a lot of women who would disagree with you.' Martha's voice was tight with anger as she watched the inspector stride down the steps and on to the road.

'He's not in the best of moods today,' the constable whispered to Ethel.

She raised her eyebrows and shared a smile with him.

'I can see that. But Martha's his match.'

A young woman stood in the doorway, regarding them with a bemused expression.

'Can I help you?' she asked.

'Please inform Mr Drysdale we wish to pay our respects,' Martha said, handing her a visiting card.

'I'm afraid Mr Drysdale is indisposed.'

The woman tried to block their entry, but Martha swept past her.

'I take it you are new here.' Martha looked her up and down with her most officious stare. 'I am usually announced by the butler. Where is he?' She stared around the hall, observing the pile of cabin trunks piled up to the left of the door.

'Mr McGregor has gone on ahead to open the London

house.'

Martha frowned. Constance, before her death, had indicated a return to London, but she hadn't given the impression it would be so soon.

'What is it, Gloria?' Archie emerged from a door further down the hall.

'I tried to tell them you weren't well enough for visitors, but they wouldn't listen.'

Leaning heavily on his walking stick, Archie shuffled towards them.

'It's quite all right. Show Miss Fairweather and her friends into the small parlour. I'll see them there. And perhaps you can bring us a pot of tea and a plate of those shortbread biscuits.'

'We are so sorry for your loss,' Martha said, once Archie had joined them in the room. 'Constance will be greatly missed.'

'Such a terrible thing to happen.' Archie eased himself into an armchair. 'We had intended to journey to London on the midday train. Our preparations had been made. The permanent staff have gone ahead, and the temporary ones dismissed. I don't know what I'll do now.'

'I hadn't realised you were intending to go to London so soon.'

'Constance insisted. She was worried because my bout of food poisoning weakened me. She wanted me to see my Harley Street doctor.' Archie's shoulders shook, and he buried his face in his hands. His stick clattered to the floor. Kirsty leaned forward, picked it up, and handed it to him. He grabbed it from her with more haste than necessary and his hand closed on the eagle-shaped handle.

'Thank you,' he said after a moment.

'My father has a similar cane. His one is a sword-stick,' Kirsty said, staring first at the cane and then Archie.

'How interesting. I can assure you that this one is a simple walking stick, to enable me to move around.' His gaze lingered on her before he looked away to reach for a handkerchief. He wiped a tear from his eye and sighed.

An awkward silence ensued until Gloria entered the room, pushing a trolley with the tea things.

'Thank you, Gloria. I don't know what I would do if you weren't here.'

'Is Gloria the only servant left?' Martha asked once the woman had left the room again.

'I'm afraid so, but she's not actually a servant. She's the nurse who has been looking after me during my illness. I've asked her to stay on until I leave. Although, if I continue to be debilitated, I might have to ask her to accompany me on the journey to London.'

'You still intend to go?'

'I'll stay until after the funeral.' He wiped another tear from his eye. 'I don't think I can remain in this house without Constance.'

'Damned women,' Hammond muttered as he and Constable Buchan set out on the next stage of their investigation. 'Why can't they be like normal women? Ones who know their place?'

Buchan knew better than to reply, though Hammond scowled with displeasure when he saw a glimmer of amusement cross the young bobby's face.

The address on the cab's registration details was a small cottage near Ninewells tram terminus. It sat back from the road, with a strip of grass at the front. A rough-hewn path at the side of the house led to a stable at the rear of the property. Hammond thumped on the door with his fist.

The woman who opened it looked like a younger version of his gran. Worn out before her time, her expression showed defeat. Worry lines crisscrossed her face, though otherwise, her features held no signs of ageing. She wiped her hands on the apron that encompassed her body.

'Police,' Hammond announced. 'Is this the abode of Douglas Paterson, cab driver?'

The woman stepped back. The worry lines intensified.

'Dougie? He's not here. What's he done? What's

happened?'

'It might be better if we came in,' Buchan said.

Hammond glowered at him, but the young constable continued.

'I'm assuming you're Mrs Paterson?'

She nodded and stepped aside to let them enter. The room she led them into was a cross between a sitting-room and a kitchen; a jawbox sink filled the window recess, a table and chairs hugged the wall at the opposite side, and two armchairs and a dilapidated sofa sat in front of the fire, which glowed red despite the heat of the day. A savoury smell wafted from the range attached to the fireplace.

Mrs Paterson gestured for them to sit, but Hammond remained standing. He didn't fancy subjecting the sofa to his weight.

'Your husband, Mrs Paterson – when did you last see him?' He signalled to Buchan to take notes.

'Yesterday, after lunch. He left for work.' Her voice sounded anxious and her eyes flitted between both men.

'And you've not seen him since.'

'No.'

'Is that usual?'

'I expected him to come home before breakfast. He works most of the night but stops for breakfast and then returns to the rank. We need every fare he can get.'

'I see. So, when he didn't return, was that a matter for you to worry about?'

'No. I just thought he'd picked up extra fares and would come home when they were completed. What's this all about? Has he been in an accident?' She swayed and panic made her breathing laboured.

Buchan took hold of her arm and lowered her into an armchair.

'You'll feel better if you sit down.'

'Not an accident, but we need to trace him,' Hammond said. 'We found his cab on the rank last night and it contained the body of a woman.'

'Body of a . . .' Mrs Paterson, unable to continue,

surveyed them with horror. 'You mean, someone *died* in his cab?'

'The dead woman was murdered.' The harshness in Hammond's voice contained no sympathy.

Mrs Paterson sagged and uttered a moan.

'You can't think Dougie had anything to do with that?' Her voice shook. 'He wouldn't hurt a fly.'

'We won't know until we talk to him, and we have to find him first.'

'I'm sorry,' Buchan said. 'This must be a shock for you.'

Hammond glared at him. The boy was getting too big for his boots. He had no right to interfere during an interrogation.

'We will need to search your house and any outbuildings, in case he is hiding here. I will also need a photograph of him.'

The woman's shoulders sagged in defeat.

'I can't afford to have photographs taken, but search where you like. You won't find him here.'

'Buchan, you do the search, while I remain here with Mrs Paterson.'

The search didn't take long and Hammond's frustration grew as he listened to Buchan's report that nothing had been found. Hammond stamped away from the house, leaving Buchan to close the gate behind them.

'We need to find that cabby before he kills someone else.'

'Yes, sir.'

45

Thursday, 9th July 1908

Kirsty arrived at the breakfast table the next morning to find her aunt reading the *Dundee Courier* with a frown on her face.

'There has been another murder,' she said without looking up from the newspaper. 'Apparently, it happened after a meeting on Tuesday.' She laid the paper on the table and fixed her eyes on Kirsty. 'Wasn't that the meeting you attended?'

'Yes, Aunt Bea.' Kirsty held her breath, anticipating her aunt's next comment.

'In the circumstances, I think you should return home. It would be safer than Dundee.'

Kirsty leaned forward and grasped both her aunt's hands in her own.

'Not yet,' she pleaded. 'I can't desert Martha when she's lost her best friend to this maniac.'

'She was a friend of Martha's?' Bea stared at Kirsty with an expression of horror on her face.

'Yes – you met her on Sunday. The lady you were sitting beside.'

'Oh, dear. Such a nice lady. I remember thinking, if every suffragette was like her, they would be much easier to accept.'

'You must see, Aunt Bea? I can't leave Martha in her hour of need. At least let me stay until after Constance's funeral.'

'I do understand. But I worry, dear.'

'I'll continue to be careful and only go out during the daytime. Please, Aunt Bea.'

'Very well. It is against my better judgement, but you can

stay here until the funeral. After that, you must return home to your parents.'

46

Kirsty completed the last stitch in the banner and held it up
for Ethel to admire.

'It's lovely,' Ethel said. 'I can sew a hem but I couldn't
do that.'

'Embroidery is the only sewing I was taught. I wouldn't
know where to start with dressmaking.'

'May I?' Martha reached for the banner, running her
hands over it. 'This will take pride of place on the wall and
we will carry it when we march.'

The bell over the shop door tinkled and the stooped figure
of a woman entered. Her clothes were grimy and a headscarf
covered her hair.

Ethel gasped when she lifted her head to look at her.

'Ma! What are you doing here?'

Margery Stewart leaned over the counter and grasped her
daughter's hands.

'I came to warn ye. Your da's on the way and he's had a
good bucket. He's raging and threatening to drag ye home by
the hair on your head. He says if ye willnae come, he'll kill
ye.'

'Lock the door, Kirsty.' Martha tossed a key to her. 'I'll
telephone the police.'

'Hurry, Kirsty! I can see him crossing the street.' Ethel
stared out of the window, feeling powerless. Kirsty rammed
the key in the lock, turned it, and shot the bolts at the top and
bottom of the door.

'He mustn't see you in here, Ma.' Ethel lifted the flap at
the end of the counter. 'Quick, hide in the back room.'

'Only if you come with me.'

'Yes,' Martha said. 'You need to be out of sight, as well.

If your father gains entry, leave by the back window and take your mother into the house.'

The door rattled as the man outside sought to enter.

'Maybe he'll go away,' Kirsty whispered.

'I think that doubtful, considering what Ethel has told me about him. I can only hope the police arrive to apprehend him.'

A face appeared at the shop window. Malevolence shone from his eyes and his brows knitted together in a ferocious scowl.

'I know ye're in there, ye wee bitch.' He banged on the glass. 'Ye canna escape me. I'm your da and ye have to do as ye're bid. If ye dinna, it'll be the worse for ye.'

Kirsty shrank back.

'Did the police say they would come?'

Martha shrugged.

'The sergeant I spoke to was noncommittal. Said most of the bobbies were out on the beat but he would try to find someone.'

Glass shattered around Kirsty's feet as the window caved in.

'Think ye could stop me from coming in, did ye? Well, ye'd best think on,' Hughie bellowed. Glass perforated his hands as he grasped the window but he paid no heed to the blood running down his wrists, soaking the cuffs of his grubby shirt.

Martha lifted the counter flap.

'Quick, get behind here.' She slammed the flap closed as Kirsty joined her behind the counter.

Hughie leaned over it, globules of spit hitting their faces as he roared, 'Where is the wee bitch?'

There was no mistaking the sound of Sergeant Edward's boots pounding on the flagstones in the corridor. Constable Buchan laid his pen on the desk and pushed the unfinished report aside. He was the only one in the constables' room, and if Edwards was looking for spare bodies, he was it. The door opened with a thud and the sergeant's bulky frame filled the open space.

'Are you the only one here?' he growled. 'I suppose you'll have to do.'

'Yes, sir.' Constable Buchan sprang to his feet. The sergeant had taken a dislike to him after Inspector Hammond had co-opted him as a detective. The sergeant looked at him with an expression of distaste on his face.

'I need someone to check out a disturbance in the Nethergate. You sure you're up to it?'

Buchan held back a retort. Disturbances had been part of his daily routine before Hammond claimed him.

'Yes, sir. If you give me the details, sir. I'll get on to it right away.'

Sergeant Edwards crossed the room and slapped a piece of paper on Buchan's desk.

'Details are on there,' he said. 'Hop to it, lad.'

The sergeant's footsteps receded as Buchan shrugged on his uniform jacket. It would be good to do real police work instead of hanging on Inspector Hammond's coat-tails and writing his reports. He finished buttoning his jacket and picked up the sheet of paper. By the time he'd finished reading, he was running up the corridor. The disturbance was at the Women's Freedom League shop, and that was where Ethel now worked.

He grabbed a bicycle leaning against the courtyard wall and pedalled through the archway to West Bell Street. The bike wobbled when he skidded around the corner leading to Barrack Street, but he managed to keep his balance. The Overgate loomed up in front of him, impeding his progress, but he pedalled through the crowds, frantically ringing the bell on the handlebars. A hansom cab blocked his way at the end of Tally Street, but that gave him time to blast twice on his whistle. There were always bobbies on the beat in the Overgate. He pushed the bike past the hansom and stared across the street.

Despair swept through him when he saw the shattered window. He was too late. Abandoning the bicycle against the church railings, he dodged between cabs, carts and carriages on the busy road. Curious onlookers clustered around the front of the shop, but he pushed past them, grabbed the window frame and clambered into the shop. Inside, Hughie Stewart was wrestling with the counter-flap while the two women behind it were attempting to keep it closed.

He grabbed Hughie. The man's eyes were bloodshot; they flashed with fury as he turned towards Buchan. He lashed out at the constable but missed his face, the blow landing on the bobby's shoulder. Buchan pinned the man's arm up his back, twisted him around and pushed him forward so that his face pressed into the counter.

'You're under arrest,' he said, 'for criminal damage, threatening behaviour, and assault of a police officer.'

By the time two constables raced over the road from the direction of the Overgate, a subdued Hughie was sitting on the floor complaining.

'I only came to take my wee lassie home. I didnae deserve this.'

47

'You're bleeding,' Martha said to Buchan after the two constables led Hugh Stewart off to the police cells.

The constable stared at his hand as if wondering how the blood got there.

'You probably cut yourself climbing in through the window.'

'It's nothing, just a scratch.' He looked around the shop. 'Miss Ethel . . . has she been harmed?'

'The back room is empty, so she must have gone out of the window as I suggested. She should be in the house by this time.'

Buchan nodded and Martha thought she detected relief in his eyes.

'You should be safe as long as Mr Stewart is under lock and key.' After a moment's hesitation, he added, 'Will you give my regards to Miss Ethel?' He placed his hand on the doorknob. 'Ah! It appears I'm locked in. Perhaps I should leave the way I entered?' He nodded at the window.

'Kirsty,' Martha said, turning to the younger woman, 'do you still have the key?'

'I put it under the counter. Give me a minute.' She picked her way through the glass splinters and sidled past Buchan and Martha. The lock clicked when she turned the key while the bolts at top and bottom screeched as she pulled them from their sockets.

'What about the window?'

'Don't worry,' Martha said. 'I'll get a carpenter to board it until we get a replacement.'

'Ladies,' Buchan said, tipping a finger to his helmet as he turned to leave.

Martha placed a hand on his arm.

'I have bandages in the house. You must let me dress that injury before you leave.' She sensed his reluctance, and added, 'I am sure your inspector wouldn't wish you to leave before assuring yourself that Mr Stewart didn't harm his daughter.'

Several women remained outside the shop to watch their exit; most of the crowd had dispersed after the policemen left with their captive. One of the stragglers stepped forward as the trio left the shop.

'Are you all right?' she asked. 'I know some people are against you suffragettes, but there's no excuse for that kind of violence.'

'Thank you for your concern,' Martha replied. 'We are fine. The only damage done is to the window.' Eager to escape curious eyes, she ushered Kirsty and Buchan into the close at the side of the shop and didn't relax until they emerged into the courtyard at the back of the building.

Aggie was washing crockery when Martha led Buchan into the kitchen.

'I believe we have bandages in one of the cupboards,' Martha said.

The maid removed her hands from the soapy water and dried them on a towel. She extracted a small box from a cupboard and handed it to Martha.

'Miss Ethel and her friend are in the drawing-room. I served them tea to calm them.' Aggie's eyes glittered with curiosity. 'Been some kind of rumpus, I was told.'

Martha opened the box and inspected the contents. Bandages, iodine, several safety-pins and a small pair of scissors nestled inside.

'You could say that,' Martha replied. 'It has left the shop with a broken window. It will need to be repaired to make sure intruders don't get in and create more damage.' She selected a bandage and two safety-pins from the box. 'Do you know any carpenters who could board it?'

'There's one in Dock Street. He's not a craftsman. Doesn't make furniture or the like, but boarding up a window should be no problem for him.'

'I want you to go to him with instructions to come to do the work at once. After that, you'll be about due to finish, so don't worry about returning. Thanks, Aggie.'

After the maid had left, Martha snipped a small piece from the end of the bandage. She wet it and dabbed at the cut on the palm of Buchan's hand.

'Aggie's a godsend, but she can be somewhat curious. I thought it best to dismiss her for the day.'

Buchan flinched as she dabbed the wet gauze on his skin.

'Hold still.'

Martha unrolled the bandage. She took her time; she wanted to find out what the police were up to and the constable might be less guarded while his wound was being dressed.

'Amelia's mother came to see me,' she said gently. 'She says Billy Murphy is still locked up.' She lifted his hand and laid the end of the bandage on his palm.

'Yes. He's being held for three of the killings.'

'But surely Billy can't be responsible if he was locked up at the time of the last murder?' She wound the bandage around his hand, pulling it tight to make him concentrate on the pain and not what she was asking.

'Inspector Hammond thinks the last murder was unconnected.' Beads of sweat stood out on his forehead.

Martha's brow puckered in a frown. She'd seen Constance with her sash wound around her neck, just as Amelia's had been.

'I don't understand,' she said. 'Constance was strangled, just like the others.' She finished wrapping the bandage and held it in place with her finger.

'Strangulation was the cause of death for the other victims, but not the last one. It was different.'

'In what way?' She picked up a safety-pin and attached it to the end of the bandage.

'The last victim was stabbed in the back. The sash was placed around her neck after her death. The inspector thinks the killer copied the other murders.'

'But surely, if she'd been stabbed, there should have been

more blood in the cab?'

'I suppose that's because the weapon was a slim blade. We nearly missed the wound, it was so small.'

'I see.' Martha frowned as she digested the information.

'If that is the case, who killed Constance?'

'The main suspect is the cabby, but we haven't found him yet.'

'All done.' Martha patted his bandaged hand. 'Now you can come and pay your respects to Ethel before you return to the station.'

As she led him to the drawing-room, she pondered the information he had provided. It made little sense for the cabby to kill Constance, and it made less sense for him to have copied the other murders. It could only be someone with inside knowledge. Someone who would have known how the other women were killed.

48

Memories of Constance plagued Martha the entire night. As she tossed and turned, unable to find the solace of sleep, visions of her friend played out behind her closed eyes. Constance chained to the railings at the prime minister's abode in Downing Street, waving her banner as she marched in the London rallies, battling with the police in front of parliament. She'd survived arrest, prison, and even forced feeding. And now, to be struck down by a murderer in Dundee, where she should have been safe. A place where suffragettes didn't experience the violence that they did in London . . . it was beyond belief. How could this happen to someone as strong and indomitable as Constance?

The steeple bells tolled eight times. She counted each chime, just as she'd done every hour through the night. Unable to sleep or rest and with no appetite for food, she forced herself out of bed to join Ethel at the breakfast table.

She caught Ethel looking at her with concern as she pushed her plate aside, untouched.

'You aren't eating this morning.' The girl's voice held a faint tinge of admonition.

'I'm not hungry. A cup of tea will suffice.'

'You usually have a good appetite. Are you unwell?'

Martha smiled. Ethel was more direct than most. She didn't believe in masking her words with flowery comments.

'I am well, Ethel, but it's kind of you to ask. I had a restless night, thinking of tomorrow's funeral.'

'You should rest. I'll see to the shop.'

'I don't think Lila intends to come in today.'

'It doesn't matter. I've a good grasp of everything now, and Kirsty can help.'

'Well, if you are sure.' Martha's brows gathered in a frown.

'Don't be daft. Of course, I'm sure.'

The house was quiet once Ethel left, though a faint clatter of pots and plates in the kitchen indicated Aggie getting on with her chores. Martha paced, unable to settle. Since Constance's death, she had tried to stay busy. She'd spent most mornings tramping Dundee's streets, handing out pamphlets, trying to blank out the sequence of events leading up to her friend's murder.

But nothing helped. Thoughts rumbled around her mind. The police were no nearer finding the killer than they had been at the start of their investigation, and she didn't believe that either Billy Murphy or the cabby was responsible. Ethel had claimed, at the beginning, that the police wouldn't put any effort into looking for the killer; but she, along with Ethel and Kirsty, had done no better. They were no nearer than the police to finding out who had committed the murders.

Frustrated, she stalked through to the dining-room, where the sheets of paper with the victims' details still lay, spread out on the table. She pulled out a chair and sat, studying each sheet. There were three, one each for Victoria, Gladys and Amelia, but nothing for Constance. Selecting a blank sheet of paper, she started to write. Maybe if she completed one for Constance, the connections might become clearer.

Tears trickled down her face as she wrote, and she brushed them away. Once she'd written the final word, she placed the sheets side-by-side and compared them. Two names stood out as being the only ones connected with all four women. Paul Anderson, the *Courier* reporter, who had summoned the cab for Constance on the evening of her death and who had been present when the first three bodies were found. The only other person with a connection was Archie, Constance's husband. He had been involved with the suffrage cause from the first day of his arrival in Dundee, with his wife.

If it was either of the two, the most likely one would be

Paul. He was an unknown quantity. A stranger to Dundee. But was that enough to make him a killer? Kirsty certainly thought he had a motive for Amelia's murder because he'd overheard the girl telling them she had seen Victoria entering the Howff the day she went missing. But thinking back, Archie had been present, too.

She shook her head. It couldn't be Archie. She'd known him too long, and he was devoted to Constance. That just left Paul. But she found it hard to believe. Perhaps she was trying to find a solution where there was none, and in the process, she was doing both men an injustice.

There was no point in presenting the police with her ideas only for them to brush her aside – yet again – as a silly woman; an annoying suffragette. That didn't mean she should do nothing. It wouldn't hurt to check things out. She could talk to Archie this morning, and once Ethel finished in the shop, they could tackle Paul together.

Decision made, she donned a cotton jacket and placed a hat on top of her curls, then left the house. Before she could change her mind, she crossed the road to where the hansom cabs waited in the rank in front of the church. After a moment's hesitation, the memory of Constance surfacing in her mind, she mounted the step and slid inside. If she was wrong about Archie, it would be safer if a cab was waiting for her departure.

Archie appeared pleased to see her.

'This is a surprise, Martha.' He smiled, leaning heavily on his stick as he led her into the drawing-room. 'As you can see, I'm still somewhat disabled.'

'I have a cab waiting so I can't stay too long. But I couldn't forgive myself if I didn't visit to find out how you are coping.' Martha sat in an armchair, spreading out her skirts. This was going to be more delicate than she had expected, and she wasn't sure how to broach it all.

'It has been difficult.' Archie's response broke through Martha's thoughts. He sat in the chair opposite her. 'I miss

Constance.' He reached into his pocket and produced a handkerchief. The movement caused his walking stick to fall to the floor.

'Don't get up,' Martha said, jumping from her seat. As she bent to reach it, a memory flashed through her mind of Kirsty saying her father had one similar, and that his was a sword-stick. Curiosity made her twist the eagle-shaped handle; it moved, exposing the slim blade.

'I thought you said this wasn't a sword-stick.'

'You shouldn't have done that.' Archie grabbed it from her.

'A thin blade killed Constance,' Martha whispered, a chill running through her. 'Oh, Archie. Tell me it wasn't you?'

He stood, towering over her. His disability shrugged off like a discarded coat. She glared at him. She mustn't display any fear; inside, she was quaking.

'What are you going to do?'

'I can't allow you to leave. You must see that.'

'How can you stop me? People know I am here, and the cabby is waiting to take me home. If I don't reappear, he will be able to testify this was the last place I was seen.'

'That can be taken care of easily enough.' Archie laughed mirthlessly. 'And don't bother screaming. No one will hear you.' He grabbed her arms, twisted them up her back and forced her to walk to the door.

She stumbled as he pushed her in front of him along a passage, through another door and down a flight of stairs, before forcing her to sit in a wooden chair. The wine cellar was dark and full of shadows. What a fool she had been to come here. Was this where it was to end?

The boarded-up window made the WFL shop darker than usual. Ethel was sweeping up glass fragments when Kirsty arrived.

'Can I help with anything?' Kirsty removed her hat and placed it on the counter.

'It's all done.' Ethel swept the glass into a shovel and emptied the contents into a bin before carrying the brush, shovel and bin through to the back room.

'Martha's taking a day off,' she said, 'and Lila won't be in. Constance's death has rocked them both.'

'How are you after the rumpus yesterday?' Kirsty joined Ethel behind the counter.

'I'm used to my da. I was more worried about you and Martha.'

'What happens when the police let him go?' Kirsty couldn't imagine herself in a similar situation to Ethel.

'Martha's worried about that, too. She's convinced me I need to leave Dundee.'

'Will you?'

'I don't want to. But if I stay, he'll wind up killing me.'

Kirsty couldn't imagine a father wanting to kill his daughter, but having seen Hughie's violence the day before, she knew Ethel's fear was genuine.

'I'll miss you.'

'Me, too.' Ethel said.

Both girls were quiet for the rest of the day. Although she tried to convince Ethel she was doing the best thing by leaving Dundee, Kirsty walked home with sadness in her heart.

49

'I'm sorry, Martha, really I am. I never wanted to harm you, but you're the final link in my plan. I have no choice.'

The rope binding Martha's wrists to the arms of the chair bit into her skin. 'Does that mean you will kill me, like the others?'

'That's a very bald way to put it. But, I suppose, you're right.' Archie sighed.

Martha stared at him. The mild-mannered man she'd known for such a long time had vanished and he appeared menacing and cruel. His personality change was inexplicable. Questions buzzed around her mind. Why would he do this? Why the other suffragettes? She had thought him sympathetic to the suffrage cause; but she'd been deluded, she saw now. She needed answers.

'Tell me, Archie – did you ever support our cause? I always assumed you were one of our more enthusiastic supporters.'

'It was never to do with the cause,' he said, looking at her straight-on. 'I believe in what you do.'

'Then why? Why kill suffragettes? And why so many?'

'It had to be suffragettes – don't you see?' Sadness flickered over Archie's face. 'And if the police and the press had recognised that earlier, I could have achieved my aim sooner. And then –' he sighed again '– some of them might still be with us.'

'Your aim, Archie?'

'Get rid of Constance, of course.'

Martha drew in her breath. It was so obvious now. Why hadn't she seen it?

'Money? This was for money, was it? So many lives, just so you could inherit Constance's fortune.'

'It was the only way. And now, it's your turn. And I'm so sorry, Martha, really, because I like you.'

'You don't have to do this, you know.'

'Oh, but I do. I need one final suffragette to complete my plan and deflect attention.'

'It doesn't have to be me.' Martha stared up at him, willing him to meet her eyes. 'We like each other . . . we could be good together.'

'Yes, we could have been good together, and you would have made an excellent lady of the house. But now? You know too much. I really am sorry.'

'That can still happen,' Martha urged. 'I would keep quiet. Nobody needs to know.'

'No. I couldn't trust you.' A sigh shuddered through him. 'Besides, I need one more to complete things.'

Martha slumped back in the chair. It was hopeless. Her time had come, and there was nothing she could do to stop it happening.

Archie climbed the stairs from the wine cellar with Martha's jacket and skirt over his arm. He needed to cover his tracks. His departure from Dundee after the funeral tomorrow mustn't give rise to suspicion.

Gloria was waiting at the top.

'What do we do now, Archie?'

He put his arm around her waist and led her to the study, where Martha's hat lay on a chair.

'Put these on,' he said, handing her the garments. 'You're the same build as Martha, and you can pull the hat forward to hide your face.'

Gloria did as he instructed her.

'What now?'

'Take the cab back to Martha's house. Then, if anyone comes looking for her, we can say she returned home.'

'What if the cabby notices I'm not Martha?'

'Cabbies never pay that much attention to their fares. Make sure your face is hidden by the hat and don't look up at him. He won't notice the difference.'

Archie spotted the indecision within Gloria but disguised his twinge of annoyance by pulling her towards him.

'It will work. You just have to be confident.'

Gloria nodded but remained looking troubled.

'After you leave the cab outside Martha's house, wait until he moves on and then walk through the Overgate with the other shoppers before you return here.'

Archie hugged her before escorting her out of the house. He assisted her into the hansom waiting at the kerb and approached the cabby to hand him the fare.

'Take Miss Fairweather home,' he said, before waving to Gloria inside. 'Until we meet again, Martha,' he called. He waited until the cab turned the corner into the Perth Road. His plan had worked perfectly; the cabby hadn't questioned a thing.

50

Thursday, 16th July 1908

'Beg pardon, Miss Kirsty, but there's someone come to see you. Says her name's Ethel.'

Kirsty laid her buttered toast on a plate and rose.

'I won't be long, Aunt Bea.'

Ethel was pacing back and forth in the hall. Her face lit up when she saw Kirsty.

'Has something happened? Is it your father?'

Ethel shook her head.

'Martha's missing,' she blurted out. 'She wasn't at home last night when I finished work and when I got up, she wasn't there. Her bed hasn't been slept in. I don't know what to do.'

'Have you told the police?'

'Police? What good will they do?' Ethel grasped Kirsty's hands. 'We have to figure out where she went, and you think better than me.'

After making her excuses to Bea, Kirsty joined Ethel and hurried to Martha's house.

'She's been going over the evidence sheets we made,' Ethel said. 'Look, she's made another one for Constance.'

Kirsty picked up the sheets of paper.

'It looks as if she's been trying to figure out who the killer is. She's scored off all the names apart from two – Paul and Archie.'

'She wouldn't confront Paul on her own,' Ethel said, 'but she trusts Archie, which means she's probably gone to see him.'

'It wouldn't be the first time a husband killed his wife,' Kirsty said, frowning. 'And, if I recall, he was at our table when Amelia told us she'd seen Victoria going into the

Howff.'

Ethel gasped.

'Does that mean Archie could be our killer and Martha's in danger?'

'We won't know if we do nothing, and Archie will be at the funeral today. If it's nothing to do with him, then no harm will be done. But if Martha is in his house, we need to find her.'

'Wait for us,' Ethel said as she climbed down from the hansom cab. 'If anyone other than me or my friend instructs you to go, you must refuse.'

'Yes, miss.' The cabby settled back on his perch and pulled the brim of his hat forward over his eyes.

Kirsty had already opened the gate and climbed the steps, but she turned to wait for Ethel. They needed to present a joint front whenever the door opened.

'Are we ready?' she asked as Ethel joined her.

'As ready as we'll ever be.'

Ethel grasped the knocker dangling from the brass lion's mouth and thumped it against the door. After a few moments, when there was no response, she thumped again.

Kirsty heaved a sigh of exasperation and grabbed the doorknob. The door swung open. She exchanged a glance with Ethel and then stepped into the hallway.

'Everyone will be at the funeral,' she whispered.

Several cabin trunks were piled up, to the left of the door.

'It looks as if Archie is ready to leave in a hurry afterwards. But it's strange the door is unlocked.' Kirsty advanced further into the hall.

'Anyone home?' Ethel's voice reverberated around the spacious hall and up the staircase.

Kirsty's heart pounded. She'd never entered a house unless she had been invited, and the intrusion felt wrong. But they had to find Martha.

'Come on,' Ethel said. 'Let's explore, while we have the chance. Archie won't return from the funeral for a few hours.'

They had only taken a couple steps when a young woman appeared at the top of the stairs.

'What are you doing in my house?' She lifted the edge of her skirt and ran down to confront them.

Kirsty gasped, struggling to find a response.

'Your house?' Ethel stepped forward, staring at Gloria. 'I thought this was Mr Drysdale's house, now that his wife is deceased. Not unless Constance bequeathed it to you?'

'Archie's not at home at the moment. He left me in charge, so I must ask you to leave.' She waved a dismissive hand at Ethel.

Fear replaced Kirsty's anxiety when she spotted the ring on Gloria's finger.

'Where did you acquire that ring?'

'It's mine. Archie gave it to me.'

'Close the door, Ethel. She's wearing Martha's ring, and I intend to find out how she came by it.'

Ethel slammed the door shut, turned the key in the lock, and pocketed it.

'Where is Martha?'

The colour drained from Gloria's face, confirming Kirsty's suspicions. Martha was here; she knew it. She just hoped they were in time. Kirsty gasped for air as she fought to control the pounding in her chest. She took several deep breaths to regain her self-control, clenching her hands to stop herself from reaching out and trying to shake the information from the woman in front of her.

'If anything's happened to Martha, I swear I will kill you.' Ethel grabbed Gloria's arm. 'She may be a lady –' she nodded her head in Kirsty's direction '– but I am not.' She twisted the arm up the woman's back, giving it an extra pull upwards in response to her squeal.

'It's nothing to do with me.' Tears streamed down Gloria's face.

'I'm not going to ask again.' Ethel increased the pressure, making Gloria yelp. 'Where's Martha? Has Archie harmed her?'

'I don't know, I swear! And when Archie finds out you've hurt me, he won't be pleased.'

'We know Martha is here.' Ethel gave the woman's arm another twist, ignoring her scream and avoiding the hand that flailed towards her.

'Grab her other arm, Kirsty. We'll make this bitch talk even if we've to half-kill her.'

Kirsty's heart thumped, but she didn't hesitate. She seized the arm trying to reach Ethel and forced it up Gloria's back. Despite never having committed a violent act in her life, Kirsty had to admit it felt good now – strong and powerful, when so often she had felt weak and helpless.

'What now?' She forced the arm further up, preventing Gloria from wriggling in their grasp.

'One of these doors must lead to the kitchen – it'll be the best place to find something to persuade her to tell us what we want to know. Maybe a carving knife to her throat will force her to talk.'

'You wouldn't?' Kirsty couldn't keep the horror out of her voice.

'Oh, but I would.'

'I don't know anything.' Tears rolled down Gloria's cheeks.

'We'll see about that.' Ethel pushed the woman in front of her, roughly, while they walked down the hall, looking for the kitchen.

The kitchen was behind the third door they tried. A large cooking range took up most of one wall; the others were lined with cupboards. Brass pans hung from hooks in the ceiling and a long, wooden table stretched down the middle of the room.

'This'll do nicely.' Ethel forced Gloria against the table. 'Grab her feet, Kirsty, and we'll hoist her on to the table, where I'll be able to carve her up proper.'

Gloria kicked and struggled against them until they were forced to push her on to her back on the floor.

'Never mind,' Ethel said, placing her knee in the woman's midriff. 'I would have preferred the table, but this'll do. Have a look around for a carving knife and I'll start.'

'You won't get away with this.' Gloria's voice came in gasps.

Ethel hitched her skirt up to her knees and straddled the woman, pinning her arms to the floor so she couldn't fight back.

'I don't see anyone stopping me. If there were any servants left in the house, they'd have appeared by now. There's only us here, and that means I can do anything I like.' Ethel smiled grimly, holding Gloria's gaze.

Kirsty's hand tightened around the shaft of the knife she'd taken from the wooden block on the sideboard. The conversational tone of Ethel's voice sounded more chilling than her earlier threats, and she wondered whether it was wise to give her the knife. Would she really use it? But, however she felt about what might be about to happen, Martha's safety had to take precedence. She handed Ethel the knife.

Ethel leaned forward and placed the flat side to Gloria's cheek.

'This carver's very sharp. It wouldn't take any strength to cut your throat. But I'm not going to do that – yet.' She emphasised the last word. 'You're going to tell me what Archie's done with Martha.' She slid the knife down the woman's cheek until it reached her chin, her tone low and steely. 'And she had better still be alive. If she's not, I'd advise you to confess your sins to your maker, because you will join her.'

Kirsty shivered. The menace in Ethel's voice chilled her. She hoped it was having the same effect on Gloria.

Fear distorted the woman's face.

'The wine cellar – Archie only locked her up to give us time to leave. He wouldn't have harmed her.'

'You may believe that, but I don't,' Ethel said. She turned to Kirsty. 'I'll stay here with her while you check the cellar. There's bound to be a door near the kitchen.'

It didn't take long for Kirsty to find the door but when

she opened it, she faced a set of stairs leading downwards into complete darkness. She returned to the kitchen.

'I need a lamp.' She checked out the shelves and found what she was looking for – a small paraffin lamp and a box of matches. She removed the glass funnel and shook the base to be sure it contained paraffin. The swishing sound inside satisfied her; she struck a match and lit the wick, waiting until it flickered to life before replacing the funnel.

She sped back to the cellar door and descended the stairs, only to be faced with another door at the bottom. This one was locked. If she'd been a man, she would have cursed, but what good would that do? Kirsty closed her eyes and took a deep breath, trying to clear the jumble of thoughts clouding her head. Would she have to return to the kitchen to search for a key? Would Archie have it with him? If it was a wine cellar, surely it must be nearby, because it wouldn't always be the same person who brought the wine up to the main house. Think, think, think! There must be a key somewhere.

Kirsty held the lamp up, inspecting the area to the left and right of the door, but there was nowhere to place a key. She raised the lamp higher and spotted it, hanging from a hook at the top of the door frame. Standing on tiptoe, she reached up and prodded it until it fell off the hook and landed on the floor with a clang.

It only took a moment to unlock the door. She held the lamp up, but all she could see were the vague outlines of wine racks stretching back into a dark, cavernous space.

'Martha,' she shouted. 'Are you here?'

'Over here.' The answering voice was faint and lacked its usual confidence. For a moment, Kirsty wasn't sure it was Martha.

She swung the oil lamp in the direction of the voice and walked towards it. The light flickered over the shadowy interior, with its rows of racks stacked with wine bottles. Kirsty directed the light down each aisle, advancing further into the cellar. A scurrying noise off to her left caused her heart to race, but she ignored the flutters and continued her search. How many more rows did this cellar contain? And where was Martha?

'Martha,' she called again.

'I'm here.' The answering voice came from the next aisle.

Kirsty rushed forward, holding the lamp up in front of her. Illuminated in its glow was Martha, bound to a chair.

'I thought it was Archie coming back. I couldn't believe it when I heard your voice – I thought I must be imagining it.'

'I'm here now. I'll soon have you free.' Untying the knots wasn't as easy as Kirsty had thought it would be. Her hands grew slippery with sweat as she pulled at the rope; she gasped as she broke a fingernail. But at last, the knots loosened, and Martha was freed.

'Ethel's upstairs in the kitchen, sitting on Gloria.' Kirsty put an arm around Martha to steady her.

'Actually, *sitting* on her?'

'That's how we found you.' Kirsty grinned, relief threatening to overwhelm her. 'Ethel persuaded her to talk.'

'I'm not sure I want to know what persuasion she used.'

'Let me just say that I now see Ethel in a whole new light. I wouldn't want to get on her wrong side.'

Martha stumbled up the stairs, her legs unsteady. Lack of food and too long in the same position had taken its toll. Emerging from the dimly lit corridor into the full brightness of the kitchen made her blink, and it was a few moments before she could focus on Ethel sitting astride Gloria. She pulled a chair over and sat beside the two women.

'I see you've met my friends,' she said, her tone conversational.

'Get this banshee off me.' Gloria glared at her.

Ethel leaned forward and placed the knife at her throat.

'Hush, now. We wouldn't want this knife to slip.'

A look of panic flitted across Gloria's face as her eyes moved between Ethel and Martha.

'I told you what you wanted to know. I helped you find

Martha.'

'That's true,' Ethel said. 'But you don't imagine that's the end of it, do you?'

Martha leaned forward.

'My friend Constance is dead, and Archie is responsible. But it's not too late to save yourself.'

'What do you mean?'

'You know what I mean. Archie is a murderer.'

'I don't know anything of the sort,' Gloria said. 'Archie wouldn't do something like that.'

'Archie told me everything before he locked me in the cellar. He confessed to killing Constance and the other suffragettes, and he intended to kill me.' Martha stared into Gloria's widening eyes. 'And how long do you think it would be before he disposed of you? You're only alive because of the alibi you gave him.'

'I don't believe you.'

'Whether you believe me or not,' Martha shrugged 'we'll be handing you over to the police while they investigate. And you will find Archie's guilt will be proved beyond doubt.'

The fight left Gloria's body and she went limp.

'I suggest you confess everything to the police unless you want to risk the hangman's noose alongside Archie.' There was no response from Gloria, but her expression told Martha what she wanted to know. She turned to Ethel. 'I think she has seen sense. You can get off her now.'

'Don't think of doing anything you'll regret. I still have the knife.' Ethel hoisted herself up and stood next to Martha.

'What happens now?' Gloria stumbled to her feet, keeping a wary eye on the knife in Ethel's hand.

'The first thing we do is find my skirt and blouse,' Martha said. 'I rather think I might shock the police if I turn up in my shift. Then we take you to meet Inspector Hammond, and you will provide him with a full confession.'

'But I haven't done anything. I can't be held responsible for Archie's actions.'

'In that case, I'm sure the inspector will make the right

decision.' Martha gave Gloria a push. 'My clothes, if you please.'

Martha glanced at herself in a mirror after she dressed. Her hair was messy, her skirt and blouse were crumpled, and she knew that her under-garments were far from fresh, but there was no time to do anything about any of that. They had to get Gloria to the police station before Archie returned and made his escape from Dundee.

'We have a problem,' Martha said as they left the house. 'Four of us won't fit into the cab.'

'There needs to be two of us to make sure Gloria doesn't run.'

'It's no problem,' Kirsty said. 'I'll walk back.'

51

Hansom cabs were built for two passengers and with three on board, there was little room for manoeuvre. Martha and Ethel shared a smile as Gloria, pinned between them, struggled to move her arms. Martha leaned in closer and nodded to Ethel to do the same.

The cabby's whip snaked over the top of their compartment to flick the horse's rear; the cab picked up speed as it rolled along Perth Road. Kirsty raised an arm and waved as they passed her walking towards the Nethergate.

Martha hadn't wanted to leave Kirsty to walk back alone, but there had been no other option. It needed two of them to make sure Gloria reached the police station, and there was no room for a fourth person in the cab. They could have drawn lots to see who travelled and who walked but the choice was obvious. Gloria was afraid of Ethel, while Martha was the one who had been imprisoned and would be making the complaint. Nevertheless, Martha worried for Kirsty's safety.

'Do you think Kirsty will be all right?' Ethel gave voice to Martha's concerns.

'I think so.' Martha lacked conviction. 'She has grown stronger since I first met her.' She recalled the innocence she had sensed in Kirsty. Her lack of understanding that women could make their own decisions and were not held in thrall to their fathers. 'I knew from the beginning that once she understood our purpose, she could be an asset to our cause.'

Beside them, Gloria wriggled to find more space.

'I can't breathe.'

'You'll breathe less if they hang you.'

Gloria lapsed into silence and stopped struggling and the horse continued clopping through the town until they turned and entered the police quadrangle through the archway.

'We've arrived,' Martha said.

Ethel dismounted first and waited for them to follow. Martha could see her poised to tackle Gloria if she attempted to escape.

'Don't even think about trying to run for it,' Martha whispered in Gloria's ear as she prodded her along the seat. 'Don't forget, she still has the knife and I rather think she might enjoy using it.'

Kirsty pushed away her disappointment as she watched the hansom cab speed along Perth Road. She had craved to be there when they confronted Inspector Hammond with Gloria, but it was not to be. She knew it made more sense for Martha and Ethel to be there, but that didn't prevent her from feeling left out.

The morning's events had been terrifying and exhilarating, making her heart thump harder than it ever had before; the drop in her spirits invoked by the normality of walking to the town ushered in, once again, her dissatisfaction with her life. With Martha and Ethel by her side, she felt like a different person. When they weren't with her, she was reminded of the reality. Her role as a dutiful daughter; the family ties that dictated how she should act; and the subservience her father expected. But above all, it was the lack of independence and the ability to make her own decisions which frustrated her the most. Martha had introduced her to a new world in the short time they'd known each other – a world she had never imagined existed.

Reaching the Nethergate, she walked past the row of hansom cabs. The WFL office across the road was closed as a mark of respect for Constance, and Martha was at the police station. That only left Aunt Bea. Her steps quickened as she turned the corner into Reform Street. Thoughts bounced around inside her head. She didn't want to return home to a continued existence as a submissive daughter. She wanted changes in her life, but how was she going to achieve them? Her parents would never understand. Sometimes she thought Aunt Bea understood but was she just seeing what she wanted to?

Kirsty opened the door and climbed the stairs, took a deep breath, and entered the sitting-room, expecting to see Aunt Bea in her usual spot. Instead, her mother's voice greeted her, stopping her in her tracks.

'Ah, there you are at last, Kirsty,' she said. 'I was just saying to Bea that it's time you returned home.'

Chief Constable Dewar glared at Inspector Hammond.

'What progress have you made in this investigation? It's time we had this killer off the streets of Dundee.'

Sweat beaded on Hammond's brow and he resisted the temptation to run a finger around his collar. Dewar was Dundee's procurator fiscal as well as chief constable, and he was responsible for the investigation. Hammond couldn't remember a time when his boss had sought active involvement in a case, so the man's fury at the failure to find the perpetrator of these murders puzzled him. Either there was a personal interest, or it must be because the last victim was more important than the others.

'It's been a difficult case to resolve, sir. We have three suspects but no evidence.'

'Are they in custody?'

'No, sir. We had one of them in custody, but we've had to release him. As I said, there's a lack of evidence and two of the men have alibis for the times of the killings. The third man has evaded capture.'

'Do they have motives?'

'Billy Murphy is the boyfriend of the third victim, but the relationship broke down when she became a suffragette. As a result, he hates suffragettes. His mother attests to him being at home at the time of the murder.'

'And the second suspect?'

'Paul Anderson. He's a reporter with the *Dundee Courier*. I'm not sure of a motive, but he's always on the scene when a murder's been committed.'

'I suppose that's a reporter's job – being on the spot when anything newsworthy happens.'

Heat built beneath Hammond's collar again. Had he been unfair in his judgement of the reporter because he'd taken a dislike to the man? Was his gut feeling wrong?

'I found it suspicious, sir.'

'What about the third suspect?'

'Douglas Paterson, the cabby in charge of the cab which contained the body of the last victim. We think he must have left Dundee – we've been unable to locate him.'

'Excuse me, sir.' Sergeant Edwards loomed in the doorway. 'But them suffragette ladies in the charge-room are getting impatient and demanding to see you. I informed them you were busy, but they be insistent.'

'Tell them to come back later.' Hammond frowned. Those damned women were determined to spoil his day.

'I told them that, but it didn't work.'

'Put the ladies in one of the interview-rooms and inform them Inspector Hammond will be with them in a few minutes,' Chief Constable Dewar snapped.

'Yes, sir.' The sergeant saluted, turned sharply, and marched along the corridor.

'Do you have a reason to keep these women waiting?' Dewar narrowed his eyes.

'I'm sorry, sir.' Hammond almost choked on his words; he wasn't sorry at all. 'But these women have been interfering in the investigation. Every time I turn around, they are at my back. They think they would make a better job than the police of finding the killer. It's not normal for women to be poking their noses into police business.'

'Then perhaps you had better talk to them and find out what they know.'

'Yes, sir.' Hammond suppressed the urge to thump his desk and swear. It wouldn't do to lose his self-control in front of the chief constable. That didn't prevent him from muttering under his breath as he strode up the corridor to the interview-rooms. Nor did it stop him from taking his anger out on Constable Buchan, when he interrupted the young bobby's lunch and rousted him from the canteen.

Martha drummed her fingers on the table. The inspector had kept them waiting for over an hour before the sergeant had shown them into this room. Her patience had worn thin some considerable time ago.

The interview-room was small, with one, tiny window, high up the wall. It reeked of stale cigarette smoke and a hint of body odour. Gloria fidgeted in the chair next to her; Ethel sat, immobile, on her other side.

'Remember, if you don't tell the police all you know, you're likely to hang alongside Archie.'

'I told you before, I don't know anything about what Archie was getting up to.'

'But you did give him a false alibi, and you know perfectly well what he did to me.' Martha turned her head to glare at Gloria. 'So, that makes you an accessory. You had better say your prayers.'

The door slammed open and thudded off the wall. Hammond strode in.

'I hope you ladies are not wasting my time.' He glowered at them from the opposite side of the table.

Martha stiffened before speaking in the most authoritative tone she could muster. 'I assure you we would never think of doing that.'

'Constable, take notes.' Hammond slumped into a chair and stared at them.

Buchan, who had followed the inspector into the room took the seat beside him, notebook at the ready.

'Well, I don't have all day. What have you come to tell me?'

'First,' Martha said, 'I want to report a crime. I was held prisoner by the man you are seeking, but have failed to find. If my friends hadn't rescued me, you would have found my body with a sash around my neck in the same fashion as the other bodies.'

'You expect me to believe that?'

'I have the two witnesses who came to my rescue. Miss Stewart, who is here in this room, and Miss Campbell, who is not present at the moment, but can be contacted. I also have this woman –' she glanced at Gloria with contempt in her eyes '– who assisted the man when he detained me. I say "detained" for want of a better word . . . he tied me to a chair in his wine cellar. To be fair, I do not think she realised what he intended to do with me. But she has been a party to Constance's murder by providing him with an alibi.'

Buchan, at the other side of the table, was writing as fast as he could. Hammond, for once, appeared speechless. After a few moments, he found his tongue.

'The man's name?'

'Archie Drysdale, husband of Constance Drysdale.'

'How do you know he was responsible for the murders?'

'He told me. No doubt, he thought he was safe because I wouldn't live to tell anyone what I knew. He committed all the murders to mask killing his wife, and he said I was going to be the last. That way, no one would suspect him and he could act the heartbroken husband.'

'You can confirm this?' Hammond turned to Gloria.

'Yes,' she said, her voice low. 'But I didn't know about the murders. I swear, I didn't.'

'You have a note of all that, constable?' Hammond leaned back in his chair.

'Yes, sir.'

'Right, then. Miss Stewart and Miss Fairweather, you may go. As for you, Miss Wallace, I will require to detain you while I investigate this further.'

'Does that mean you believe us?' Martha demanded.

'I didn't say that. What I said, was that I will need to investigate your claims.'

Half an hour later, Hammond, pleased with his handling of Gloria's interrogation, left the interview-room and strode towards his office. She hadn't taken long to tell him everything he needed to know, though he'd had to apply some pressure.

'Attend to the paperwork and get her locked up,' he'd instructed Buchan. 'Then report to me in my office.'

No doubt Buchan was, at this moment, escorting a tearful Gloria to the women's cells underneath the police station.

The staccato sound of Hammond's footsteps echoed through the building, heralding a warning to any bobbies in the duty-room that it was time for them to look busy. Cigarette smoke tainted the air as he passed along the corridor to his own office.

Pushing the door open, he was met by the sight of Dewar sitting at the desk, reading the case files. If anyone else apart from the chief constable had been in his chair, going through his files, Hammond would have given them short shrift. Instead, he bit his lip to prevent any caustic remarks escaping.

'Sir,' he said before Dewar castigated him again. 'We've had a breakthrough. My constable is escorting a female suspect to the cells as I speak.'

'A woman, you say? I wasn't expecting that.'

'She's the killer's accomplice, sir. She's confessed and given us his name.'

'Well, man – get on with it. Which one of these is the murderer?' Dewar gestured to the files.

'None of them, sir. Our killer is the husband of the last victim, Constance Drysdale. He's currently attending her funeral.'

Silence descended on the room. The chief constable scratched his chin while he thought.

'You realise this will have to be handled carefully,' he said, after a moment. 'Archie Drysdale is a man of substance. We cannot afford any mistakes.'

'Yes, sir. That's why I intend to seek an arrest warrant from the court before detaining him.'

'Good thinking,' Dewar said.

'I'll need access to my desk to complete the application, sir.' Hammond suppressed a smile as he watched the chief constable vacate his chair.

'Keep me informed,' Dewar said, as he left the room.

'Yes, sir.'

Hammond busied himself with the paperwork, which he planned to present to the sheriff to request the warrant. He smiled to himself as he wrote. The case was solved, and he had a killer to bring into custody.

The sheriff had needed little persuading to issue the arrest warrant, and it now nestled in Inspector Hammond's breast pocket. Meanwhile, Buchan had done a good job in rustling up some bobbies glad to escape the boredom of the beat. A squad had been dispatched by the time Hammond returned from the court, and a police wagon awaited his return.

The wagon rattled its way to the cemetery, while Hammond fidgeted and tapped his fingers on the wooden seat. If the funeral was over, they would miss their chance of an easy arrest. With Drysdale's resources, he would have no trouble fleeing Dundee.

Bursting out of the van, Hammond strode through the cemetery gates, passing several mourners on the way. More people, dressed in customary black, were clustered on a knoll in the graveyard. Followed by Buchan, he strode over the grass to join them. They had almost reached the group when the grief-stricken young man throwing a rose into the grave looked up. An expression of alarm crossed his face. The inspector instinctively broke into a jog. The young man took several steps backwards and Hammond thought he was going to run.

'Hoi!' he shouted. 'Drysdale. We want a word with you.'

The young man hesitated then ran, dodging between the headstones in his flight. On his approach to the cemetery gates, he changed direction when he saw the police constables clustered there.

The inspector was out of breath by this time, so he stopped and waited while the assembled bobbies chased their quarry through the graveyard. It didn't take long before they bundled Archie into the police wagon.

'Good lad,' he said to a breathless Buchan on his return.

Buchan grinned and handed him a sword and its sheath.

'Took this sword-stick off him,' he said. 'He was brandishing it at us when we caught him. Do you think it might be the weapon he used on his wife?'

'Good lad,' Hammond repeated. The sword-stick, combined with Gloria's confession, would be enough to make sure the man kept a date with the hangman.

52

Friday, 17th July 1908

'It's that reporter,' Aggie announced. The dry tone of her voice expressed her displeasure. 'Ye'd think he'd know not to call at this unearthly hour.'

'It is after nine o'clock.'

Martha laid her cup in the saucer and wiped her mouth with a napkin.

'I've shown him into the drawing-room and told him he'd have to wait until ye're ready.'

'Thank you,' Martha said, but Aggie was already on her way back to the kitchen.

Paul was staring out of the window when Martha joined him in the drawing-room.

'You see all sorts from here,' he said, not lifting his eyes from the busy street below.

'Why have you come?' Martha crossed the room and stood next to him.

'I brought you this.' He handed her a copy of the *Dundee Courier*. 'It's hot off the press – I thought you'd want a copy.'

She unfolded it and walked over to the table, where she could lay it flat.

'Page five,' Paul said, following her.

'Our news is always on page five. Do you think your editor keeps that space for us?'

'If he had his way, he wouldn't give you any space. But news is news, and he can't ignore it.'

Paul stood behind her as she turned the pages. He was so close she felt his breath on the back of her neck.

'I'll get Ethel,' Martha said, moving away from him. 'I am sure she will want to read this.'

She was relieved to see that Paul had returned to his stance at the window when she arrived back a few moments later, Ethel in tow.

'*Dundee Killer Apprehended,*' she read aloud. '*The honourable Archibald Drysdale arrested and charged with the murder of his wife. Other charges are being brought. Dundee women can now walk the streets in safety.*' She finished up her summary of the short piece.

'I would have thought they'd have printed more,' Ethel said. 'And you notice there's no mention of suffragettes.'

'The piece I wrote contained more information and said Drysdale was charged with the murder of suffragettes, but my editor cut it.'

'At least the police arrested him. I wasn't sure they were going to when we left the police station yesterday.'

'What were you doing there before the arrest?'

Martha sensed the arousal of Paul's reporter's instincts, but she had no intention of informing him what had happened to her over the preceding two days. He might find out from the police, but she was sure they wouldn't want to admit suffragettes had any hand in solving their case. They would want to keep the glory of catching a killer all to themselves.

Despair had been Kirsty's constant companion since her mother's visit yesterday. This was to be her last day with Aunt Bea, and she felt she was sliding back into the lethargy that had claimed her since Ailsa's birth.

Gone was the energy and joy of the past three weeks, when she had come to realise there was more to life than the existence she had previously led. How she wished she had Ethel's resilience.

She finished brushing her hair although it hadn't eradicated the tangles from the unruly auburn curls which fell to her shoulders.

She didn't care. Nor did she care that the blouse she had pulled on was the same one she'd worn yesterday. What was the point of it all?

A tap at her bedroom door was followed by Ruthie's voice.

'Your aunt is wondering whether you're ready for breakfast.'

Kirsty didn't feel ready, but she crossed to the door and opened it.

'Are you feeling well, miss?' Ruthie's concerned face peered at her.

'I'm all right.' Kirsty forced a smile.

'I'll let your aunt know you're on your way.' With a last, anxious glance, Ruthie scurried away.

At the breakfast table, Kirsty forced herself to eat a spoonful of porridge and spent the rest of the time pushing her spoon around the plate.

Aunt Bea had finished eating before Kirsty's arrival and sat studying the local newspaper.

'I see they have caught the man who was killing those women. The streets will be safer now.'

Kirsty's mind flashed back to yesterday's events, and the thrill of helping to unveil Archie as the killer. Aunt Bea and her parents would be horrified if they knew of her part in the affair. However, she had no intention of telling them.

'In that case, you no longer need to worry when I go out alone.' She pushed her plate aside.

Bea folded the newspaper with deliberate fingers and did not look at Kirsty as she spoke.

'As you are returning home tomorrow, your safety is guaranteed.'

'I'm not ready to go home yet, Aunt Bea. Can't I stay a little longer?' Kirsty tried but failed to keep the desperation out of her voice.

'I have loved having you here, my dear, and I wish I could say "yes". But I cannot go against your parents' wishes. You must see that.'

'Yes, of course, Aunt Bea.'

'Perhaps you should visit your friends today, say your farewells.'

'Yes,' Kirsty mumbled, despair sweeping over her again. Once she was ensconced at home, she would never see them again. Her father would make sure of that.

Lila looked up from sorting leaflets as Martha and Ethel entered the WFL shop.

'You're early this morning,' Martha said, pocketing the key she had intended to use. 'I thought you might want some time off after Constance's funeral.'

'I expected to see you there yesterday.' Lila raised a questioning eyebrow.

'I am afraid I was otherwise engaged.' Martha shared a glance with Ethel, resisting the urge to elaborate on the activities of the day before. 'How was it? Was there a big turn out?'

'You could say it was eventful,' Lila said. 'And not like any other I have attended.'

Martha and Ethel shared another glance and Lila finished collating the leaflets, setting them to one side.

'Poor Constance, thank goodness she wasn't there to see it happen.'

Martha guessed what Lila was about to tell them, but didn't want to interrupt.

'Did you know the police turned up to arrest Archie? It caused quite a rumpus.' Lila's voice faltered. 'I never thought for a moment he would do anything to harm her. They seemed such a devoted couple.'

'I think Archie may have had money troubles.'

'That's no excuse for what he did.'

'So, what happened? When did the police arrive?'

'Thankfully, it was when people were dispersing. The coffin had been lowered into the lair and the minister had finished saying his piece. Some of us remained for a few moments at the end. That was when police officers came storming into the cemetery. Archie took one look at them and took to his heels. It was pandemonium after that – they were chasing him between the headstones, can you picture it? Absurd! We didn't realise what was happening, and only found out afterwards that he had been charged with Constance's murder.' Lila wiped tears from her eyes. 'Poor Constance, it would have broken her heart if she'd lived to see it.'

It was afternoon before Kirsty summoned up the courage to go to the WFL shop to inform Ethel and Martha of her imminent return home. When she arrived, she found Ethel bubbling with excitement because she'd been left in charge.

'Lila had to go home,' Ethel said. 'She was fine when she got here this morning, but as the day went on, she couldn't stop talking about Constance. I thought she was going to break down. Martha must have thought so as well because she told her it was too soon after the funeral for her to be here.' Ethel did a little jig. 'She left me in charge.'

'Did Martha go home, too?'

'She's gone out with leaflets. You know what Martha's like. The cause has to continue.'

'Hasn't she been affected by what Archie did to her?'

'Martha's tougher than she looks.' Ethel laughed. 'It's as if it never happened.'

Kirsty's admiration for both Ethel and Martha increased. Why couldn't she be more like them? And what would they think of her when she told them she had to give in to her parents' demands? They would assume she was a weakling. And, Kirsty thought, they would be right.

She resisted the urge to tell Ethel, unwilling to dampen her friend's excitement over her new responsibilities. It was better to wait until Martha returned, and inform them both at the same time.

53

Saturday, 18th July 1908

Kirsty paced her bedroom, worrying about the decision she had made after leaving Martha and Ethel yesterday. Her suitcase was packed and, from now on, her life would change. Martha had assured her the women who were part of the cause regarded themselves as sisters, and a bed or a meal was always available for anyone in need. But she knew she would never again live the life of comfort and luxury to which she'd been accustomed. She hoped she had the strength to cope.

The temptation to leave without saying a word to anyone had been strong, but her sense of loyalty was stronger. First, she would tell Aunt Bea; after that, she had to break the news to her parents. She shuddered at the thought of the task. Her father was bound to do his best to prevent her departure; she would have to remain firm.

After what felt like an eternity, she heard movement downstairs. The clatter of pans in the kitchen meant cook was preparing breakfast.

Kirsty closed her eyes, took a deep breath, straightened her blouse and smoothed her skirt.

'Courage,' she told herself. She was going to need it.

The breakfast-room was empty, though the table was laid with china and cutlery. The porridge urn stood on the sideboard, alongside a bowl waiting to be filled with boiled eggs, and a silver ashet waiting for the contents to be brought through. Kirsty wondered whether it would be bacon or kidneys this morning.

'I thought I heard you come downstairs,' Bea said, bustling through the door.

'Aunt Bea,' Kirsty said. She wanted to get this over

without delay. 'I've made a decision.'

'And what would that be?' Her aunt's expression was guarded.

'I do not intend to return home.'

'You know I can't allow you to live here, Kirsty – as much as I would like to. Your father will never permit it.'

'I know.' Kirsty grasped her aunt's hands. 'But you know how much I suffer, having to watch Ailsa being brought up by my mother. I can't live there any longer under the pretence I'm her sister. It's better I cut the ties now.'

'What will you do? Where will you go?'

'My mind is made up to leave Dundee, with Ethel. Her home circumstances are difficult, and she is in fear of her life from her father. She's been offered a way of escape, and I intend to accompany her.'

'I see.' Bea was silent for a moment. 'Do you have somewhere to go?'

'Martha can arrange for us to go to one of the league's safe houses. She's already making the arrangements for Ethel.'

'Where?'

'I'm not sure yet. Either Edinburgh, Glasgow or Aberdeen. Far enough away so Ethel will be safe.'

'Your father will never approve this.' Bea's voice expressed sadness, and Kirsty thought she detected a note of sympathy.

'I won't allow him to stop me,' Kirsty said. 'When I go home this afternoon, I intend to inform him of my decision, so please don't tell him before that.'

'He may force you to stay. You are only a girl and not yet of age. What can you do to stop him?'

'I'm going to ask Martha and Ethel to come with me for support. I'm sure they'll agree.'

'I will come with you, as well. I may not be able to go against your father's wishes, but I can try to prevent him from forcing his will on you.'

'I appreciate that, Aunt Bea.'

'There is a condition.'

Kirsty's spirits sank, bringing her back to the gravity of her circumstances, despite the relief Bea's reaction and the act of confiding, had brought. Perhaps her aunt was not as supportive as she had imagined.

'A condition?'

'Yes. I wish to meet Martha and Ethel, to assure myself that you are being realistic and will not come to harm. We will call on them later this morning. And now, we must partake of breakfast.'

Both of them made a pretence at eating, and cook scowled when she removed dishes still containing much of the food. Kirsty, in particular, had barely eaten more than a mouthful. Now, she watched the clock and paced the room, but the hands barely moved.

'Stop pacing and be patient, Kirsty,' her aunt said, after a time. 'It is not socially acceptable to call on anyone before ten in the morning.'

Despite her admonition, Kirsty could see her aunt was nervous, as well, but she contained herself until the last chime of ten on the grandfather clock at the head of the stairs.

Bea crossed to the mantelpiece and tugged the tasselled bell-pull.

'Bring me my hat, jacket and gloves,' she instructed Ruthie, who appeared in the doorway. 'Kirsty and I will be out for a time, but tell your mother we will require a light luncheon at one o'clock.'

'Yes, miss.' Ruthie scampered off to do Bea's bidding.

Kirsty ran upstairs to collect her own jacket and hat. Her heart was thumping at the prospect of her aunt quizzing Martha and Ethel about their plans.

Martha ushered Kirsty and her aunt into the drawing-room. They completed the formalities and sat down.

'My niece has informed me she intends to leave Dundee with her friend Ethel,' Bea said. 'And, though I do not approve, she seems determined. So, I felt the need to check the arrangements.'

Martha looked across at Kirsty.

'Is this what you want?'

'Yes.'

'In that case, I will send my maid to fetch Ethel from the shop downstairs, so we can discuss the plans together.'

While they waited for Ethel to join them, Martha explained to Bea, 'Ethel is in training to be an organiser and I will do my best to arrange something similar for Kirsty.'

'I haven't told Ethel I want to leave Dundee with her, so it may come as a surprise.' Kirsty chewed her bottom lip.

Bea sighed. 'How can you be sure she will want you to accompany her?'

'There's no doubt in my mind that she'll welcome my company.' Kirsty stiffened.

'You sent for me?' Ethel said, entering the room.

'Sit down, Ethel. Kirsty has something to tell you.'

'I've decided . . .' Kirsty hesitated, a sudden, last-minute doubt creeping into her mind. What if Ethel didn't want her? She shrugged the thought from her mind and started again. 'I have decided to leave Dundee with you, rather than return home.'

'What?' Ethel's eyes widened. 'You want to come with me? Why? You have a nice home, and I don't know what's in store for me after I leave Dundee. Why give that up to come with me?'

'I have my reasons. I know life will be more difficult, but if you can survive, so can I.'

'If you're sure, I'd love to have you come with me. It'll be an adventure!'

'A rather risky adventure.' Bea's voice was dry. 'How will you both survive? Where will you live? What happens when your money runs out?'

'It is not my place to encourage Kirsty to leave home,' Martha interrupted, 'but I can provide reassurance that the league provides support. We have members nationwide, and there will always be someone to ensure her wellbeing.'

'I've made my decision.' Kirsty ignored the niggle of

doubt at the back of her mind and made her voice firmer than she felt. How would she survive, really?

'Our cause is a sisterhood. We look after each other. No suffragette ever wants for a bed or food – there is always someone to provide. As for money, Ethel will receive a small wage as an organiser. Not enough to live extravagantly, but enough to survive.' Martha paused and turned to address Kirsty. 'If you are firm in your wish to leave Dundee with Ethel, then you must realise that life will not be as comfortable as that to which you have been accustomed.'

Kirsty grasped her aunt's hands.

'I'm determined to leave with Ethel. I hope you won't put obstacles in my way.'

'I see your mind is made up.' Bea sighed. 'But you still have to face your father this afternoon and tell him your decision.'

'I'm not looking forward to it, but I can't leave without telling him. That would be dishonest.'

'I will come with you for support, but do not expect me to go against your father's wishes.'

'In that case,' Martha said, 'Ethel and I will come along to provide support, as well. I will arrange for a carriage to take us all there together.'

Kirsty's head buzzed as they walked along the street, away from Martha's home and the WFL shop below. She had no idea what the future held for her, but she'd made her decision and there was no going back.

Aunt Bea stopped halfway up Reform Street, in front of the Bank of Scotland.

'I have business requiring attention. It won't take long.' She gestured for Kirsty to follow her into the bank, whereupon a teller hurried over immediately.

'Ah, Mrs Hunter, what can I do for you?'

'I believe the manager has some forms requiring a signature.'

'I will inform him you are here.'

The manager, an officious, bald-headed, little man, rose

from his chair to greet them as they entered his office.

'I have the paperwork right here,' he said, 'as you instructed. Now, if the young lady will append her signature, everything will be set up.'

Mystified, Kirsty signed the form as she was bid. The manager blotted the signature and handed her a bank passbook.

'You may use this in any branch,' he said, before rising to show them out.

'What was all that about?' Kirsty asked once they were outside in the street again.

'I will not see you destitute, Kirsty. I could not have that on my conscience, so I have set up a small monthly allowance for you. It will be enough to keep you from starvation. But on no account are you to tell your father I have done this. Not a word, Kirsty.'

Kirsty stammered her thanks. Was it possible her aunt had foreseen her decision before she knew it herself? Puzzled, she walked up the street in a daze.

54

The carriage arrived at two o'clock. A four-wheeler with plenty of room inside. Martha and Ethel were already ensconced in the interior as Kirsty and her aunt climbed in.

All the way to Broughty Ferry, Kirsty's heart thumped so loudly she feared the others might hear it. It was with trepidation that she dismounted when they arrived.

Her mother welcomed them and, though she made no comment, Kirsty could tell she was surprised by Martha and Ethel's presence.

'I thought you might like to meet Kirsty's friends, Martha and Ethel,' Bea said, as she peeled off her gloves.

Ellen Campbell shook their hands before leading them into the drawing-room. Martha and Ethel perched on a sofa, while Bea chose an armchair. Kirsty followed them but stopped in the doorway to catch her breath as the familiarity struck her with a pang of dismay. After she left, she would never see this room or this house again. She shrugged it off; she couldn't afford to change her mind now and be sucked back into the misery of remaining in this place. With a heavy heart, she entered and sat beside Martha and Ethel on the sofa.

Kirsty's pulse raced as she heard her father's footsteps approach the door. It opened and there he stood, older and more tired than she remembered, as if he had aged over the short time she'd been away. A smile lit up his face as his eyes met hers.

'Ah, Kirsty! You've regained your senses and come home.'

Kirsty rose from her seat. She had never confronted her father in the past, but now her decision was made, she had to stay resolute.

'These are my friends, Martha and Ethel.'

Robert Campbell nodded to them.

'I am pleased to meet you. Friends of Kirsty are welcome here.'

Kirsty noted his voice lacked warmth and recognised his words were merely a polite form of greeting. He had always been suspicious of anyone she met who was not part of the family circle.

'I need to speak with you and Mother in private,' she said.

He raised his eyebrows.

'If you will excuse us for a few moments, please, ladies.'

Martha and Ethel nodded their assent. Although they said nothing, Kirsty could see encouragement reflected in their eyes. She wished they could be with her when she broke the news of her departure to her father, but that was impossible. This was something she had to do on her own. She squared her shoulders and followed her parents to her father's study.

'Well, what is so important it can't wait? I hope you have not formed a liaison with a young man during your holiday in Dundee.'

Kirsty thought she detected a note of worry in his voice, but that didn't prevent her surge of anger at his lack of trust.

'You need have no fear on that score.' She could not suppress the bitterness in her voice. He still assumed she lacked morals and needed protection from men. She drew a deep breath before continuing. 'I wanted you to know that I am a suffragette and I intend to leave home.' There, it was out.

Robert, taken by surprise, clenched his hands into fists and took a step towards her. For a moment, Kirsty thought he intended to strike her, but the moment passed, and Kirsty felt herself breathe again.

'A suffragette? What nonsense is this, Kirsty? I forbid it.'

'You can't. My mind is made up. I'm a suffragette, and I intend to leave home to devote myself to the cause.'

'Women will never be allowed to vote.' Robert stopped to draw breath. 'What on earth would a silly girl like you do with a vote?'

'Use it to make life better for women.'

'There is nothing wrong with women's lives. They are looked after and cared for. They do not have to tolerate the worries which plague men.'

'Don't you see? That's the problem! Men treat us like children. We're not free. We are beholden to them, for everything. And we're not allowed to make our own decisions or live the lives we want to. I want to help change all that, and give women freedom and the lives they deserve.'

'Freedom? You have freedom. You have always had freedom. I have never stopped you doing what you wished to do.'

'That's not true. Just this minute, you've forbidden me to be a suffragette, and for years, I've had to be the perfect daughter.'

'Perfect? Have you forgotten your misdemeanour?'

'My misdemeanour?' Kirsty's anger increased. 'Is that what you call it? No! I haven't forgotten! Though that's not how I would describe it.' Kirsty's voice broke as she thought of Ailsa, playing in the nursery.

'My mind is made up.' She stiffened. 'I am a suffragette, whether you like it or not.'

'I will not allow it. This insanity must stop.' His voice was hard with anger. 'You are my daughter. I have a responsibility for your care. If you will not listen to reason, I will have you committed to the insane asylum for your own protection.'

'Robert!' Ellen Campbell gasped, laying a restraining hand on his arm.

'You call that protecting me?' Kirsty laughed. 'I would call it one more example of men inflicting their will on women.'

'You think I won't do it?' Robert shook his wife's hand off and took a step towards Kirsty.

'On the contrary, I believe you, Father. But what would all your fine friends say about you and your mad daughter, if you did? Mother would never be able to show her face in public again – you would destroy her as well, and all because you want to control me. Well, I'm not having it. I *am* a suffragette, and I *am* leaving home to live my life, independent of you and your control.'

'I will not tolerate a suffragette in the family.' Her father's voice exploded with rage. 'If you leave, know that you will never return.'

Kirsty's anger built to an unsustainable level. She grabbed the door handle and jerked the door open before running into the hall and out of the house.

'That's fine with me,' she muttered, even though her heart felt as if it was shattering into tiny pieces.

The thump of the front door slamming behind her rang in her ears with a finality that brought her to a sudden halt. She would never walk through that door, ever again. Never see her mother again. Worst of all, she would never see Ailsa again. A sob caught in the back of her throat. But still, her anger simmered. She knew she had done what was right, but she also knew that she would always feel the pain of what she had left behind.

She leaned on the balustrade at the bottom of the steps leading up to the house and allowed her tears to flow. It didn't alleviate the pain she felt in her heart, caused by leaving Ailsa behind, but it did relieve the angry tension consuming her. An anger which surprised her with its intensity. She'd never experienced anything like it before.

55

'She is upset. Go after her,' Bea Hunter urged from the doorway, where she had positioned herself after Kirsty left the room with her parents. 'I will stay here and see if I can save the situation. It has obviously not gone well.'

Martha reached the hall as Kirsty barged through the front door.

'Come, Ethel,' she said. 'Kirsty needs us.' Clutching the hem of her skirt so she didn't trip, Martha raced after the distraught form of her young friend. By the time she and Ethel caught up with Kirsty, she was leaning against the balustrade, sobbing.

'We must get you home.' Martha led Kirsty over to the carriage and helped her inside, gesturing to Ethel to follow her. Martha climbed in to join them once both girls were settled.

'I'm sorry to be a bother to you,' Kirsty said, with a smile which didn't quite succeed, as she wiped tears from her cheeks with a handkerchief.

Ethel slung an arm around Kirsty's shoulder and hugged her while Martha leaned forward from the seat opposite. Kirsty kept her eyes on the direction the coach was travelling and did not look back at the house she was leaving forever.

'Was it very traumatic?' Martha grasped Kirsty's hand.

'It wasn't pleasant. I don't know what my father will do. He forbade me to be a suffragette – he expected me to obey him.' Tears glistened on Kirsty's eyelashes. 'But I defied him, and he threatened to put me in an asylum.'

'Can he do that?' Ethel asked.

'I don't know.'

'He would need to convince a doctor that your mind was disturbed.' Martha tightened her grasp on Kirsty's hands.

'That might not be so easy.'

'No doubt he would say I was hysterical.' A single tear rolled down Kirsty's cheek. 'He brought up what he calls my "misdemeanour". He'd use that, as well.'

'Your misdemeanour? What do you mean?'

Kirsty twisted the handkerchief around her fingers.

'I have a child,' she said at last. 'A daughter. Ailsa.' Her voice was so low, Martha had to strain to hear it. 'But I'm not allowed to acknowledge her, and that's agony. My mother is bringing her up as my sister.' Kirsty gulped in air as if she hadn't breathed for days. 'But she's not my sister. She's *mine.*'

Ethel pulled Kirsty into her arms and shushed her while her friend sobbed into her shoulder, releasing years of held-back pain and anguish.

After a few moments, Kirsty looked up.

'You must think me terrible, but it wasn't my fault. He was a family friend, and he forced himself on me. My father blames me.'

Martha's mind whirled. This was something she hadn't anticipated.

'This changes things, Kirsty. Your father could make a case you were in moral danger, and that would be enough for a doctor to commit you to the asylum. We cannot let that happen. We must stop at your aunt's house to collect your belongings and you will spend tonight with me. But there is one thing I must know first, and that is how you feel about leaving your daughter behind.'

'That's my main reason for deciding to leave. I can no longer tolerate living in the same house as Ailsa and being unable to be a mother to her. Even if I did claim her, what life would she have as my illegitimate child?' Kirsty struggled for breath. 'It's far better for both her and me that I remove myself from her life.'

'Very well,' Martha said, satisfied that Kirsty had reached her decision with reason. 'Tomorrow, we will make plans for your departure from Dundee.'

56

Sunday, 19th July 1908

Kirsty woke before Ethel. She had found it peculiar but strangely comforting to share a room with her friend. Downstairs, she could hear sounds of movement. She slid out of the bed and shrugged a robe around her shoulders. Raindrops trickled down the window. The summer heatwave had ended, at last. Was the change of weather an omen, signalling the change in her own life? Kirsty stared out to the glistening streets below. So much had happened since yesterday; her life would never be the same again.

A woman stopped in front of the church steeple and looked up towards the window. Kirsty started. It was Aunt Bea. Her aunt crossed the road. She was coming here. Kirsty grabbed her clothes and pulled them on hurriedly. Aunt Bea never visited anyone before ten in the morning. What had happened to make her break her own, strict rules?

Ethel raised her head from the pillow as Kirsty's fingers fumbled with the buttons of her blouse. She buttoned the final one before grabbing a hairbrush and dragging it roughly through her curls.

'What's the hurry? Has something happened?' Ethel dug her elbows into the pillow and pushed herself up.

'My aunt's heading in this direction. I spotted her in the street.'

'So? She probably wants to check you're all right.'

'You don't understand – Aunt Bea never leaves the house this early; she thinks it a mortal sin to call on anyone before ten. Something must have brought her here.'

'I'll come downstairs with you.' Ethel swung her legs out of bed.

'Can't wait, sorry – see you down there.' Kirsty ran

through the door, letting it slam behind her. She was out of breath by the time she reached the drawing-room, where Aunt Bea and Martha were deep in conversation.

'What's happened?'

Bea rose from her chair and hurried across the room to her niece.

'Your father is furious, and I felt it necessary to come and warn you.'

'Warn me of what?'

'He intends to have you incarcerated in a lunatic asylum and plans to arrange for a physician to detain you there. Your mother tried to talk him out of it, but she has been unsuccessful, and, of course, he never listens to me.' Bea stopped and drew breath. 'I cannot stand back and see you locked up in an asylum, Kirsty. I had to warn you.'

'How much time do I have?'

'He has arranged an appointment with the physician from Dundee District Asylum for later this morning. You are safe until after church comes out.'

'Pack your belongings,' Martha said. 'We must act quickly.'

Bea leaned forward to embrace Kirsty.

'I will go now. It would not be wise for me to know where you are going.'

'Thank you, Aunt Bea. I'll never forget what you've done for me.' Tears gathered in the corners of Kirsty's eyes as she watched her aunt leave, and she brushed them away with an impatient hand.

'Where will I go?' she asked Martha.

'Leave that to me. There is a safe house with Miss McGregor at Inverkeilor. You and Ethel can stay there for a few days, which will give me time to make arrangements for you to travel to Edinburgh.'

Kirsty rushed upstairs.

'We're leaving this morning,' she said, starting to throw her clothes into a valise.

'This morning?' Ethel's eyes widened.

'Yes,' Martha confirmed, entering the room. 'I have

found a carpetbag for your belongings, Ethel, and I've ordered a carriage to take you both to Inverkeilor. The faster I get you girls out of Dundee, the better.'

'Why are we going to Inverkeilor, wherever that is? I thought we were going to Edinburgh or Glasgow.' Ethel placed her few possessions in the carpetbag.

'We have to get Kirsty to safety quickly, and you will be safe at Abbethune House,' Martha said. 'But within the week, you will be on your way to Edinburgh.'

Half an hour later, the packing was completed. Both girls took a last look around the room which had been their haven, then hurried out to the carriage waiting at the kerb.

Kirsty's heart thumped as she stepped out of the close and on to the pavement, but a nervous glance along the street reassured her that her father wasn't lying in wait for her. Her skirt caught around her feet as she jumped into the carriage with unseemly haste. Ethel and Martha followed after her, both looking anxious.

Kirsty's eyes flicked back and forth as they sped through the streets of Dundee and she only breathed easily again once they were rumbling through the countryside. She was heading for safety and freedom; towards a destiny she felt was preordained. But it was a destiny which was to take her into the unknown, and who knew what dangers she might find along the way.

Kirsty settled back in her seat. For the first time in her life, she realised she felt free, and as long as Ethel was with her, she didn't care how dangerous her destiny would turn out to be.

Historical End Note

A plethora of women's groups and societies arose during the mid-1800s to advocate women's suffrage; the right to vote for parliamentary members who would address issues that concerned women. Many of these groups have faded from history, but they formed the background to the three main suffrage societies which arose at the end of the 19th century and the beginning of the 20th century. These groups, detailed in the order they came into being, are as follows.

The National Union of Women's Suffrage Societies (NUWSS)

The NUWSS was formed in 1897, when several suffrage organisations banded together to present a common front in the pursuit of women's suffrage. Millicent Fawcett was a prominent member of the NUWSS and, in 1907, became its president. The aim of the society was to secure the vote by passive and diplomatic means, such as peaceful protests and petitioning the government. NUWSS members were known as suffragists and they abhorred the violent tactics that developed with the formation of new suffrage societies.

Women's Social and Political Union (WSPU)

The WSPU was founded in 1903, at a small gathering of women at Emmeline Pankhurst's home in Manchester. It remained a small society until the adoption of militant tactics in 1905, after which it was to become the largest and best-known organisation in Britain fighting for women's suffrage. The Pankhursts remained in charge and operated the WSPU as an army; their members were expected to obey orders without question and weren't allowed to make independent decisions. Their motto was 'Deeds not Words'. With the increase in support and membership, they moved their headquarters from Manchester to London in 1906, and the first branch in Dundee was opened the same year.

The first militant act recorded was when Christabel Pankhurst spat on a policeman, and she and Annie Kenney fought against their arrest. Christabel and Annie were the first suffragettes to be sentenced to seven days in Strangeways Prison, in 1905.

Women's Freedom League (WFL)

The WFL was formed in 1907, after some members of the WSPU became dissatisfied with the autocratic nature of the organisation. These members proposed that the WSPU should be run on more democratic lines but this was resisted. Among some of the more prominent WSPU members who were instrumental in founding the WFL were; Charlotte Despard, Teresa Billington-Greig, and Emmeline Pethick-Lawrence. Charlotte Despard became president of the WFL.

The league never became as large an organisation as the WSPU, but it had a strong base in Scotland. Why this should be the case is unknown, though it has been speculated that it might be because the Scots are an independent race and they didn't take kindly to the autocratic rule of the Pankhursts. Several notable WSPU members in Scotland were expelled by the Pankhursts for not following orders; some of these women found a home with the WFL.

The WFL continued to be run on democratic lines. They supported a militant approach to the fight for the suffrage cause but did not favour the extreme militant methods of the WSPU, which involved a risk to life with fire-raising and bombing.

Women's Suffrage in Scotland

Similar to the situation nationally, before the formation of the main suffrage societies, there were various groups supporting women's rights. However, the NUWSS and

WSPU remained based in England, though two of the Scottish societies for women's suffrage (one in Glasgow and the other in Edinburgh) affiliated to the NUWSS in 1903. It was only later that branches of the main societies were opened in Scotland. The WFL Centre opened at Gordon Street, Glasgow, in 1907. The WSPU opened a branch in Dundee in 1906, and their Scottish headquarters in January 1908, at 141 Bath Street, Glasgow. In 1909, the Scottish Federation of Suffrage Societies formed under the NUWSS umbrella. They had a branch office at 12 Meadowside, Dundee.

At the time this book takes place, the WFL and WSPU were operating in Dundee. The WSPU had premises at 61 Nethergate, in a building shared with a cabinet maker, an artist, a plumber, and a tobacco pipe manufacturer. There is less certainty about the WFL headquarters, and references have been made to Lila Clunas's house at 1 Blackness Avenue and a possible office at 5 Cowgate, at a later date. For the purposes of the story, I have appropriated the shop premises of C.S. Scott, the tobacconist, at 88 Nethergate, for WFL headquarters, and given Martha the house above the shop.

After 1905, suffragettes became involved in militant activities in London, initially creating disturbances and accosting members of the government. Over the years, as they became more frustrated, this escalated into fire-raising and planting bombs. The escalation took longer in Scotland, although militant suffragettes travelled regularly from Scottish towns to London to take part during the earlier years. The first time that suffragettes were imprisoned was in 1905, after which it became a regular occurrence. No suffragettes were sent to prison in Scotland (although many Scottish suffragettes were imprisoned in London) before 1909, when the first suffragettes were sentenced to prison by a Dundee court. Likewise, women were being force-fed in Holloway prison from 1909, whereas the first person to be force-fed in Scotland was Ethel Moorhead in Calton Prison, Edinburgh, on February 21, 1914.

The suffragettes in this book are members of the WFL, which allows them to have militant tendencies without the restrictions imposed by the WSPU.

Also by Chris Longmuir

DUNDEE CRIME SERIES

Night Watcher
Dead Wood
Missing Believed Dead

KIRSTY CAMPBELL MYSTERIES

Devil's Porridge
The Death Game
Death of a Doxy

SUFFRAGETTE MYSTERIES

Dangerous Destiny

HISTORICAL SAGAS

A Salt Splashed Cradle

NONFICTION

Nuts & Bolts of Self-Publishing

CHRIS LONGMUIR

Chris Longmuir was born in Wiltshire and now lives in Angus. Her family moved to Scotland when she was two. After leaving school at fifteen, Chris worked in shops, offices, mills and factories, and was a bus conductor for a spell, before working as a social worker for Angus Council (latterly serving as Assistant Principal Officer for Adoption and Fostering).

Chris is a member of the Society of Authors, the Crime Writers Association and the Scottish Association of Writers. She writes short stories, articles and crime novels, and has won numerous awards. Her first published book, Dead Wood, won the Dundee International Book Prize and was published by Polygon. She designed her own website and confesses to being a techno-geek who builds computers in her spare time.

http://www.chrislongmuir.co.uk